JESSIKA GREWE GLOVER

*For Coco, who started writing this book by my side, and for Fiona,
who helped me finish it.
And for every woman who felt she wasn't enough.*

CHAPTER ONE

The first few feeding sessions were hardest to drown out the sound of a body in motion. A body knowing its life hangs on a peculiar balance. Her thumping heartbeat moved in waves as she walked through the sterile foyer and into the feeding room. She squinted at the change in lighting. Most donors were comfortable, I have found, with soft, low lighting, yet not too dim as to make it intimate. She clocked each seating option, careful calculation in her eyes noting the chaise and low stool, the small sectional sofa, the two armchairs and matching ottomans, the counter stools perched at the kitchen island.

Her heart sped as she turned to me. They were always anxious the first few sessions, never knowing what questions should be asked and just how dangerous I was. Heat radiated off her, the scent of her toiletries a powdery green almost masking the fear exuding from her underarms. After several centuries, I still hated to admit I craved that scent of fear. Even more so, I craved the way they always tried to mask it.

"Please choose where you would like to sit," I told her, waving an arm at the room proper. "As I said in our interview, I always start my new donors with an inner arm feeding, so you should be fairly comfortable anywhere."

She unconsciously pulled her long hair into a low tail with a tie from her wrist. My eyes locked on the spot the circulation moved back to the area. She sat on a tufted leather armchair, dropping her handbag on the wood floor next to her. Her heartrate was so high, my own ears began to throb with the sound. I hadn't eaten in the weeks I went through the hiring process after my last donor left town. I took artificial adrenaline the night before so as to not shake in the presence of fresh blood. There were two main points I hammered on.

One: to make my donors as comfortable as possible, treating them as valuable employees being paid handsomely for my nutritional needs. Two: make absolutely certain candidates and then donors are one hundred percent aware that this is my life, not a sexual fetish. If anyone makes it awkward, they leave, and the contract is invalidated.

I motioned for her to lean back as I gathered a caddy of supplies and took my seat in the chair next to hers. I never much cared for this particular seating arrangement, but most donors chose this one for the first session or so. It must have a sense of safety and autonomy in it. This donor, the first I'd had in quite some time, seemed to value her autonomy above all else.

"Ophelia James," she'd offered during her second in-person interview five days prior. Placing feelers out with contacts and businesses I know was how I always found donors. One couldn't simply place an ad asking for someone to blood let. That's an invitation for the mad fetishists to come knocking. I vetted any inquiries fully before a first video conference interview, then made sure I met them in person. Everyone's body chemistry is different, and I was easily put off by people's scents. Hers seemed to call to me, making me instantly hand over a contract stating she would be paid 1000 pounds per week to start, doubling after six months, and she would get an additional 500 pounds if I needed to feed more than once a week. She took the paper from me, meeting my eyes in a show of conviction I rarely saw.

"Javier Eneide," I said, passing a rollerball pen to her waiting fingers.

CHAPTER TWO

OPHELIA

The club chair seemed the safest bet. A sofa would have been too intimate to start this odd job I had taken. The bar stool looked purgatorial, and the chaise a bit like I had a fainting spell during high tea. Truly, I didn't mind where I sat as I considered myself lucky to have been recommended for the job by a former personal trainer. One I used to love going to back when it wasn't a hand-to-mouth financial situation as I tried to start my business. Before I sold off my car and rather impressive handbag collection when my company went under the previous year, thanks to that abomination of an ex. It didn't hurt that this new "boss" was not hard to look at. He rolled the short sleeve of my T-shirt up and wiped the inner arm with alcohol. It felt clinical.

"I always remind my donors in the first session that I will not put up with any sexual misconduct. I am aware my kind are swathed in lore and overly sexualized. This is a business arrangement for my own feeding." He met my eyes.

"Believe me," I said with a bitter edge, "the last thing on my mind is sex. I am trying to start a business."

He nodded, allowing the alcohol to dry on my skin.

"Why the elbow?" I asked.

"It feels safer I am told," he admitted. "Plus, we do not yet know if you will scar." I started. "It will heal, of course. A bit like Botox." He gave me a small smile, two elongated canines peeking out between his lips. "You'll have a bit of redness and swelling at first, but it will be shiny and smoother than before."

"Oh, in that case, I have a list of places you can feed from."

He laughed at the poor attempt at a joke, but I stepped on my own toe to keep from feeling stupid. He opened his mouth wider. "Here. Touch the points so you know what will be piercing your skin."

I brushed my hands on my sweatpants before lifting the pad of my index finger to the tips of his fangs. *Fangs*, I said to myself in disbelief. Not that vampires were a far-fetched concept. Vampire mythology has been in every culture since the dawn of time. Why wouldn't they be real? But still…fangs. They felt as sharp as needles, but heavy. He had explained that feedings can cause arousal in donors. It was part of the predator process. He also explained that as an adult, I could contain my reaction to it and be professional. He switched on classical music and tapped my arm once.

"Ready?" he asked. I nodded, and before I could do anything else, his mouth closed over my inner elbow.

Pressure and stabbing made me gasp. He pulled out and looked to me, his hazel eyes glassy.

"Are you all right?"

I thought so. I was dizzy, but a quick self-scan told me I was fine. At my nod, he bit down again. This time there was little pain as his teeth sunk into the same holes. Then he began to suck.

My stomach turned over. I'd lost my business almost a year before and taking odd freelance design jobs since led to this situation. This prostitution of my life force. I was disgusted. Sickened by the soft mewling of his mouth on my arm and the drain I felt. Anger flared in my cheeks, hot and ready to flee. How had I stooped so low that I was selling my blood? Dragging pain tugged at my arm, keeping my anger a living flame. Equal parts of me hurt and wanted to lash out in anger. Until he swallowed a larger mouthful and that pain and anger changed into something else. The drag of teeth in flesh felt silken and warm. That warmth traveled through me, flooding my belly. *Oh*, I thought. I tried not to squirm. His eyes flashed to mine, and he lifted his mouth from my arm.

"That's enough for the first time." He began cleaning the wound and dressing it. I found it hard to look anywhere but the gauze pad. "I will see you again next week. Loads of iron rich foods and vitamin C, yeah?"

"What do you eat in between sessions?" I found myself asking. I knew I was the sole donor. He was meticulous about keeping trust between himself and his donor, but surely one must need to eat more than once per week?

"I can take animal blood. It doesn't sustain me the same, but it keeps the hunger pangs at bay." His eyes crinkled at the edges, and he winked.

Session three. I felt like I might be able to tune out the bizarre reaction I had to the feeding. I knew he had said people react to the sensation differently, and becoming aroused is normal. I knew he said it's because he's essentially a predator and that sort of reaction keeps prey docile. I just thought I would be exempt from it. Seeing as I could not even fathom any form of sex right now that doesn't involve my own fingers or Voltaire, my trusty vibrator who felt like a new partner every time I switched between his twenty-seven settings. Regardless, I put on baggy trousers today with my white vest, hoping the airy outfit would give me breathing room in my nether regions. I really needed the money this gig paid, so I would do what I could to curb this inconvenient reaction.

There was a cushion on the armchair today I hadn't noticed before. It was a black and cream print, and I couldn't decide if it went with the room or not. I noticed Javier was wearing a type of running jacket rather than the button downs I'd seen the other times we had met. It's funny when you see someone outside of how you typically picture them. Their persona takes on a more multidimensional look. The black jacket matched the new cushion, so everything started coming together. If I focused on the design of the room and my boss, I might be able to ignore the feeding reaction.

"Are you Argentinian?" I blurted out as he swabbed my arm. He snorted a laugh that seemed so genuine, I knew I'd surprised him.

"Why do you ask?" He looked up briefly, blotting my alcohol-damp skin with gauze. The previous bite marks had healed shiny and fresh, but the phantom scar of them was ultrasensitive. Even the swipe of gauze sent a buzz south. I swallowed and shifted.

"Your surname," I said.

He lowered his mouth to my inner elbow, and I was glad we didn't start somewhere else. The neck, wrist, even inner thigh were all possibilities, which would give him more pull, but we wouldn't utilize those until much later. I assumed after the six-month probation mark ended.

"My surname? Eneide is Italian." His fangs pierced the skin, and I involuntarily lifted my hips. He ignored it, and I tried to as well. That first pull felt like I'd hit the slick bit on a downhill ski slope.

"Yes, but it's also used in Germany, and your given name is Javier, which is Spanish." I felt his sucking pause, the press of his lips on my skin soft. "Argentina has a lot of people of

Italian and German descent, and as it's a Spanish speaking country, I thought perhaps that explained the names."

He pulled his mouth away, fangs sliding out slowly. I watched, half in horror as my blood coated the ivory tips.

"That is a fair assessment," he admitted. His words slurred ever so slightly. "I have spent many years in Argentina. As you may have suspected, my kind live long lives, and must adapt and change with our times and surroundings." He plunged back in, and I gasped. He patted my knee in what may have been an apology or a calming gesture. The sucking ensued. Thoughts swirled, yet I had trouble snatching one to ground me.

"Okay," I said after a good five minutes. "That whole adaptation thing makes perfect sense. But do any of your names mean anything? Culturally?"

He chuckled and coughed a little. I realized it might be off putting expecting him to answer like we were having pasta at a business lunch. Honestly, I was curious, and I was really trying to quell the blood rushing to my groin. Which I was one hundred percent certain he could feel or smell or whatever it was vampires did. When he came off my arm again, he smiled at me, closed lipped.

"All of my names mean something." His thumb swiped at his lips, probably checking for smears of me. Thank God for baggy trousers. "Until a few years ago, I was in Argentina for over thirty years. Before that, I was in Brazil, Spain, San Francisco, and many other places."

"Are you Italian?" There was no way to know based on accent as I have detected so many different nuances in his speech; his accent was untraceable. Not that I was an expert but having run a boutique city hotel for the better part of a decade put me in contact with people from every dialect.

"I...yes. I am."

"But Javier..."

He laughed, sticking supplies back in the caddy. "A name given to me by someone special almost three centuries ago. In Spain. You are a curious woman, Ophelia."

I felt embarrassed and ducked my head. "I'm sorry. Was it weird that I was asking questions whilst you fed?"

"Not at all. It was refreshing actually. As long as it wasn't strange or frightening to you that I have to pull my teeth out of you to answer." The vernacular "pull my teeth out of you" was a hot bucket of pitch to my core I did not welcome at all. He turned away, and I knew he sensed it. His shoulders tensed under that fitted fabric of his jacket.

"No, I found it interesting."

He nodded once, still turned from me. His dark hair had threads of gray in it, which I found oddly more attractive than a solid and youthful color. The shiny glow of youth was not what I was attracted to. The patina of experience, knowledge, and living lured me more. Which I sincerely hoped would not be an issue in this case. Internally, I chastised myself for thinking it.

"Is the reaction you are having to the feeding going to be a problem?" His words were clipped, and to me, sounded like he was on the verge of anger.

I reared back, off balance from blood loss and swinging a too-large handbag onto my shoulder. My cheeks must have been a thousand shades of red. I really needed a drink, and so I pulled my phone out to text my best mate, if for nothing else other than to stop my first response, which was to tell him to fuck off. My days of allowing myself to cow to a man were over. They were over when I finally had the nerve to walk out on Connor that last time. I vowed to never let a man tell me how I felt or needed to behave. My mum and dad had such a healthy, loving relationship, it was high time I valued myself enough to seek one out. Though not any time soon since I truly did not have the time.

"Not at all," I answered instead, sweet and final. The notification for my weekly thousand pounds, showed on my phone screen before I made it past the threshold of his door. We were professionals.

It must have been the embarrassed anger, but today's feeding left me dizzier than before. By the time I'd had one drink in me at The Botanist, I needed to put my stiletto heels onto Sascha's seat. I had changed into my business attire after the session, done with the sloppy sweats and the uncomfortably wet crotch I walked away with. My non-disclosure agreement made it so that I couldn't talk about my new "job", but I had to tell my best friend why I was so run down. And able to finally afford a round of drinks somewhere other than Wetherspoon's.

"No offence, Lily," Sascha said, tucking a long silver lock of my hair behind my ear. That streak had started the day my ex admitted to cheating on me and turned into a solid argent reminder of my fragility the day I had to tell my staff the hotel was bankrupt. I'd thought about dying it. Actually, I had dyed it a few colors in the past, but I'd decided ultimately it was a mark of who I was and what I had survived. It was just me. Sascha touched the tip of my nose like she had been doing since we were kids. "You look super peaky. I know Voltaire has been good to you, but I think you might need a bit more than his silicone tongue these days."

"Are you suggesting his twenty-seven settings aren't enough?" I asked, hand to my chest. "One makes a sucking motion, and is designed to feel—"

"Sorry to interrupt," a voice said from behind my shoulder. I closed my eyes once, knowing he had overheard the conversation. "I was waiting on my drink and saw you here and didn't want it to be awkward if I didn't say hello."

So, it was less awkward to walk into the middle of a girly chat about vibrators simulating oral? I asked myself. Sascha made no attempt to not laugh openly. She held out her hand for Javier to shake.

"Sascha," she said with her tongue between her teeth. "Lily's most revered and beautiful best mate." She winked at him from behind the fall of her pointed black fringe which hung over the buzzed undercut of her hair. The wink caught the light from an overhead chandelier, glinting off her eyebrow ring.

"Javi," he said, taking her hand. "Ophelia's employer." He addressed Sascha with a polite smile, but I didn't miss the tiny twitch of his lips at me. I raised an eyebrow at him in challenge, because this was my table. My time. My best mate. Okay, so yes to all of that, but it was still so embarrassing. Javier pointed in the other direction and simply walked away without another word.

Wherever he had gone to fetch his drink was not nearly far enough. I could not believe he had to hear about Voltaire's many settings after the "reaction" he'd referred to today. Humiliated was not even close to describing how I felt. Of course, Sascha would not let it drop. She lasted all of thirty seconds, most of which was spent swallowing a sip of her drink.

"HR frustrations, then?" she asked, lips smiling against her sidecar. As unpredictable as Sascha was in her career moves, wardrobe, hairstyles, and lovers, two things she was utterly predictable for: always pushing the envelope on an uncomfortable topic, and her drinks. Sidecar September through November, gin cranberry in December, dry January, regrettable espresso martini February, gin and slimline tonic in the spring, mojitos in summer. Plus, prosecco anytime.

"Javi is one lovely specimen to be working...under." If she only knew I literally did work under him. Though not in the way she suggested. The feel of his mouth pulling blood from my veins flashed over me. I broke out in a sweat but rolled my eyes at my friend. I really needed to check myself with these flashbacks. They could be as intense as the feeding itself. Like the aftershocks of a major earthquake.

"Look, if our food doesn't arrive soon," I said, quickly fanning myself with the drinks menu, "I'll have to beg off. It's been a long day."

"Oh! Sorry! That's what I meant to tell you before Daddy Sharp Teeth graced our presence."

"Sharp teeth?" I panicked, thinking she knew.

"Haven't you noticed? He has those super-hot, youthful canines. Along with the silver-streaked hair, he's almost as hot as you." She flicked my nose again. I rolled my eyes but descended on the shared starters as they were placed on the table. "Anyhoo. My investors came through. They are a go to stick some cash in our knickers for upping the arthouse vibe of the new hotel."

I whooshed a breath and took a long plug of my own gin and tonic. I could have cried. We had been working for months on these investors, wanting to give our new boutique hotel a different style to most in town. It was two a penny here to find hotels which were comfortable. Hotels which were stylish and classy. Classic. It was a hard press to find one which could bring in a more design savvy crowd. Those who would appreciate the same sort of place in London or Bristol but have business here in Exeter. Between my design background and Sascha's business skills, we were a good team. The bloody pandemic was not kind to boutique hotels though. The high of new business possibility carried me home, hopeful and finally feeling secure.

In my bed a couple hours later, I spread all the hotel partners' contracts out. The NDA I'd signed with Javier—Javi—peeked out as well. It was interesting to me that he introduced himself to Sascha as Javi, as though we were casual enough colleagues to use nicknames. This NDA and the question *"Is the reaction you are having to the feeding going to be a problem?"* proved we were very much not on casual terms. His teeth, gleaming with my fresh blood, flashed in my mind, and the pounding started in my core again. I placed the contracts on the nightstand and sat back, watching rain slide down the windowpanes. I could see him in my memory. The hazel of his eyes became dark and murky when he looked up while sucking on my arm. Did *he* have reactions to feeding or was it just his prey? The rain kept a steady pace on my window, the sound an echo of my heart and core pounding in synch. I started to reach for Voltaire but became impatient and wiggled from my pajamas, dipping my fingers along my wet crease. What would it feel like to touch myself while he fed? To ease that ache that was becoming a disability. I honestly was having trouble walking out the bloody door afterward. Not that I would ever tell him that. God. So much blood rushed to my clit every time those fangs sank in. What must it feel like for him to feed from my inner thigh? *Oh God*, I thought. *I am really not supposed to be thinking this way.* My fingers curved into my opening and pushed, bruising my G-spot. I bit my lip, tasting blood. The metallic tang had me pump harder, until I came with a huff of dissatisfaction. Sascha was probably right. Voltaire and I were an item past its sell-by date. I needed someone real.

OPHELIA

Pigeons scattered where students walked through the high street in town that first week of classes in the local university. Stands lined the curbs, selling all sorts of produce and dairy items to locals, while others capitalized on what students needed, moving into halls on campus. I held a plum, fresh and taut in my hand, debating how many I would go through before they became a gnarled mess on my counter. The kale and Swiss chard peeking out from my market bag begged I show it the same mercy. I counted the coins in my hand and passed a couple pounds to the grocer, dropping two plums into my bag, letting them pillow between leafy-green veg. One more stop before I dropped into my favorite Sunday tea shop for prosecco and avo toast. The dairy farmers were behind the butcher stand, and I needed eggs. Hurrying past the coolers full of meat, I missed a step and collided into a solid body.

"Steady on." *Oh, for the love of Christ.*

"Javier," I said, my face smooshed into his shirt. I could taste his...whatever he used to smell so fucking good. Like grapefruit and pine or something. I was in so much trouble. My hands found purchase on his chest, and I pushed off, regaining my balance on the cobbled street. His face looked amused as he crossed his arms. "I was just getting eggs."

"Eggs, kale, plums," he said, taking a brown paper bag from the butcher and thanking him. "Glad you are taking your iron intake seriously." His accent hit the r in seriously like a d and it made my toes curl. I muttered something vaguely intelligible. "You should pick up a bottle of red as well. Or is gin your drink of choice?"

I looked up, trying to take the measure of the conversation. Was he being friendly, sussing out my lifestyle and eating habits, or stalking me? I shut that last one down as we were in a small university city. It is not uncommon to run into people every day. Plus, he probably just needed to make sure I didn't end up in A & E with anemia.

"Mostly wine. Gin when it's been a trying day. Or when Sascha is hitting it hard."

He walked to the dairy grocer with me and watched as I paid for my eggs. An arm snaked around my waist, startling me. I spun and was face to face with my ex. The sight had me jump back, crashing into Javier, who I knew could hear my heart raging in my chest.

"Lily," Connor said with a bright smile. To his credit it was his true smile. One I hadn't seen in years. Probably the one he gave to his lovers when he met them. I always got the leftovers. The forced smile and cocky grins. "You are a creature of habit. Every Sunday on the green, Lily gets her veg."

My mouth worked to respond but kept snagging on the fact that he didn't live here, and if he took the train two hours from London simply to corner me at the farmers' market, something was up. My heart sped up. Connor always made things complicated. The way I fell for him. The way we fought. The way I hated him and loved him and let him walk all over me. Until I didn't. When I decided to leave him, I closed the book on him. For good. So why was he back here, and why was my heart telling me to run? Tentative fingers pressed into my lower back, and I remembered Javier was still there. My shoulders dropped. At least it was someone else. Someone to keep me from breaking down, or worse, jumping back into bed with the man I really did not want to take Voltaire's place. I wished Sascha was with me, but she never got up before noon on a Sunday.

"Hiya, mate," Connor said, sticking out his hand at Javier. "Connor. Lily's partner."

"Javier. And no, I don't think you are."

Woah. This could get ugly quickly. Especially if Connor was on something. It was early on a Sunday, but who knew with him. He laughed instead, and there it was. His cocky smile. He ran a hand over his bristled face. The facial hair that hid his unimpressive jawline.

"Come again? You new in town? Come from Poland or something, *Javier*?"

"Connor." My voice held a warning. Fucks sake. He tried to grab at my hand, but Javier stepped in front of me.

"Ms. James did not say you could touch her, and seeing as she nearly went into cardiac arrest when you ambushed her, I would say she does not welcome it. I understand you may have had a history together, but that is all it is." Javier spoke with lethal quiet. People buzzed around us. The dairy grocer was openly staring, a glass jug of milk held midair. It was as though time froze. No one but Sascha had ever stood up for me. Not since my parents died. The color on Connor's fair skin rose, making the mole near his temple stand out.

"Lily," he said. "Let's talk, love."

"I'm done talking, Connor. If you come near me again, I will get the police involved. Again."

"Lil—"

"That's your cue, *mate*," Javier said.

Connor gave me one last pleading glance before turning

on his purposefully scuffed All Saints boots and strode up Queen's Street.

Javier watched him go for a full minute before turning to me. "I take it things did not end well?"

I shook my head, feeling lightheaded. Maybe I wasn't getting enough iron, because I felt faint. Javier moved us back toward the avo toast sanctuary and sat me on the edge of a picnic bench. A waiter started to say something but was silenced by a look from my employer. I put my head between my knees.

"It's been over a long, long time. I don't know why he's here."

Javier squatted down to hear me better. I told him briefly how bad it had been. The career ramifications of leaving Connor. How he review-bombed me on every website. How he destroyed my credit. Things I'd only ever told Sascha. But it seemed worth saying because Connor was a leech. He wouldn't have shown up just for a quick fuck, and there was no way he would think I would take him back at this point.

"That's why you applied for the position I offered," Javier stated. I nodded, my hair falling over my denim clad knees. "I will walk you home if that was where you were going."

Well, I was now that Fuckface Connor invaded my space. I cast one longing look toward the avo toast that would not be had and told Javier I was ready.

The sun hadn't shown face in eight days, leaving my hair and temper in a state of perpetual static. The plus side was that the new windows on the hotel had been installed last week. The clarity in the glass reflected each slow slide of raindrop, casting the entire library sitting room of the hotel in a cascade of light, as though standing within a glass of champagne. Though the building would not see proper guests for a few months more, some childish whinge within me wanted to create a bit of early Christmas magic here. If only in one room. It was silly, really. Perhaps because my flat was such a disappointment, I was ready to create some magic somewhere else. Tomorrow, the floors would be buffed and polished, removing the grit of sanded, reclaimed wood. I stood watching the rain, thankful to be in a progressive chapter of my life. A small part of me kept whispering that I wasn't as progressive as I could be, given that I was a weekly, sometimes twice weekly, meal for a vampire. And that immediately after said mealtimes, I would touch myself until I came. Was I getting paid to pleasure myself? I shook my head, clearing the thought. Of course not. I was solving a complication of my contracted terms. That was all.

But you enjoy it, that same whisper said. *You get a rush thinking of your next appointment. You ride Voltaire, wishing it were Javier's face, fangs and all, clamped around your pussy.* The thought clouded my vision, and had me cross my legs at the ankles, putting pressure on my throbbing wanny. It started two weeks prior. Four feedings to be exact. Javier had asked me to come in two extra times and I was quick to agree because it was an extra grand, which went direct into my savings.

"Ophelia." I turned at the voice, pulling myself out of my addled thoughts. My architect and liaison to the city planning commission stood in the doorway to the library. His sandy hair was matted with rain. I watched as beads of it ran down his neck and into his slashed T-shirt. He always looked more like he was on the set of some high-level fashion show rather than the everyday tasks he performed for me. I wondered what his proclivities were and had to mentally slap myself for considering it since we were working together. *Christ's sake, Ophelia. Get your head on straight.*

"Pete. Hi."

He stepped toward me, handing over a file. "Final approval on the windows upstairs. Last major hurdle before you can have a soft opening." The words "soft opening" sent me right back to the unscrupulous train of thoughts I had been having. "You all right?"

"Yeah, yeah. Haven't eaten today," I said, which wasn't a lie, but not the whole truth, of course. I propped the papers on the sideboard and read through, signing off. "Can't believe it's actually happening."

"You should celebrate. You've worked hard on this place." I waved off the compliment. "I'm serious. Even with your experience running a hotel, you were able to transform this place in record time. Let me take you out for a drink to celebrate."

"What? Now?" I looked at my phone for the time.

"I've got the time, and you need a nibble anyway." It was midafternoon, and my appointment with Javier wasn't for another three hours. I agreed, grabbing my coat and leaving the light on in the foyer before stepping out into the December afternoon.

One drink turned to three drinks and a shared bit of ceviche, which was not enough to soak up any alcohol. The old personal trainer who had recommended me to Javier had also been the one to put Pete's and my professional networks together. I really owed him a lot. It was such a shame he had moved away a few months back.

Even though drinks with Pete ran later than I'd thought, still, I arrived at Javier's on time. He gave me a slight smile as I walked in, a glimpse of fang poking through. I realized he rarely smiled with both sides of his mouth. One day I would ask him if the scar he had on the left happened before or after he'd turned. One day, I'd ask him how he had turned. It was none of my business, but I was a curious woman.

I dumped my bag on the floor near the couch, and he picked it up as he always did. He always said that in his culture, it was bad luck to leave a handbag on the floor. A new hook had been installed on the wall by the door since our second appointment, and that was where he hung my bag every time. It was almost...sweet.

"Javier," I began but noticed an odd, almost angry look on his face. I stepped back involuntarily. His nostrils twitched like he was...sniffing me. My body and mind froze. I had never been caught in what I imagined was his predator's missile lock. I couldn't bring myself to move.

"You were drinking?" he asked, fangs showing fully as though they had elongated in the brief moment between my being on one side of the door to this side.

"I had drinks with my architect to celebrate signing the last city commission forms." It was like I was programed to only answer his question. Nothing more. He stepped forward, nostrils still flared, his mossy hazel eyes far darker than they had ever been. Dark blue veins pulsed along his chiseled cheek bones looking like firing neurons.

"Did he harm you?" How did he know it was a "he"? I couldn't ask that because I was still ensnared.

"No!" it came out harsher than I'd intended, but for Christ's sake. His shoulders relaxed but his eyes and the veins along his cheeks were still evidence of the demon within him. And I was still trapped.

"Forgive me. His scent is all over you, and something in it triggered a memory. Plus, I scent...something else."

Oh my god, I thought. *He can smell my arousal from earlier.* And maybe the spike of arousal when one of us made a vibrator joke and I was just tipsy enough to mention Voltaire. Pete laughed and told me he had his own Voltaire, though sadly, his was not named. His toy, however, he used to give himself a prostate orgasm and I, of course, asked for every detail. I am a curious woman. So, it was no doubt Javier could smell the pool of wetness I had accumulated over the course of a rather horny day. I narrowed my eyes looking at Javier, getting angry that I was standing like a duck in an oil spill. He seemed to notice and blinked his eyes several times.

"Please do not do that again," I said with enough venom he looked slightly repentant. "I do not want to feel threatened and unable to move when I come here."

Javier was silent but went to the kitchen and brought me a bottle of fizzy water.

"Like you, I have a short temper," he said softly. "My behavior was unacceptable, however. I apologize."

I accepted the water and apology with a curt nod before settling on the far side of the sofa without thinking of it. He cocked his head to the side, and I simply went with my error in seating. If it could be called an error.

"And please. Whomever you were with. Be careful."

I wanted to roll my eyes, but his words slid through me, causing me to nod and change the subject.

"I am planning a small soft opening in two weeks. A Christmas party for friends and coworkers. Since I haven't got any family apart from Sascha, I thought it would be a fun way to show the hotel. Would you like to come?"

He looked confused for a brief second, quickly rearranging his expression to the cool, blandly friendly mask I most often saw. "Send me the date and time, and I will have a look at my schedule."

I scoffed and started rolling up my sleeve. "I'm not asking you to help me move a sofa, Javier. It's a Christmas party. Whether you are able to make it or not is irrelevant. I asked if you would like to come."

"Yes. Also, please, call me Javi." He sat beside me, pulling his sterilizing supplies. I realized after the first few times that this was all for show. His saliva itself was sterilizing, so I put my hand on him.

"You don't have to do that; I know it's unnecessary." He seemed to wrestle with something before placing the kit on the floor.

"I was going to ask if it would be all right with you if I took from another vein today." My breath quickened immediately. I hated that he could hear that. "Specifically, the neck, as I feel your arms might need a rest. And I might need something more free flowing."

My heart kicked up and his eyes flew to my chest, rising and falling under the button-down shirt and balconette bra I wore. Was I ready for the neck? Based on the fact that mere mention of it sent my mind back to last night's fantasy of his mouth over my entire body, I was either completely ready, or never would be. So, I nodded and waved my hand as though he asked if he could take the extra chair at my table.

"That's fine." I knew from previous conversations that I had to undress that side of my top half in case there was any dripping. Slipping my arm from the unbuttoned half of my shirt, I attempted conversation. "Why not have me call you Javi from the beginning? You introduced yourself to Sascha as Javi."

He smirked a bit. "Why not have me call you Lily?"

I bristled at the question. "Only Sascha calls me Lily. It was my parents' nickname for me."

"And that desperate looking boy from the market?"

Fucking Connor.

"My ex. Connor. He is well aware no one but Sascha calls me Lily. I believe that was for your benefit." I rolled my eyes, and Javi made a sort of guttural "ah" sound from deep in his throat, which sounded like it would feel glorious on other parts of me.

"Then I will only call you Ophelia. But you can call me Javi." He winked, and I smiled for him, because the wink was rather adorable on his serious vampire-about-to-feed face. Plus, the way *Ophelia* ran off his tongue made me want to feel it everywhere. *Christ's sake, Ophelia.*

He motioned for me to rest my head back against the cushions in the corner of the sectional. I did so, awkwardly, trying to figure out where my hands should go. He leaned over me slowly, his eyes never leaving mine, gauging my anxiety level, I assumed. The hazel seemed to move from green to brown and back again, a fluid change I would bet mimicked his mood and temperament.

"I am going to hold your head with my hand to keep you supported. If it is too much, tap me three times. Okay?"

"Yes," I breathed.

His chest pressed against mine, the soft knit of his T-shirt like phantom fingers on my exposed skin. Dear God. I have never before been so aware of a T-shirt on my skin. His hand, as promised, slipped behind my head. I knew he was sniffing me, and I wondered what it was he was working out. The wonder ceased when the points of his teeth dragged along the taut side of my neck. A fuse was lit under me, crackling in a line where his teeth grazed. For the first time, I could feel his heartbeat against my chest. I closed my eyes and counted the beats, realizing they were in accord with mine. His heart beat as fast as mine. I couldn't start thinking that meant anything other than he was hungry and finally getting blood from a free-flowing vein. The points of his teeth scraped at my neck, teasing the skin. My hips lifted, finding them flush against his. I expected him to adjust but realized there was nowhere for him to go, and I couldn't bring myself to lower mine. He murmured a "ready?", lips on my skin like a kiss.

I didn't have time to answer as the heat of his mouth opened against my neck and his fangs pierced my skin. I screamed out, a flash of pain making me grasp his sides. His hand tightened around the base of my skull. I knew he could break my neck. Crush me. Tear my throat out and lap every ounce of my blood for hours. I knew he could kill me and bring me back, a demon inside me as well. Yet, I knew he wouldn't, and so I relaxed my grip on him where my long nails had made him bleed. A sound of a starving man fed rumbled against me when the sucking began. My breasts swelled in answer, wishing he could take from them. Wishing he could feed from every part of me. My hips pushed up, not even realizing what I was doing. He paused his sucking, tongue circling around the bite marks. I whimpered, and he bit back down, a long, hard pull sending stars across my eyes. There was no sterile room. No kitchen filled with various types of waters. No employer and employee. There was simply Javier, latched on to my neck, making me feel vibrations in the universe I'd never been privy to. My hips were bucking, and I may have voided my contract because I had little control over myself in that moment and he was not stopping me. Slowly, his knee pushed my own apart to allow him better access to my throat. I opened for him, his knee moving further past the hem of my skirt, stopping just before my wet groin.

He knew the reaction I had to the feedings, so I was no longer embarrassed. When his knee touched my crotch, I gasped. He groaned, sucking at the neck wound harder. My nails dug back into his tight skin. I lifted, rubbing his knee with the exposed parts of me. My underwear had shifted to the side, my bare flesh against his trousered knee. His suckling changed to a rhythmic rolling in time with my heart. There was not one part of me that was not bursting with sensation. His whole body sank into the rhythm, his knee rubbing against me. My hands still clasped his sides, anchoring me against him as I rode his knee, wetness seeping from the side of my pants and onto his trousers.

"Do you feed off everything?" I found myself asking, breathless and in motion. He groaned into me, pulling his fangs out so just the tips remained against my heated, bloodied skin.

"I feed off every bodily fluid that isn't waste." His head remained where it was. I knew he was not done feeding, but his body still rocked against me. My stomach dropped. "Your arousal fluid, menstrual blood, semen. All of it." His teeth slid back in, and I nearly choked on the orgasm that ripped through me. He pulled away quickly. I didn't realize he was on the other side of the room, facing away from me.

"I'm sorry," I said. Because we both knew it was not my fault, but I had also pushed the boundaries.

"No," he said, voice like frost. "I lost control a bit. I am sorry. As something has shifted between us, I am happy to release you from our agreement. With severance pay, of course."

"What?" I tugged my skirt down and buttoned my top. "Javi, I..."

He looked up at me, an odd, darkened look on him.

"I need the money." It wasn't technically true anymore, but it helped. He held my stare for a moment before muttering a "very well". I stood, taking a swig of my fizzy water, feeling uncomfortable with stickiness between my legs.

"Also," I said, clearing my throat. "I don't mind. I, um, enjoyed it. I enjoy it."

"You should go." He was still facing away, his words spoken with a look over his shoulder.

What the fuck. Fuck him.

I stormed from the room, slamming the door behind me. Of all the things that have made me uncomfortable in this arrangement, those last three words tipped the scales.

She might be my ruination.

CHAPTER FIVE

OPHELIA

When I first met Connor, we were at uni. He, a transplant from up north. I, a newly orphaned eighteen-year-old with a small life insurance payout and enough funds to cover my education. He made me giggle and stay out too late snogging in people's gardens. He was new and everything I wished I could be. Free, charming, and had everyone, men, women, professors, all wrapped around his finger. We became iconic. Ophelia and Connor. A love story in D minor.

It took me years to notice the way he'd call me crazy for suggesting he was seeing other people. The way he'd kiss the top of my head and laugh, telling me I had a vivid imagination. The way he would tell me to just go back to sleep when I could see the glow of his phone as he texted other people all night long. *Just a friend* was uttered more times than I could count.

A couple of years after we moved to London, my career managing a hotel booming, a woman walked into my workplace, asking to see me. She sat in my office and told me my partner had been fucking her for a year. She told me how he liked it and how he told her about me and said I was abusive, and he wanted to leave but couldn't because I was the bread winner. She said they often had others as well and she never wanted to tell him no.

I walked out of my job, took a train back to my hometown, and started over. He followed, of course. He said it was all my vivid imagination That a crazy bitch from his work was stalking him. I believed him for a day. I let him into my bed. I let him into my head. Until Sascha pulled the duvet from our bodies and told him if she ever saw his skinny face near me again, she would make him wish he had been eaten alive by rabid crows.

Connor became my control. The measure upon which I gauged other men and what I wanted or needed from them. I vowed, Sascha as my witness, shots of cheap tequila our holy sacrament, that not only would I never let Connor into my head again, I would never let a man make me feel less than. I would never laugh again at a joke made at my expense or back down from a gut feeling. If that meant I was single the rest of my life, then so be it. Walking out of Javier's, having rubbed the most intimate parts of me against him, whilst he drank my blood and groaned, then being told to leave? I was not going to lay down for that.

I showed up for our next feeding, not a minute late, dressed in my work attire with my sleeve rolled to the elbow. I let him feed without interaction, watched for the funds to transfer to my account, and left again. Javier was my job. He didn't have to occupy space in my head. He tried to speak, and I put my earbuds in, volume up. He looked at me, his brows pinched in a sort of consternation. Did he feel the need to control me or this arrangement? Or was he sorry for how he reacted? I didn't stick around to ask. I was the ATM, the vending machine. I got paid to give him what he needed. Not. A. Damned. Thing. More.

CHAPTER SIX

Typically, I would not have chased down a donor who was not in compliance. If they couldn't control themselves and did not wish to see me for our scheduled appointments, I must move on. In some cases, it was a matter of life and death. Not for me, of course, but if I went too long without human blood, my sanity slipped, and humans around me were a never-ending buffet. It had been quite some time since I'd sunk to that base level. In fact, I believed it was toward the end of the Great War when I'd last fallen victim to my inner demon.

Europe had been on the verge of total starvation. America had stepped in to fight, yet food was scarce to begin with, and the provisions brought by the Americans quickly ran out. Tanks and motorized vehicles began replacing horses and furred cavalry, causing scores of dead animals to spread disease. I lost eight donors to disease. Two I let go as their own nutrition was not being met. I fought. I lay in trenches with dying men, the stench of blood, viscera, and death a shawl over my person for months. I pushed at my hunger, wanting only to help end the blasted war.

One day, our position was compromised. A small battalion descended on us, and my blood hunger made me the most formidable opponent. The most precious soldier. Until my own men turned against me, and I could no longer keep my gorging to the enemy. From those ghastly trenches full of shit and bodies, I emerged to terrorize the French countryside. My reign lasted a little over a month until a fellow vampire caught wind of my actions and came to secure me. He chained me in his cellar, in a place far removed from civilization, until I was fully under control.

So, I did not take my margin of humanity lightly. When I barked at Ophelia to take care of her needs after seeing the thick wetness spread across her leggings, I knew she might leave. Especially as she had stopped speaking to me because of the day I encouraged her to ride my knee. Half of me wanted her to leave; I'd never been one to react to my donors, regardless of their reactions to me. The squirming and heat in her cheeks, I'd been turning the other cheek to—literally. Smelling her arousal drip from her and spread over those bone shard-colored leggings? I was teetering on the knife point of tearing through the crotch of them and sucking every fluid from her warm sex. I told her to just touch herself. And take care of herself whilst I fed. She was offended. Not by the actual directive, but the tone I'd used. Just as she was that day she rode my knee and I had to pull away because I had cum in my trousers. She hadn't known that though. She hadn't known I used the damned tone because it was me who was having an issue. I should have let her go. I simply couldn't.

The fact that Ophelia was professional enough to agree to come back gave me hope for both of us. Both of our livelihoods depended on this working relationship. She did not think it would be necessary to service herself whilst I fed, though the offer stood. I would not be offended nor put off if it kept our agreement in terms. She arrived today a minute before our time, which in Ophelia time, was late. She was breathless and pulling a blazer from her shoulders though the air was starting to move into the bitter stage of autumn.

"I'm sorry, I had to take the train from Bristol, and one was broken down, so there were loads of people and stops." She caught her breath and smiled. "I had a successful meeting with my investors, and we found several artists who agree to show their work in the hotel. Hence the uptight outfit." She gestured to her fitted dress and heels. I turned from the doorway with what may have seemed indifference. She flung her bag down and flopped into the armchair. I handed her a bottle of water, which she downed in three gulps. "Thank you."

The faint trace of sweat radiated from her, and I took my time swabbing her arm, readying myself for our first session since I noticed the change. I needed to make totally certain I didn't make her feel uncomfortable. I lifted her forearm to my mouth, asking the question with my eyes. She nodded and watched me plunge into her skin. The slap of her thighs clamping together startled me, though I merely slowed my pace, massaging the skin of her bicep. The blood flowed into my mouth freely, as though it were missing the journey. Her breathing began to keep pace with my suckling, her hips rolling with each inhale. I slid my eyes to her lap, where her fingers toyed with the hem of her skirt. A drop of blood escaped, so I let my tongue dart out to lick it before it dripped. She squeezed her eyes shut and seemed to take another deep breath before moving her fingers under the black material that kept my sight from devouring her whole.

"I'm sorry," she whispered.

I could hear the wet invasion of her fingers as she touched herself. Each slip a sort of waterboarding to my sanity. I squeezed her knee with my free hand attempting to say there was no need to apologize. The contact made us both gasp, so I slowed my sucking as her movements sped up. Had the arm of her chair not been blocking me, she would have been able to see the painful erection I had jamming itself against my trousers.

I wanted nothing more than to let it out and pump myself while suckling her soaked clit and feeding from the apex of her thighs. I wanted to feel the hot blood run messy down my chest and watch her look at me in horror and desire, until we were both blood drunk. Instead, I applied pressure to her bite, and cleaned her up as she rode the final waves of orgasm. I immediately moved to the kitchen and stood behind the counter, filling a glass for her with fizzy water and pushing over a few bits of dark chocolate. She sat there still, her face in one hand, the other hand curled in on itself, still glistening with her cum. I cleared my throat.

"I am humiliated, Javier," she said, not looking at me.

"Please do not be. I offered for a reason."

She was nodding. When I felt my own inappropriate reaction was under control, I walked to her with a baby wipe and cleaned her hand. Each finger was coated, thus I made a point of removing evidence of anything from them. She watched, an expression near to horror on her face, melting into one of acceptance.

"This is a partnership, Ophelia."

CHAPTER SEVEN

OPHELIA

I walked out of Javier's, sticky and lightheaded. I had never even touched myself like that in front of my ex or any partner for that matter. Javier and I both needed the partnership to work. I understood why he suggested it and why I didn't offer much resistance when my core started pounding. What sent me over the edge was once his tongue licked the blood droplet. It was either touch myself or wait and watch the cum run down my thighs. I could have sworn the feeding took longer than usual. Almost as if he had slowed the process to watch me. What a ridiculous thought to have. But then, the way he cleaned my fingers...there was a palpable hunger in his eyes as he wiped each digit, the evidence of my own desire absorbed by the cloth. What had I gotten myself into?

To top off the awkwardness of the evening, I had scheduled drinks with Sascha directly after my session with Javier. I walked into Lovely Lola's, nearly turning my ankle on a cobble, which had the audacity to catch my five-inch studded Valentinos. Shoes which were a relic from a bygone era. Or a bygone financial situation.

Think positively, Ophelia, I told myself, ducking into the vaguely pink lighting and out of the building rain. *You are so close to getting it all again. So close.*

Sascha sat at the first high table, blocking my view of with whom she sat. Probably some attention seeker. God forbid a woman should be alone in a bar for five minutes without a man to accost her. I ordered a G&T before making my way to the table. Once in view, I sloshed a bit of spirits from my cut-glass tumbler.

"Connor, what are you doing here?"

"Having a drink with Sascha," he answered, holding up a watered-down whiskey, which looked cloudy in the rose-tinted room.

Sascha pushed her elbow into me, but it did nothing to temper my annoyance. Why hadn't she told him to fuck off as she normally did?

"Sit down, Lily love," Connor said, smothering a burp.

My stomach roiled seeing it. Nothing was more unattractive than Connor off his rocks pissed, burping. Compared to my experience a quarter hour earlier, I was failing to see what I ever saw in Connor to begin with. An admittedly thin penis, classic narcissistic personality, and daily drinking was less than what I would look for in a partner. Yet I'd wasted eight years of my life with him.

"Why are you here, Connor?" Two sips of gin, and I was feeling the blood loss. Plus, the fury at this skinny-necked excuse for a man in front of me. He had been attractive to me once upon a time. A catalogue face and catwalk body, catching eyes wherever he went. Yet each time I discovered he'd taken another stranger to bed, it was like a chisel filed off his attractiveness, leaving the withered shell of male beauty. All I saw now was excuses, lies, and self-indulgence in a jacket he probably couldn't afford. I palmed a bunch of Marcona almonds from Sascha's dish and chewed so that I wouldn't say what was on the tip of my tongue. He burped again, looking slightly green and panicked.

"I saw Sascha walking and joined her here while waiting for you."

"Here!" I yelled through the almonds. "Why are you in town?"

Honestly, I don't think the question was intelligible, but I managed to spray him with Spanish salted almonds, and my meaning was clear enough. He patted his face with a cocktail serviette, and there was a gurgling just under the sound of Phoebe Bridgers crooning from the speakers. Sascha and I loved it here early in the evenings because the music was fab. The owner kept it chill until the students came round wanting a club atmosphere.

"I miss you," he said, though again there was a gurgling. I rolled my eyes and chugged my drink so I didn't throw it at him. No sense wasting good local gin. The gurgling sounded again, louder, and Connor's face looked like unsalted butter. "Excuse me," he said and left the table in a rush.

"You finished?" Sascha asked me, and I realized then she had been unusually quiet for my best mate.

I nodded yes but grabbed the rest of the almonds.

"Good." She hopped from the stool, her slight height only helped a tad by platform boots. I followed her out the door. "Because I dumped like four doses of laxative in his whiskey the moment we sat down. He'll be shitting himself for days."

"Sasch!" I knocked her on the shoulder. "That's illegal!"

She made a dismissive gesture and kept walking.

"Why did you even have that much laxative on you?"

"One, because I have it on hand if I need to slim down quickly for an event." She held up her hand to cut off the lecture she knew I'd give. "Two, when you told me Dickface was in town, Lily, I wanted to make him hurt. Like, flaming arsehole hurt. Because he was a flaming arsehole to you. In more ways than one."

I let out a bubble of laughter I had needed to release for days. It shook me and followed us into the small Indian restaurant where she steered us. "The last place he will look for us right now is an Indian." She winked and I slumped in my seat, wishing I could tell her about Javier. About the fact that I was still sticky and unsatisfied, thinking of my boss' teeth in me while I rode my own fingers in front of him. Next to him. Wishing his fingers, his mouth, his fucking fangs, were attached to my wanny.

"You getting sick, Lil?"

I cracked a poppadum and spooned some chutney onto it.

"No, just tired, I think. Went from the meeting in Bristol to my job with Javier. Then seeing Dickface didn't help."

"Okay. 'Cause you look like you're feeling poorly." She was eying me suspiciously, and I wondered if she could see right through to my filthy knickers. "Javi treats you all right? He's not a monster?"

I snorted, covering my mouth, lest I spray more food across a table. I said he was a perfectly professional boss. What I didn't say to her was that he was professional apart from drinking my blood in an incredibly sensual way, which wasn't allowed to be sexual, yet I'd orgasmed and had the excess fluid wiped from my fingers by him. Just not a monster. Monsters were rarely the ones with fangs and complicated pasts. Monsters were the pretty ones who fed you platitudes and lies until you didn't have a clear notion of who you once were.

"Okay, well, then no more booze for us tonight. We've got suits to woo in the morning." She held up a glass of fizzy water.

"Permits were filed this afternoon. Ready for the fun part?" I asked, smiling at her.

She nodded once and touched the tip of my nose. We were going to take our lives back. Or mine at least. Sascha always had a second income and was independently wealthy thanks to a family with legitimate claims to the patent on several items half the world used in their daily lives.

"To the fun part." The chime of our glasses clinking rang in the din of the small restaurant, muffled by the sizzling curries brought to our table. To many more tomorrows labeled as "the fun part".

Cathedral Yard was the view from the hotel's front windows, and it always gave me a bit of a giggle. Seeing as I moved from working in a building that had once been a rectory, to a job feeding a vampire, the juxtaposition was comedic. Not that the Church of England isn't just as sordid in its history as I assumed Javier had been. Yesterday, Sascha and I had stayed late, decorating the library and foyer for the holiday party. She talked me down from regretting the party all together.

"There are only two working toilets," I argued. "And what if catering needs the kitchen? The kitchen is not ready. It's just this bloody room."

She laughed and strung a garland of stars around my neck, pulling me in to flick my nose. "It's not a grand opening, Lily. It's an early Christmas party. Like a pre-Christmas, Christmas party, seeing as it's a month before Christmas. You and me and thirty of our closest friends."

"You're my only close friend. Everyone else is like a base level friend." I took the garland and hung it over the evergreen-swagged mantel. Light caught on the points of stars, reminding me of Javier's fang tips when he allowed them to show. I felt a swish in my gut. Sascha looked at me and smirked.

"Javi coming?" she asked.

I wanted to shoot her a seething glare, but that would have been too much of a protest. Instead, I shrugged, turning to adjust one of the heavy sapphire draperies where it had gotten caught on a chair leg.

"You know who is coming, though I haven't worked out yet if it's a good thing?" I perched on the arm of the chair and waited for her answer.

"Pete."

"He's our architect. Why wouldn't it be a good thing? Plus, he's really lovely when you get his work hat off."

She twitched her lips and pushed a pointed strand of black hair behind her ear, where I noticed a new piercing on her rook. "You know I get gut feelings about people. He seems…off. Like he's hiding something."

We turned out the lights, leaving the room in a state of waiting, like the opening scene of The Nutcracker. I turned up my collar as we stepped out on the path separating the hotel from the green in front of the cathedral.

I would have liked to say Sascha was paranoid or even overprotective of me, but truthfully, she really did have a good radar on anything dodgy. Why she had no suspicious feelings about Javier was beyond me. He was a vampire, for Christ's sake.

In the mottled light of night, the monolith that was Exeter Cathedral loomed, dark and ominous, casting us in puzzle pieces of dark and light. Such Goliath beauty always made me wary. In my experience, things of sculpted, forcefully hewn exquisiteness never held up to that which had natural elegance. Something I wished I'd seen in Connor. Especially considering both my mum and dad were organically winsome people. Neither had to try hard to be lovely. They simply were. Javier was a vampire and not what one might deem as natural, yet his features, from the dimpled chin to the spears of lines from his hazel eyes, were gorgeous in and of themselves.

The skin on the back of my neck prickled with alarm as we made our way across the yard toward the high street and city center. I wouldn't be moving from my rough, student let flat until January, when a new flat just opposite the hotel would be ready. However, I did take advantage of Sascha's hospitality and had been staying on in her guest room. Once I knew I was moving back up in the ranks of my own head, I caved and agreed to move in with her. Had I been too stubborn the past couple of years? Probably. Did I need to prove to myself I was more than capable of reinventing my career and life and thus suffering the late-night drinking games and parties of my young neighbors? Of course. But I was done suffering. And Sascha's guest mattress was heavenly. A relative haven after always feeling on edge where I had been living.

The prickling sensation did not ease up after turning up Keep Street where my best mate lived. She and I gave each other a quick side eye, and I knew she felt it too. That heaviness in the air when something just wasn't right. I cursed myself for not being in better shape. For feeling like my thighs were a shade too big and weak.

The street inclined, forcing us to push harder to crest it. My phone was tucked in my jacket pocket, keeping it out of the cold and wet. Sascha's was in hand ready to fire off a call. Headlights blinded us, and the sound of tires on a rain-soaked street drowned out the sound we should have heard. The tapping of shoes on concrete. A woman's heeled boot or a man's dress shoes. Pressure built behind my eyes in an inevitable feeling of attack.

Sascha was down before I registered her moving. A snarl rent the night. I spun, breathing an erratic metronome I could not tame as I sought what we were dealing with. In the streetlamp-dappled darkness, a figure crouched over Sascha on the icy concrete. My feet rooted to the spot, a trap of enthrallment I had felt once before. Something keeping me from getting to my favorite person. Sascha kicked up a platform boot landing the blow. A blur of movement told me the attacker had fled. I reached down with a shaking hand and pulled Sascha to her feet. She had a hand to her neck, and it came away with blood. My stomach dropped. I yanked her back to the pavement and continued stomping at breakneck speed until we were locked behind her door, draperies drawn, alarm set.

I poured from the kettle, watching the tea bags float, hoping I hadn't caused the attack. It didn't look or feel like Javier. It didn't smell like Javier. I blinked, wondering when I'd begun to recognize his scent. He smelled bright and green and just a little musky. Like having a lie in on a summer morning in Spain.

Christ, Ophelia, I thought.

The smell of whatever had attacked Sascha was more like cologne. Like something expensive yet obvious. A designer poster on a counter in John Lewis. I set the mug down in front of Sascha. She held her phone, camera lens turned around, as she blotted the wound on her neck. It had looked torn and ghastly in the flickering lights along the street. Now it was slightly raised but closed. Not even puckered. Her eyes met mine.

"Care to tell me what you know, Lily?" Her voice was steely, not accusatory. I sat hard on a Philip Stark Ghost Chair, wondering if anyone found them comfortable. "I have been mugged before. My handbag has been stolen. I've had my drink tampered with. I've been pushed around at a club. I have never, until tonight, been followed from work to home and had my neck torn open, only for it to heal in the span of ten minutes. While I am hard pressed to send into gasps and tremors, you tend to be more easily spooked. And you aren't. Not enough. So, let's start with what you know, Lil."

Everything in this flat was too white. My eyes burned looking for a place to focus. Focus and tell her what I was under no circumstances allowed to tell. Even though the thing I am not allowed to talk about just threatened her life. Bloody hell.

"Give me a sec, Sasch," I said, darting to the guest room with my phone in hand.

Was that you? I texted Javier, wanting him to say yes. Wanting him to say no.

Was that me what, Ophelia?

I strummed my fingers on the edge of the bed, toeing off my boots and socks, the adrenaline finally wearing off. I found a spot just above the automatic roman shade over the window and focused on it.

We were followed home, and Sascha was attacked.

Attacked how? May I call you?

I exhaled and punched his contact instead. He picked up immediately. "Are either of you hurt?"

"Well, I'm not, and though there were clearly bite marks on her at the scene, it is just shiny and blood smeared now."

I heard him swear in Spanish on the other end. Something relaxed in me knowing it truly was not him. But somehow there was another of his kind in my town. Following me.

"I assume the person was not identified?" he asked.

I laughed in a dark burst. "That was not a person," I snapped. There was silence on the other end. "No, I did not see a face. It was a man. His shoes were something with a hard sole. As in not trainers. They made tapping or clicking noises." Not that that was helpful, but it was something I noticed. "Sascha is asking what I know. She suspects something."

"What have you told her?" he asked, voice light.

"Nothing. I came into the other room to ask what *you* know. I signed an NDA, remember?"

"Somehow I thought you would have told her," he admitted. "I didn't think you two kept secrets."

I scrubbed a hand over my face. We didn't keep secrets, but a contract is a contract.

"Is she stable?"

I was nodding, which he couldn't see.

"Yeah, just angry." I heard him chuckle. "Javier?" There was an mmm sound on the other end. "She can't turn, right?"

"Have you?" he asked. I rolled my eyes. "No, Ophelia. She cannot turn unless she is drained until the brink of death and there is an exchange of fluids before she's reborn." I shuddered, feeling nauseous. He continued, "Make sure your doors are locked. Call me if anything untoward occurs. Any hour. And I will see you tomorrow night. Yes?"

"You're coming?" I asked, feeling slightly stupid.

"I said I would. Now it also seems prudent I am there." Ah, then not for the party or me. For the investigation. "Good night, Ophelia. And if you think it wise, you may tell Sascha about our arrangement. If it seems an issue, please let me know so I can arrange to leave town. Yes?"

"Okay," I mumbled. "Okay."

I sat with my hand on my forehead, feeling like I had spent the night under a bottle of vodka. Seeing as all I had to drink all day was copious amounts of Earl Gray, and I have a hard and fast anti-vodka rule, I blamed stress. The door cracked open, Sascha standing there, half dressed. Our eyes held, and I opened my mouth to speak.

"Vampire?" she asked. My mouth fell open, but I nodded. "You don't have to speak if it will breach your NDA. I heard you mention it."

I scooted over on the bed, and pulled the covers back, making room for her. We lay facing one another like we had done for decades. Sisters when neither of us had a biological one. Her neck was clean. She had removed her makeup and cleaned all the blood, a fresh T-shirt, looking like it belonged to someone else, over her.

"I wondered about Javi," she said. "That wasn't Javi though."

"No." I pulled the duvet up under my chin. She did the same.

"Did you know who that was? You can just say yes or no."

"No. Neither did Javier."

"Do you feed Javi?" I looked toward the window over her shoulder. "Lil."

"I do. I make pots of money for it. He's very professional." The phrase "you should go" rang through my head, making feel like throwing something.

"I'm jealous," she said with a wicked grin. "I mean, what I just had happen did not feel good. But Javi's mouth on me..." I pulled my hand out and playfully punched her shoulder. She laughed. "I knew vampires were real. I swore I saw one feeding at a club once in Ibiza. It was intense. But here? It seems so...boring here. Like there's literally nothing to do in Exeter."

"We need to be careful, Sasch. I think whoever followed us tonight was not interested in getting us off club style. I think it was more a drain us and toss us into the hedges near the castle wall."

We both shivered.

"What did Javi say?" she asked.

"He will see us tomorrow. And to call if anything weird happens."

"He did not say 'weird'," she said.

"No. He said 'untoward'." I laughed scrunching the pillow to my face.

She flicked off the light, and we chatted, drifting off like we were twenty again. I dreamt of footsteps. Footsteps echoing on pavement. Down flagstone halls. Across wood floors. Footsteps trailing me everywhere I went. I woke covered in sweat, yesterday's makeup a skid mark across the pillow and Sascha not in bed.

OPHELIA

My office behind the reception desk at the hotel was mostly bare. A desk I'd bought from an estate sale, coupled with a Ghost chair pilfered from Sascha's dinner party for twelve set up, and a strange painting from my parents' house I'd never been able to part with was all there was.

I sat, my legs stretched out in front of me in an unattractive position so as to not crease my dress. The party was set to begin in moments, but my mind was whirling with dread. Would the building hold? Would the plumbing keep up? Was the vegan option also gluten free, killing two birds? I couldn't remember if I'd asked that of the caterers. Would Connor somehow show up and ruin it? And mostly, were we safe? I hated admitting I was afraid to walk home alone.

When the music began playing, that was my cue to head out. Sascha was waiting, drink in hand, talking to a couple of friends from uni and an investor. I spotted Pete across the room, chatting with Angela, an old friend of my mum's, who lived only an hour or so away in Plymouth.

I nabbed a coupe of champagne from a passing tray and raised the glass to them. I started to make my way over but heard the door open directly behind me and saw Javier walk in.

His hair was perfectly in place, like a living shadow. He wore a black suit, black shirt. I pulled another glass and handed it to him, careful to not jostle too much and spill on my own emerald-green velvet dress. We walked into the room, wordless and slightly awkward. I moved to Angela, leaning in for a kiss on both cheeks, and introduced Javier.

"I've just met your architect, Ophelia, love. Seems a good lad," Angela said, face flushed from champagne, though she'd likely only been there a quarter hour. "Oh, where's he gone?" She looked around. "Never mind."

She patted my hand and walked to the tray of nibbles, grabbing an ornament filled with cranberry cocktail as she went. When we came up with the idea for the cute drinks, it never occurred to me just how ridiculous people would look drinking direct from the Christmas balls. The forethought had been emptying them into glasses. As I looked about the room, there were many sets of mouths, plugging from Christmas ornaments. I shook my head.

"You can never plan for everything, can you?" Sascha asked from behind me, following my gaze. "Hallo, Javi," she said, leaning over for a double cheek kiss. "You smell divine. Arancia di Capri?" she asked.

He nodded with a sniff of a laugh. "Are you well?" he asked her. His eyes locked on to her neck, which sent a strange zing of jealousy through me. I was never jealous of Sascha. Ever. She waved him off and drank a large sip.

"Not like I've never been bitten before." She winked.

He laughed, draining his glass. He seemed...nervous. His eyes moved about the room.

"Doesn't Lily look exquisite tonight, Javi?" Sascha asked.

I choked on a pomegranate seed in my drink and stared daggers at her. Javier kept looking around, turning this way and that. He set the empty glass down on a passing tray and walked off, shoulders stiff.

"Sasch!"

She smirked and swaggered away.

I moved through the crowd, tidying as I went, answering questions about the opening, accepting congratulations, and finally, sneaking to a corner to shove three brie and prosciutto pastries in my mouth before I passed out from hunger. A low chuckle sounded from the corridor. I had moved a bookcase to block the part of the hall which was off limits. Pete stood in the narrow space between the wall and bookcase, arms crossed.

"A wee bit hungry?" he asked, eyes twinkling.

I laughed, dabbing the party from my lips, and taking a swig of wine. "I need to stop going all day without eating," I told him, leaning against the damask papered wall.

"I haven't eaten since last night either. Makes the alcohol go straight to the head." He mimed getting hit in the head. He took a step toward me, and I froze.

Click. Click. Hard soled shoes on flagstone floors.

My hand shook on my glass, and I dropped my cocktail serviette. "Here, let me," he said bending to pick it up. As he rose and balled the dirty serviette in his hand, I caught a whiff of his cologne, and my body locked in a familiar feeling of imprisonment. Pete. My architect. He had been the vampire who attacked us? Pete with his easy smile and bawdy jokes?

"You are looking a bit peaky, Ophelia," he said, reaching a hand to me and feeling my cheeks with the back of his hand.

"I'm fine," I gritted out with extreme effort. He moved closer, running his hand on my face and neck, his thumb pressing on my jugular.

"Shall I take you home? I think maybe you've had too much to drink. I'll just let them know."

My feet would not move, so all I could do was drop my glass and listen as it shattered at my feet. Sparkling wine and shards of glass sprayed up my legs, splinters embedding themselves into my bare legs and feet. Tears ran down my face in pain, yet I still could not move. Warmth dribbled down my shins from the tiny assailants in my skin. The sound drew other footsteps and without warning, Pete was gone, and I tumbled forward. The effort my body had been putting into getting away from him launched me forward when his pull ceased. I fell into the empty bookcase, my toe crunching on glass beneath my shoe. Javier and Sascha grabbed my elbows and led me to my office. They shut the door behind us, and when Javier leaned over me, I knew he was scenting Pete.

"Pietro Alfonsi," Javier growled. I didn't know speech could come through an animalistic sound like that. Sascha was wiping blood from my legs with a baby wipe from my desk drawer, plucking glass where she found it. "I knew I smelled him the day you came in after a drink with him."

"Pete?" Sascha asked, acting surprised.

I nodded, finally able to use my voice again. She had been cagey all day, snapping at me and slipping out for more breaks than we had time to take. I blamed it on nerves, but truly Sascha was not acting like Sascha. Even her surprise seemed false.

"What does he want?" I asked.

Javier tipped my chin up, probably checking if I had been hurt. "Me. He wants me."

Quiet fell on us.

"I hired him on recommendation from the same acquaintance who led me to you," I said, numb and cold. Javier's cheeks hollowed as he whispered something that sounded like a prayer.

"I need to get back to the party," I said. Both of them protested, yet I left the office anyway, knowing Pete wouldn't be there. I walked back out, drink in hand, ready to close the night and thank everyone for coming.

"We are having a long chat back at mine tonight. Both of you." Sascha indicated both Javier and me with her accusatory finger. Only Sascha would deign to spell out orders to a vampire. I gave a final wave, paid the caterers, and the three of us walked in the fairy-lit hush across Cathedral Yard toward Sascha's. Only tonight, it didn't feel so frightening.

"I think we should drink," Sascha announced, pulling a bottle of prosecco from the wine chiller. Normally I would tease her about prosecco being below her pay grade, despite both of us agreeing that we preferred it over most sparkling. Instead, I sat slumped on the twill of her overstuffed sofa and grunted. I didn't know if drinking more was a good idea. I didn't know if Javier being there was a good idea. So, I held out my hand for the glass when it was offered. The street beyond Sascha's lay silent. The occasional car drove past. The wind tinkered in the trees, a sort of jam session in the midnight hour. She switched on low-fi music, setting the bass to high and volume low.

Sascha downed her glass in one long sip, refilling it immediately. I had started to suspect maybe she self-medicated with alcohol. She fell onto the side of the sofa nearest Javier and snapped her fingers, the sound of her long nails like an alien insect.

"You want answers," Javier said matter-of-factly. He leaned back, crossing one wing-tip boot over a black knee.

Looks mattered to me. I could admit that. Style mattered. I liked design, what could I say? Javier never looked scruffy or unkempt. He was a specimen of a man. In his black-on-black attire, with those gorgeous dress boots, I was only keeping my drool at bay because I was tired, and fucking Pete had enthralled me. I was also increasingly worried about the elfin woman next to me on her third glass of Italian sparkling.

"I'd also like to not have glass in my legs and my best mate's throat not bitten, but sure, answers." I waved him on. Sascha's eyes took on the glassy effect they got when she was about ten minutes from crashing, so these answers either needed to be quick or she would get a morning recap.

"Pietro—Pete as you know him—was my friend for years. Centuries." Javier took a sip and watched the light dance in the bubbles of the glass. "Truth be told, he is what we would always call a leech. A sort of parasite that clings to the stronger of us. Though, as you may have noticed, he can be quite charming. Funny even." Javier cleared his throat and rolled his eyes. "We had a falling out about a hundred years ago. His political leanings were quite different from mine, and yet we both fell in love with the same woman. She was like us—"

"A vampire, you mean, or Italian?" Sascha asked with a slur.

"Vampire, yes." Javier sipped his drink. "She was working to undermine the Germans before the Great War. Years before, when unrest was only just beginning. She—" He cleared his throat and drank the rest of his drink. Sascha filled it again, ever the hostess. "She loved me. We had been married. I will spare you every detail."

Sascha leaned over, eyes a shade brighter, and said she would like every detail. I shushed her.

Javier carried on, "She did not love Pietro, despite stringing him along for months. It was not nice, but she was convinced he was hiding intelligence. She was correct in that. However, in finding him out, he inadvertently got her killed. Her cover was compromised, and I pulled her out, but he alerted authorities, thinking they would bring us to him for questioning. We were ambushed outside of Sarajevo."

"I thought you were hard to kill," I asked.

He met my eyes. "Hard, yes. Impossible? Nothing a blade severing the head and a bit of fire won't take care of." Sascha whistled. "Pietro blamed me. I'm sure he is aware it was more by his hand. We have made it a point to not cross paths since, but I have recently been endowed with Alicia's vast estate. As I said, she was my wife." He waved his hand dismissively.

"This is why I don't trust people," Sascha said, leaning further forward. Her hair was finger-waved, silent-film-star style, the silver of her frock a stark contrast. "Then they try to tell you you're wrong—just like Fuckface did to you and Shitmonger did to me. It's a constant cycle with men!" She shook her head and stood, muttering how every man is a cliché, then she walked from the living room and put herself to bed. Javier and I sat in silence for a beat too long.

"I take it she had a rough relationship?" he asked. I hadn't expected that angle of question.

"Her fiancé had an affair. She found out about it, he swore up and down it wouldn't continue, she was his one and only—you know the story. Then she learned to read his tells. She was so in love with him, she let it go. Months and months. She would be able to see the way his eyes moved when he was lying or the way he acted after seeing his— whatever—mistress. She finally left, and she's so good at sussing out men's rubbish now, it's scary. It's as though her heartbreak unlocked a superpower. She knew Pete was dodgy."

The flat was silent for a few long moments. My fingers fidgeted with the hem of my dress, pressing the velvet and releasing.

"You did look extraordinary tonight. You do, rather. Apologies for not saying so earlier. I knew he was around and couldn't distract myself."

His comment made me pause, glass to lips. I realized I

didn't want any more of the wine, and I set it aside. Why would saying I looked nice distract him?

"I can heal the glass cuts for you if you'd like."

I agreed and he kneeled on the carpet in front of me, then pierced his thumb on his incisor, allowing blood to well up. Each place he touched the blood, from my knees down to the arches of my feet, the cuts healed, glass even popping from the top layer of skin. His head at my legs, pressing his blood to my skin brought a wave of heat over me. His body tensed where I could feel his shoulder against mine.

"So, what do we do about Pete?" I asked, trying to not sound breathless. Wetness pooled in the thin hammock of my thong.

"I need to keep you close. I haven't sorted out all the details yet, I'm afraid."

"How close?" I asked, immediately regretting it.

His eyes looked up, dark lashes casting shadows in the room lit by only one wall sconce. He didn't answer, merely kept his eyes on me, his hand still wrapped around my ankle.

"Do you need to feed, Javier?" His hand squeezed and he shut his eyes. Eyes which had taken on a green glow I had told myself I'd previously imagined. "We missed yesterday. I missed yesterday," I corrected. "You can feed now if you need to."

"Please call me Javi." His voice was strained. I sat up a bit straighter and looked down at him. The cuff of his hand moved up from my ankle, palms sliding over my calf and knee where my dress bunched. "Are you certain?" he asked, thumb sweeping the divot of my inner thigh. My core pounded and nipples peaked.

"I'm sure, Javi," I answered, opening my legs wider, not really knowing what I was doing. I only knew he had said once he could feed from my inner thigh, and that was what I wanted now. He stood, and I felt embarrassed until he held his hand to me and led me to my room.

"I think privacy would benefit us both, no?"

It was then I saw the bulge in his suit trousers. My mouth went dry thinking he was turned on by me. Or the prospect of my blood, anyway. I sat on the edge of the bed, bare feet touching tip toes to the rug beneath them. I once again opened my legs, and he knelt between them, slowly pushing my dress up until it was a top, ruched around my waist.

"I would, perhaps suggest removing the undergarment. It might..." He didn't have to finish. I wiggled myself from them, feeling all at once self-conscious. Ever so slowly, he lowered his mouth toward my tense inner thigh. "Relax," he murmured, thumb massaging the tensed muscle.

How was I supposed to relax? I thought of running water and balmy seas. Warm sand and—I don't know if the probe of his teeth or the hot press of his mouth assaulted me first, but I swear my heart stopped.

He sucked hard, and I felt a warm rush through my veins and from my pussy. He exhaled, forehead pressing to my thigh. Both hands were touching me. One stayed near his mouth, massaging the skin more. The other rested on my opposite hip, his thumb stroking the crease of my hip. I wanted that thumb further in. I wanted his mouth further in. I threw my head back, chest rising and falling. He pulled his teeth from me, blood dripping down my leg. I knew the edge of the bedding was soaked with my cum. I knew he could smell it. There was a sheen in his eyes. They were a backlit screen, glowing in the dimmed room. His body moved in closer like he would press his shoulder into me. Instead, I grabbed his hair, fingers twining through the dark mass, then pushed him back in. Whatever gave me the prowess to be so bold was answered by his not leaving. The deep pull had my fingers digging into the base of his skull, bringing his head nearly flush with my dripping sex. The thumb moved to my center and drew a quick line up my crease. I swallowed a gasp, still wanting to be as quiet as possible, though I knew Sascha would be asleep until noon.

It was the first time he had touched me. Deliberately touched me in a sexual way. Sure, there had been times I could have sworn he felt it too. Needed it too. But he never gave it to me. He told me to leave. But here, now, his head between my legs, teeth in my artery, his thumb touched me once. It was a question. A request for permission to proceed. Or that was what I was telling myself.

"More," I said, feeling the thumb flick at my clit.

Oh my fucking God.

The lights had to have stuttered because there were bursts everywhere. The pull of my blood through his mouth matched the rhythm of his thumb along my seam. He ran his tongue in circles as his fangs dismounted from my artery. His eyes were a brilliant olive. A candle in a stained-glass window. I had never seen them that way before. Maybe they had never been so blood drunk. Or lust driven. He brought his thumb to his bloodied mouth and licked my cum from it. My vision swirled; the dark room had flashes of light and pockets of hot and cold.

"More," I repeated, my hand on the top of his head, ability to form coherent speech, gone. "Feed off it all."

His snarl sent a throb through me. He latched on like the demon his kind were portrayed as being. His hot tongue became pointed and hard, probing me, snaking up the recesses of me. Pushing in and out. How could a tongue change? Each time he pulled away a bit, I could see it hissing out, as though it begged for me too.

My back hit the mattress at the same time his hands yanked me to him harder. This is what people died for. Teeth grazed the sides of my labia in a friction which made me shake. Had the flat been on fire, I would not have noticed it. All the rapture was in the space between his mouth and my greedy cunt. The straps of my dress fell, exposing my breasts. My free hand stroked my own nipple, desperate for any and all traction. Part of me knew I would regret this come morning. The other part knew I would never know anything like this and would always want it. He consumed me. Lapping, suckling, pulling my hips closer so he could angle me better into him. From the base of my spine, like the first few sips of champagne, I felt a rising tingle. I moved my hips up and down along his lips, his fangs, his hot, pointed tongue, until the throb and tingle ran like rushing water, sweeping me away. I knew he was feasting on the amount of cum I released. I could see the glimmer off his bronze skin and felt a long release and dribble of blood before I collapsed and he sighed, contented and fed.

Long moments we stayed like that. His head lay against my thigh. My hand on his head, his on my hips. The rise and fall of his chest touched me, and I realized I'd never felt him breathe so much.

"Javi?"

He turned slightly. The sight of my wetness coating his skin, had me tighten again. He stroked the top of my leg.

"How did you become what you are?"

He sighed.

"My village was raided by catholic missionaries. We were of a secular culture deep in the mountains. My father sent me to find help as our people burned. I was found by a solider who promised aid if I would allow him a sip of my blood. I was frantic. I worried for my mother and brothers. I agreed. He drained me and fed me his blood. I was reborn alone on a rocky mountainside and returned to my village to find it totally desolate. As though no one had ever been there. Someone called to me from the last cottage. A young man like me. I saw at once he had met my same fate. We became brothers and grew up in this new life together. So to speak."

I hadn't realized I was combing my fingers through his hair until he stopped talking and looked up at me.

"This arrangement has changed," he said. "I believe for both of us. Enlighten me with your thoughts."

I propped myself on my elbows, still completely exposed. I looked at him, crouched between my legs, offering me every chance to get out. To get away. I knew he wasn't like Connor or Sascha's ex. I knew he wasn't a Pete or a cliché. He was someone else. Something else.

"I struggled with whether my arrangement with you made me feel..."

"Like a prostitute?" he asked. I nodded. "I don't want you to feel that way."

I pulled my fingertips all the way through his hair and over his ears. His eyes closed once. "I decided it didn't. I had decided I could feed myself and feed you. I could enjoy myself and make this work. I decided I liked it. And I wanted it. This." I gestured to him. To my naked lower torso. "All of it."

He was silent. Breathing and staring off. I could see the faint glow of his eyes in the nearly full dark.

"I want it too," he whispered. "God help me, but I do."

I might have been convinced Pietro was in town simply to rankle me or even to make amends after all these years. Not that I would acquiesce to anything resembling amenability when it came to him. A century later, and Alicia's death still hung heavy on my shoulders. Did I love her still? I supposed I always would. She was my first love. The only human I had felt the need to turn into this thing I am. And she loved it. Loved being a vampire. Loved the endless nights and thrill of the chase when we hunted. She was a predator, and I never made the mistake of underestimating her or her bloodlust. Still, I loved her.

I am a different man now, however. The things I find solace in, the things I find important in my own world and that which lies beyond my personal borders, have changed over this century. So, while I may always love Alicia, I no longer pined for her, nor felt the sting of her loss. Perhaps that made me more of a monster, but I have learned to live comfortably with my inner demons. Pietro, though, had never learned how to keep his in check. Once on a path of his twisted choosing, he couldn't be convinced to veer off course. He already attacked Ophelia's friend and clearly had designs on Ophelia herself. What I had to figure out is what his true end game was. And if he thought I would let him anywhere near Ophelia again, he would be paying a very steep price for that ignorance.

I had left Sascha's flat not long after I fed. This arrangement had gone so very differently than I had anticipated. I'd never wanted my donors before. My control was what had kept me alive all these years and losing it over a donor, no matter how attractive they were, no matter how sexually reactive they were to me, had never been an option. So, I kept asking myself, why now? Why Ophelia? Why did I feel the need to tear through walls when I thought of her or to find relief with my own goddamned hand every time she left our appointments? Last night was the last straw. Of course, things had been changing for weeks. Allowing her to ride my knee as I fed from her neck and let my chest lay against her peaked nipples was a true turning point. Physically so. Last night though, made this thing between us wholly different.

I was able to scent her arousal even as I healed the cuts in her legs. Even as my body heated from the anger I felt toward Pietro. She had only to open her legs so slightly as she asked if I needed to feed, and I knew we were colliding—a star collision—and only time would tell if our collision was world ending or world making. When she sat and rucked up her dress, baring herself to me like it was the most natural thing ever, I would have done anything for her. I would have worshipped her and not fed. I would have killed for her. And that thought alone was why I'd left soon after feeding. I needed my head sorted out, and staying between Ophelia's wet thighs, as they still pulsed with blood and want, my own arousal nowhere near sated, would make it impossible.

Half of me expected Pietro to be waiting for me outside the terraced flat block. But he was biding his time, which worried me more. The keypad on my front door was as loud as a siren in the late hour when I let myself back into my house. Ophelia always used the courtyard entrance, where my feeding room was. Looking around the interior of my townhome, I realized how perfect it was. How spotless and outfitted in minimalist designer bits and bobs I'd curated over the years. A Louis Vuitton Damier trunk, a mid-20th century Balmain train case I left open and filled with antique books. A custom-made Givenchy chess set I'd commissioned from Givenchy himself in the late 1950s. It was supposed to have been a gift for a colleague I'd met at Le Sorbonne, but he had inadvertently found out what I am, and I had been forced to use a glamour on him. So, the chess set remained in my possession, a cheeky reminder that I was always one move away from being in check. This home of mine had not seen a visitor in many years. Neither had my last home, nor the one before that. I was lonely. That thought made me stop in my tracks.

I looked into the mercury glass mirror, its red leucite edges casting an ominous glow to my face and how it distorted in the foggy reflection. I was not born too dissimilar to how I look now. I remember my mother's hazel eyes and my father's black hair. His chiseled jaw that sat ever so slightly off center. My mother would grab his chin and shake it when she was trying not to laugh at him. Of course, years of being the evolved predator I am had honed my features. Smoothed the lines of human strife from my skin, healed the freckles and scars. But I was still in the body of a human. I had just forgotten the emotional needs of humanity for so long, I wasn't certain I knew how to tap back into them. The first step was going to have to be how I approached this thing with Ophelia.

The steam from my too long shower blew from the bathroom when I came out, fogging my bedroom windows. I only ever used the heating to ensure my pipes didn't freeze, so my home was often a temperature that would be considered uncomfortably cold for a human. Steam met the frost laying thick on the glass, and I saw a notification on my phone cast a glow against the play of ice and heat.

Checking you made it home.

My long dead heart did a small skip that was so foreign to me. I sat heavily on the side of my bed, the towel around my hips opening.

Not that you can't defend yourself, Ophelia texted. *But you know, with Pete the Prick out and about, I wanted to check. X*

I smiled to myself, thinking of her flustered and typing out the text. She was probably in bed herself. Probably just got out of her own shower, the heating in Sascha's flat too high, so Ophelia was likely wearing only minimal clothing. I felt as though I could picture her small breasts peeking through a thin top. I could picture her knees bent, phone propped against them. Her scent was still all over me. My cock was hard, standing at attention, warring with the beating of my chest for the rush of blood in my body.

Safe and sound, Ophelia, I texted her, grabbing hold of my cock and squeezing.

I swear I can hear your accent even in the way you typed my name, she wrote.

I exhaled, pumping my hand, and hit the voice recorder on my phone.

"Ophelia," I said into it, slowing the syllables, and knowing my voice shook with the restraint of my building orgasm.

Jesus, Javi. I smiled at that. *I guess I'll see you next Thursday unless you need to feed before that.*

My hand tripped up reading that. I worked my hand harder, slipping over the head of my cock, imagining Ophelia's hand in its place. Her mouth, hot and eager. I wanted to tangle my hand in her mass of brown hair and hold her over me while she sucked. I spurt into my hand, quickly gathering the towel to wipe up. I really needed to get ahold of myself. Thursday was a long way away. My mouth went dry and thirsty thinking of the length of time.

If you have time, I find I am perhaps needing an extra feeding or so this week. It was a very good thing I had plenty of money, because clearly my food budget was the equivalent of eating at Michelin starred restaurants a few times a week. But she was worth it all.

Yeah, no worries. Monday, okay? I can be there early afternoon. I'll text.

Perfect. Thank you.

Okay, OMG this is going to be so awkward...

Yes? I was intrigued and yet somehow knew what she was going to ask.

Do you think we will be as...intense as tonight?

It can be as intense as you want, Ophelia. I find I am at your mercy.

Goodnight, Javi.

"Goodnight, Ophelia," I said into the voice recorder. I swore I could feel her shiver. God help me.

Sunday was quiet. Peeling cathedral bells punctuated each hour I sat in a café window, sipping an herbal tea blend I'd found recently. Anything I could find to ingest and seem more human, the more time it bought me in each location. My laptop ran cameras of the perimeter of my home, alerting me if someone were to come sniffing around. I tossed round the idea of putting security outside of Sascha's to keep them both safe too, but I had a feeling both women would find it a gross invasion of privacy. And it was. Because I knew I would be watching. I walked by their flat early this morning, checking for a vampire scent that wasn't mine, and it all seemed clear. Hopefully, the fact that I had walked them home and stayed a while, leaving my scent all over Ophelia, had warned them off. Ophelia's scent was all over me too, and none of the four showers I'd taken since leaving her eliminated it. And I wanted to get straight back to her.

A blur moved across the wet glass. I straightened and shut my laptop, turning toward the door. Though a rustic beam blocked my full view, it was obvious Pietro had entered. He slunk to the seat across from me and grabbed my tea, taking a healthy gulp.

"God, I don't know how you stomach that swill," he said, spitting into my cup. "Javi."

I sat back with a smile and crossed my arms over my chest. "Pietro. Say your piece and leave my town."

"Your town!" He laughed, slapping the worn wood table. "That's a good one, old friend. I cannot leave until my contract is fulfilled with Ophelia's hotel." He reached across as though to touch my chin. I grabbed his hand and snapped the wrist first left then right, watching the blood drain from his face. He would heal, but I had meant to hurt him.

"You don't need that money. You will release her from the contract and leave before there's not enough left of you to sprinkle over the river."

He shook with a disturbing mix of pain and amusement, cradling his wrist.

"That's where you're wrong. I do need the money, and you need my help."

I stood, lifted my bag and computer, and pushed out of the café before we caused a scene at eight on a Sunday morning. He followed me through the tight alley and past the high street.

"Before you attempt to rope me into another of your schemes like two centuries past, know that perhaps had you come to me before infiltrating my donor and attacking her friend, I may have listened. But as you have proven time and again, Pietro, you rush in and do the wrong thing with questionable intentions. Get. Out."

He looked at me then, the early winter light revealing the soft lines we had to earn over the course of many lifetimes. A slow, almost apologetic grin tugged at the corners of his mouth.

"I think, my friend, you have no idea what you have gotten yourself into."

"I am about to get myself into your chest cavity. Leave Exeter, Pietro."

"As you wish," he said with a bow and retreated the way we had come.

My fingers itched to text Ophelia. Instead, I rushed home and sucked down a bag of spare blood I kept in the fridge. Through a gag, I managed to get it down. Something was happening, and I needed more strength than I was willing to allow my gracious donor to provide. If Pietro truly thought he was here to help me, whether or not he needed money as he claimed, then there was something afoot. Perhaps I should have waited to listen, but everything about him rankled me. And no matter what the nucleus of the issue was, Pietro's way was to send me through seven rings of rubbish to get to it. No. I would have to figure this out on my own.

CHAPTER TEN

OPHELIA

"Deal me in," Pete said, his eyes hooded as he looked at the hand he held. "I am ready for this round."

I watched Sascha plug from her sidecar, and I tipped my head to the side, noting she was off her calendar drink. And I worried. She had insisted I was wrong. Her eyes became clouded when I said it was December, not September. Each shrug of her bare shoulder as she typed out texts to some new friend with benefits had her increasingly agitated. To the point I didn't know why she insisted we come to this Boomer club. Sascha's smile was low and deliberate, like she was plotting. Her foot tapped the marble floor, the gold capped tip of her stiletto bootie mimicked the sound of an exoskeleton on a windowsill. I shuddered, thinking I should have told Javi I was coming along. It had seemed so sudden, Sascha wanting to meet Pete after her distrust of him. After his attack on both her and me. Based on her vengeful nature, I figured she was angling for retribution. Even Sascha wasn't reckless enough to take on a vampire alone. Yet here I was with her, unable to watch her go alone. If I did text Javi, he'd be here faster than I could dip to the loo, and there would be trouble.

"How does one get invited to a private club, Pete?" she asked him, laying a card on the table and picking one up. I lost track of the game, happy to sit and watch. His movements were labored as though he were taking as long as possible to complete each task. It reminded me of the police dramas where someone would have a person stay on their mobile long enough to track the phone. Dread scratched its nails on the inside of my gut.

"You're here are you not, Sascha?" he answered, smirking and laying three cards down. "I have been a member here for many years." He adjusted his tie and licked his bottom lip, a flash of fang showing. In my periphery, I saw Sascha's shoulders raise, the fine dark hairs on her arms standing on end. It seemed every other person in the club had blinders on. No one paid us any mind, though we were the youngest and making the most noise. I wondered if Pete had enthralled the lot of them.

"Sasch," I said, laying a hand on hers. Her eyes snapped to me, anger flashing and ebbing. "Come with me to the loo?"

She narrowed those bright blue eyes at me and looked as though she considered not accompanying me, which would break our girl code. Something was definitely up with her.

"Go on, ladies. I'll order us another round." As we passed, Pete's hand shot out and grabbed Sascha's wrist. She snatched it back but seemed to relax just as quickly. "Don't be long."

Gold seashells covered the walls in a damask pattern. The low lighting cast an eerie glow over us, but I spun us both toward the mirror. Sascha's eyes looked overly bright, pupils blown. I yanked at the high neck on her dress, walking around her. She slapped me off.

"What the fuck, Lily?"

"They must be here," I muttered, lifting her bare arms. I knelt down and ducked under her short skirt. "

"Ophelia!" She clamped her knees together, nearly missing braining me with her muscular thighs. "What in the actual fuck? You want to go down on me, you have every opportunity."

I flushed. Perhaps I had been a bit invasive. But she hadn't called me my given name since we were fourteen.

"Take your hands off me, Ophelia, or I swear to fucking God, I will hit you."

I realized then my hands were still on her upper thighs. I pulled them away, and then I felt it. The raised flesh, smoother than the rest of her thigh, which had gooseflesh over it. She knew I'd felt it too because she bolted back and hit the wall.

"Do not touch me again."

"Sasch," I said, holding up my hands in surrender. "I won't touch you. But talk to me. When did it start? What is he doing to you?"

She laughed in an ugly snort.

"He?" She cackled. "Likely what Javi is doing to you. Only one of us gets paid. And I can tell you, Lily pet, I am not the whore."

My head felt like it blew back. Her words hit me in a thousand streaks of lightning.

"Sascha," I whispered. I knew this wasn't my best mate. She would never say that to me. She would never think it. It did not stop the hurt it caused.

"I think you should find a new place to live," she said. "I am not keen to have my extracurriculars under a microscope."

My heart dropped at her statement.

"To-tonight?" I asked, voice small and detached.

She nodded once. My head spun. I still did not want to leave Sascha here on her own with Pete, yet there was no reason to stay. I pushed out the doors and made my way directly to the front, leaving my coat at the coat check.

My heel caught between the cobble, tearing it from the sole. The sting of gravel on my palms sobered me from the displacement of my conversation with Sascha. I pulled both shoes off, the ice coated street doing nothing to improve my building fury. Sascha was a volatile personality. Other people may not have noticed the little changes in her the past week or so. Others may not have, but I should have. The secretive texts as though she were sixteen again. The excess alcohol and almost no food. The passive aggressive comments. I should have known.

So, that was what happened when one was enthralled by a vampire? I knew Javi had never used any sort of compulsion on me because I never felt the need to snap. I felt that pull toward him. The ache in my core and the urge to touch myself. Or him. But not in a fanatic sort of way. Not the glazed, dead-eyed way Sascha was tonight. I wiped my palms on my dress, forgetting I'd left my coat inside, and swore. It was fucking freezing out, flurries of snow caressing my face in a way I would have loved had I been wearing shoes and a coat. I pulled my phone out to call a car as there was no way I would make it back—where? Oh God. I could sleep at the hotel, but I didn't have my keys with me. They were back at Sascha's, and I was not about to step foot in there unwelcome. Every second I dithered, my fingers froze more. I pulled up my messages.

Would you mind if I slept on the couch in your place—where we have our appointments? I felt stupid, immediately wishing I'd had another option. I had never seen his proper home. I had never been invited. A giggle escaped me because I had not been invited to a vampire's home. Oh, the irony.

Of course. Are you well? Came Javi's response.

I opened the rideshare app, plugging in his address and where I was. The private club was in a posh residential area in the adjacent town.

I'm not sure. I need to get out of the cold. I'll be to yours as soon as the rideshare picks me up.

"Lily," a voice beamed from behind me. I swiveled on my frozen, bare heel. Connor stood, leaning against a streetlamp. "Who kicked you out of bed?"

I backed up a few steps, clouded with an unholy stew of mixed emotions. Relief I might have a ride. Need for familiarity I'd just lost with Sascha. Anger because of everything Connor had done to me. On top of it all, a prickling unease, wondering why he was there. In that moment. My phone buzzed.

Where are you? The question was instant. Like he'd known.

My fingers were too frozen to type. Connor's footsteps shuffled forward. I'd always hated the way he shuffled. Too lazy even to pick up his feet when he walked. I dropped a pin of my location in the text. Every pore on my skin vacillated between hot and cold.

"Lily, Lily." Connor reached his hand out, and I reared back, stumbling. Had I still been in heels, I might have fallen. He chuckled. The sound of lighter footsteps came from the next street. The echo bounced between buildings, disorienting me to which direction they were.

The app wasn't loading. I looked over my shoulder and began walking backward.

"Good night, Connor. I only broke my heel."

A female laugh pinged from building to building. The unease gave way to mild panic. I was not alone.

"You should probably go," I told my ex.

He rolled his eyes at me. The same look he used to give me when I asked who he was texting. My stomach rolled. I realized then that whatever nostalgia I ever had about Connor, was ash on the wind. Not only was I over him, but I was also thoroughly disgusted by him. I didn't know if I could completely trust Javier. I didn't know if I wanted more from him than the blurred lines of our agreement. What I did know was that even with fangs and death on his ledger, he didn't strike dread in me the way Connor did in that moment.

"Ophelia," a female voice sang. No face nor body matched the call, its musical tone a bouncing ball in the night. Connor stood between me and the stairs to the club I'd exited. A club that should have had a man outside. Would I make it back inside? Surely Sascha was still my friend enough to give me safe haven.

"Ophelia. A Lily, I'm told!" The glee in the tone masked something else. If I looked down at myself, I was sure I would see the rapid flutter of my heart against my ribs. "A flower! Like a violet. How doth that line go?" Something dragged along the stone wall of a building. I thought it was to my right, but the way the street sat, each gust of snowy wind shifted the sounds.

"*A violet in the youth of primy nature*," she sang. I was too out of my wits to be annoyed she was quoting Hamlet at me. Normally I'd have sniffed a half laugh and turned away. "This flower...this *Lily*..." Her voice became softer. "*The perfume and suppliance of a minute; no more!*"

I was shoved back, hands gripping my shoulders as I kicked out with unfeeling bare feet. The shoes I'd had in my grasp flew.

"Ssh, ssh, Lily," Connor whispered in my ear. He was too close. His breath acrid. "You'll be all right, love." Tires blew snow and at once, Connor's hands dropped from me. A snarl rent the night, car door slamming. He turned and clicked his tongue at me, parting his two fingers and sticking a limp tongue between them. "Next time, love," he said, and took off at a run. The female was nowhere in sight. Her song-like voice merely history.

Seconds ticked by. Movements and activities fit within the time without my acknowledging their existence. Walking to the car on frozen feet. Javi's hair tickled my cheek as he bent over me, clipping my seatbelt in. His hands grabbed mine, and he swore. Not a breath later, my burning fingers were wrapped in something soft and warm. Two doors closed and the car was moving. I looked at my driver. He sat, shirtless, one hand on the wheel, another fiddling with the heat controls.

"Where's your shirt?" I slurred, lips numb from cold and shock. His eyes glanced down at my hands and the jumper cocooning them. "Ah. Thanks."

He nodded. "Were you harmed?"

I shook my head no. We walked in the side door to the same townhouse to which I arrived once or twice a week. Javi keyed in a code and motioned for me to go in ahead. He dropped his wallet on a sideboard in the entryway. A domestic human act which eased me. Lights flicked on, showing a minimalist sitting room, adorned with fashion books and what looked like runway photography from maybe the 1960s. I knew I would want a better look when I could feel my feet and hands again. I followed Javi because I didn't know what else to do. Plus, I could admit I liked the way the muscles shifted in his back as he walked. I was cold, not blind. Really, I could think of a fantastic way to warm up...

"Tea?" he asked.

Internally, I sulked. I guess tea would help too. I flexed my fingers, the throbbing of circulation coming back.

"Feel like telling me what happened? Apart from that boy from the market?"

I almost laughed at that. It seemed just shy of a jealous remark, though I suppose that was my wishful brain. Even if it had been one, it wasn't jealous in the way Connor used to make them. The way he'd pick apart a man I had spoken to. Connor would comment on his clothes while he peeled mine off. He would comment on the size of the man's penis while he stroked himself, wanting me to watch. He'd ask if the man could do what he was doing as he tongue-fucked me, never realizing I needed my clit touched. I would drag a finger up myself so he wouldn't know he wasn't making me cum. I shook my head, flashbacks of Connor fading. Ash on the wind. Javi was looking at me.

"Sascha is enthralled—or whatever you call it—by Pete," I told him. "I probably should have told you where we were going."

"You probably shouldn't do or tell me anything you don't want to. Though, if it makes you feel safer, please let me know."

I smiled, looking down into the tea in my hands.

"It's an herbal blend," he explained, a hint of pink staining his cheeks. "I can pick up your PG Tips tomorrow if you'd like. This is the only blend I can stomach."

It tasted of sunshine. Like a day spent in the heat on a tiled rooftop, lazing in the sun. And somehow of calming plants and lullabies. I was definitely not opposed. Especially as it tasted how I could imagine it would taste to kiss Javi. His eyes shot to mine, like he'd heard that thought.

"Sascha kicked me out. My keys to the hotel are in her flat. I was so upset, I left my coat in that horrid club."

"Did you leave your shoes as well?" His mouth quirked up on one side.

"I—never mind. I don't know why Connor was there. He was acting strangely. More so than he used to. I don't know why he's here at all, actually. This is my town. He is from New Castle. He and I moved to London after uni, and he has never had any intention of leaving."

"Until you left," Javi said, eyebrows raised as he sipped his tea.

I waved him off. "The only damage I did in leaving him was to his ego."

Javi tipped his head to the side. The glossy black of his

cabinets and appliances gleamed in the low lighting, giving Javi a halo, like a fallen angel. I felt filthy in comparison with my dirty, bare feet and now grimy ivory dress.

"Is there a shower I can use in the—" I waved my hand because I had no idea what to call that part of his house.

"I call it the office." He shrugged. "Mainly for tax reasons, mind. Yes. There's a shower, however, I have a guest room with an ensuite. It's far more comfortable than the sofa in the office."

I opened my mouth to half-heartedly protest.

"There's a tub," he said.

All protests died in my mouth, thinking about how poorly my feet felt and how much I wanted to soak. "If it's not an imposition."

"Were it an imposition I was opposed to, I wouldn't have offered." He placed his empty cup in the dishwasher, another oddly domestic act I was at odds with given he was a vampire. Who didn't eat. Or rather, who ate me. I put my head in my hand, the thought embarrassing me. I wanted very much to feel that pointed tongue move its tip along me again. I wanted to feel his fingers massaging the blood in my skin as he sucked and drank from me. I stood, teetering as though I'd had a few too many. Javi stayed turned from me, his back rising and falling with quickened breaths. He could scent my arousal. Shit. This was a nearly impossible situation.

"I'll have that bath now, thanks." How I managed to say that without my voice giving out, I will never know.

He walked out of the kitchen wordlessly, assuming I would follow. As I closed the door to what would be my room for the night, I called him back.

"Javi." He half turned in the narrow hall. "Thank you for this. I was stuck. I was in trouble, actually," I said, realizing I didn't know what was about to happen to me on that street.

"I really could have been hurt and I don't know who that woman was."

"What woman?" he asked, carefully. I told him the sing song of her voice and how she quoted Hamlet and kept to the shadows. He leaned in and smelled me.

"Regardless," I said to break the tension, "you truly came through for me. And I appreciate it."

"Of course." He carried on down the hall, and I watched him move through the dim lights, like he controlled the shadows within. "You are welcome to stay as long as you need. You are safe here."

Safe. From his kind. From my ex. From my best friend in the whole world who called me a whore and kicked me out of her flat, knowing I had nowhere to go. Safe.

Once I heard the intimate sounds of Ophelia stepping into the bath, I began searching online for traces of Pietro. While I was not one to scoff at coincidence, for I had lived far too long to think everything is a calculated cog in the machine, tonight's incident was no coincidence. That boy, with whom Ophelia once shared a life, was just as enthralled as Ophelia tells me Sascha was. However, the scent of vampire on Connor—saying his name made claws break free from my fingers—was not Pietro. It was female. And ancient.

There was a soft splash from the bathroom, followed by the light scent of heated skin and sandalwood. She had sat in my kitchen and fought a building arousal. I'd nearly cracked my mug trying to restrain myself from laying her over the counter and tasting her again. I wanted to hear her yelp at the cold press of marble under her. I needed to feed but wouldn't dream of asking when she'd had a shock like she had tonight.

As I looked at the rapidly changing searches I ran, I slipped my hand into my trousers. This ache was one I hadn't felt in years. Decades even. If not more. My cock was so hard, the fabric of my trousers was in danger of tearing. Based on her scent earlier, Ophelia would not even mind if I joined her in the bath. I would bet she was so wet, the bathwater would do nothing to keep her from being slick and ready for me. Christ, I really must focus.

A search blinked and cloned itself, adding satellite results in every corner of my screen.

Couple vanishing in Croatia, bodies found weeks later, drained of blood.

CEO of executive transportation corporation found empty of blood; his accounts transferred to offshore bank. Government coverup.

Then a photo. The profile of a woman, glossy hair pulled into a tight chignon. A face I would know anywhere. At any time. However impossible. Because the face is one that belongs to a dead woman. A twice dead woman. Who should have been burned and scattered these past hundred odd years. Alicia.

I stood so quickly, the chair blew back, knocking into my leucite coffee table. I walked down the hall as Ophelia came to the door of the guest room, a towel tucked under her pinkened arms.

"Is everything okay?" she asked.

Her full brows were cinched together, and I wanted to smooth them out. Tell her it was all fine and lay her down and drink from her. Her eyes dropped to my waist and lower, where I'm sure she saw the hard press of my cock, which hadn't disappeared in my surprise at seeing Alicia. She bit her lip, and it took everything in me to not slam her into the wall, my cock, fangs, and fingers finding themselves deep inside her.

"Did you see the woman you heard tonight?" I asked her, taking a step forward as though I had no control over my body. She shook her head. "What did she say to you?"

"She called me Lily," she said with a sneer. "And recited a line from Hamlet about the impermanence of...me." She scrubbed a hand over her face. Something primal in me burned hearing that. Like the mention of Alicia threatening Ophelia ignited a part of me I'd never known existed. "Who did you—"

I stepped to her and caught her face in my hand, claiming her lips, all in one move. Something I had wanted to do for as long as I'd known her. She melted into me instantly. Her lips tasted almost as sweet as her sex. She ran her tongue along the seam of my mouth, as though asking to be let in. I met her tongue with my own, tasting the tea she drank and the hot breath of what made her who she was. I pulled away, regretting the confused look it put on her face.

"Was that o—" I started, but she was the one who grabbed the back of my head this time. Such strength in someone so small. Her fingers dug into the base of my skull, like they had when I last fed from her thighs and cunt.

"Are you going to tell me who that was tonight?" she asked, her forehead pressed to mine.

My fingers trailed up under her towel of their own volition. The closer I came to her apex, the more she clenched her thighs together, and I felt the heat of her wetness against my hand. I growled deep in my chest. The monster I was begged to be unleashed. She moaned.

"Just fucking tell me who it was, Javi," she said. That voice coming out of her was at least three octaves lower than her own.

I smiled, moving my fingers like I was tuning a delicate violin. Her hips bucked. She made a choked sound.

"I want to feel you soak my hand," I told her instead. "I want so much of your cum on me, I can call it a feeding." To get my point across, I pulled my hand away, causing her to whimper. "Impatient, Ophelia." I pulled my fingers apart, showing her how her cum stretched between them, before sucking the slick from my fingers. Her mouth dropped open, and she stepped back, raising an eyebrow at me.

"Who was it, Javi?" she asked, taking one more step backward into her room. I prowled after, my fangs descending, fully locked on my prey. She pressed her thighs together. No fear. Only animalistic desire radiated from her.

"I want to drink your cum, Ophelia," I said, letting her see me pierce my tongue with my incisor before leaning forward to kiss her, my blood mingling with her saliva. Her pupils were blown. I knew she was almost out of her mind with want. I knew, because, even beyond the fact that my monster wanted out to play, I was just about out of my own head, needing her. She looked down at my trousers again. I cocked my head to the side and pulled my belt out, pushing my trousers down before stepping from them. The length of me pushed, showing every ridge through my briefs. "Think of how you'll feel when I drink from your cunt."

She pulled the towel off, showing me her flushed, naked body. I hissed, claws poking through my fingertips. A strangled sound of alarm came from the object of my want. I willed the razor-sharp nails to retract, but she surprised me and grabbed my hand, making me scratch down her stomach. It was my turn to choke on a whimper.

"I will play this game all night, Javi." She dropped my hand and palmed her own breast, moving her hand to play between her thighs. I dived my hand into her wet hair and pulled her head back until her neck was taut. She smiled at me. "I am not consenting until you tell me what had you upset."

This ridiculous, stubborn woman. I wanted to rip out her throat and drink until I brought her back so I could fuck her into eternity. Instead, I smiled at her myself. She touched the tips of my teeth, the taste and smell of her cum washing through me.

"This game is rather fun," I said, arcing my hips so she could feel me press into her naked flesh. She swallowed, barely contained lust leaking through her pores. "Before I tell you," I said, loosening my grip on her. "I want you to know that whatever you want to do from here is fine and justified. You want to walk out, you walk out. Know that what I want —what every part of me, the ancient and demonic, human, and male—is to have you. Here. Tonight. I want to make you orgasm so hard, time ceases to exist." I squeezed her ass, running a claw up her crack. She shuddered.

"Tell me," she whispered, two fingers racing up the length of my fabric-covered cock.

"Connor smelled like vampire."

"Pete?" she asked me, her fingers falling from my cock. I leaned in to kiss her lightly, needing a taste once more before she pulled away.

"No." I stroked her face, leaning her upright. She pursed her lips, seeming so much like that cautious entrepreneur I met months ago. "I wasn't sure at first because the scent has changed over the years. But I found hidden articles online. Investigative reports and photos. Pietro, yes. But he's not alone."

"Javi." It was a demand.

I placed a kiss on her collar bone. I could see the desire fade between us. In a moment she would realize she was naked and be embarrassed and I didn't know if she would want to give me that intimacy again. I was too broken. Too full of secrets and history.

"I found a recent photo of Alicia," I admitted.

She looked thoughtful for a second, then stiffened, stepping back.

"Your wife." It wasn't a question. She knew the answer. If Alicia were not dead—true death—then she was my wife still. As much as I did not wish it to be so. Ophelia's eyes roved the room, from the sheer white blind to the glass door to the toilet. I reached for her towel and handed it to her. "I will still be your donor. But I will not be"—she swirled her hand in the air, holding the towel to her with the other—"involved with someone's husband. That is a character flaw I do not possess."

I sat on the edge of the ivory sherpa chair beside her bed. "I understand. Though please know that she has not been my wife for a century."

She sat on her bed and put a hand on my back.

"You haven't seen her in a century. You loved her once. I know how that goes. What if you see her and it's love all over again?" Her point was valid though not a factor for me.

"There is no altruistic reason for someone to fake her own death and simply walk away from her husband. Of all *my* character flaws, Ophelia, one I too do not possess is infidelity. It is also one I won't excuse. And believe me, much happens in a century." I stood, gathering up my discarded trousers. However, did I think I would have a night with Ophelia without her knowing what we faced? "I won't attempt to be anything but the person paying you for your service. You are welcome to stay here as long as you need. I'll leave you alone." Inside me, burning began. A sick, oily ooze of anger and despair. Still, I walked from that room, leaving her to process.

It was too late to try to sort out why Alicia was back, and why she was coming after me. What game was being played that used my best mate and my ex? Had Connor shown up here before becoming enthralled, or had he been approached before leaving London? If the latter, there was more of a long game being played than simply knocking obstacles from a path to Javier.

I wanted Javier. He wanted me. That much was obvious to us both and likely every vampire within sniffing distance of us. I ached for him to be touching me more. I ached for his teeth and claws. Claws! Those were new and, oh, dear God, did I want to have them scratch at me.

Telling Javi I would not bed him felt like eating stones. It went against everything I had been craving. Yet, I meant what I'd said. Pursuing someone else's spouse is a red ledger marker against my integrity. One I had no intention of forging. Fissures of anger bubbled up inside me because of how aroused I was. With a huff, I flung myself into bed, too irritated to even use my own fingers. Maybe if Voltaire had been with me, I could have had a smidgen of relief.

Somewhere deep in the bowels of this townhouse, I heard a growl and what sounded like a hand hitting a wall. Part of me hoped he was as frustrated as I was, and part of me knew this was not his doing either. Part of me also had a feeling that growl was the result of him taking himself in hand and finding an angry sort of release. That thought had me pulling my duvet between my legs so I could rub myself along the cotton. Would he have been naked, standing in the shower, his long fingers wrapped around what looked to be a sizeable cock? Would his fangs have been out, as he pumped himself? I worked the duvet between my lips and knew I was groaning, thinking of Javier jerking himself off. Would his fangs pierce his lip? The taste of his blood still remained in my mouth. Eddies of pleasure pushed in like high tide. Would he smear his tip with precum. God, I wanted to lick that from him and taste him like he's tasted me. I could feed off him almost as well as he feeds from me. My hands shook where they clenched the increasingly wet duvet. When he growled and hit the wall, would he have let himself ejaculate all over the shower, or was it oozing between his fingers? I rocked on the duvet one last time as I had an unsatisfying orgasm.

When I was little, my parents would have me say my prayers before bed, though I knew they were not religious.

"Thank God for Mummy and Daddy. Thank God for Pebbles, my labradoodle cuddly toy." Tonight, as I drifted into an uneasy sleep, I found myself praying a different sort of gospel.

"Fuck you, Alicia, may you burn in hell. Fuck you, Pete, I want you dead and buried. Fuck you, Connor, for everything you've done to me."

Anger of this magnitude did always exhaust me.

The cold locked inside my bones. It felt like far too much trouble to light a fire in my office when I was in and out and the only one in the hotel. Maybe I should have felt uncomfortable here alone. Seeing as Sascha was enthralled by Pete, my bloody architect who obviously had access to the building. However, I really just wanted to get to work. As I ran numbers through Excel and worked on my new press kit on my other monitor, I didn't have room for how Sascha would pull out of Pete's bullshit. Or when Alicia would make her next move. I had a business to launch, with rooms already booked for Valentine's Day in less than two months. And between then and now was Christmas and New Year's. New Year's Eve, when Sascha and I would dress up in inappropriately revealing clothing to take a train to the shores of Devon and sit near the cliffs above the Jurassic Coast, passing a bottle of prosecco between us. It had been our tradition going on four years, and I just wished I would have known last year was the last.

Christmas was not an easy season for me, which is why I tried to keep myself busy. Sure, I was invited to Sascha's parents' house. Sure, I exchanged gifts with my best friend. Since my parents died, I lost that passion for Christmas. I tried to be "normal" with Connor a couple years in a row, but it always ended with me in tears, because I couldn't cook roast dinner. And I missed my mum. The way she always got me new slippers to open Christmas Eve, and how she always made the perfect Yule log and accepted the unwritten rule that an entire half was for me alone. I missed my dad and how he knew exactly what to buy Mum and me every year without asking. I missed how up until I was eighteen, he would still tickle the bottoms of my feet on his five o'clock shadow. His hands, nails often painted black, held my feet, and he laughed alongside me. Christmas was a dark reminder of all I'd lost, wrapped in strings of twinkling lights. This year, it seemed, as Christmas Eve was two days away, I wouldn't even have Sascha, and things were so awkward between Javier and me. He walked me to Sascha's flat this morning so I could pack my things before she got home, but we did not speak other than what was necessary.

My teacup rattled with the vibration of my phone.

Ciao, Ophelia, the text read. *Sascha, Pietro, and I would like to invite you and my husband for drinks in the private room at Club EX tonight! Dress appropriately or you won't be allowed in. 23:00.*

I closed my eyes and leaned my head back against the top of my desk chair. At least Club EX would be busy, unlike that awful, stuffy private grandad den from last night. I was so bloody tired, all I wanted to do was crawl into bed after dinner and sleep through stupid Christmas. And not have to get dressed up for the third time in a week. I lifted my head to the sound of another text.

I assume you received a similar text? Javier asked, sending a screen shot of basically the same invite.

Yes.

I could go alone and see what they want.

No. I want to be there. I want to look them all in the eyes and see why they are fucking up my life.

That came out angrier than I'd wanted, but it was the truth. I tidied up my office and locked up the hotel, knowing that between the lack of motivation for anything business related during the holidays and my own distracted brain, I wouldn't get anything else done. Plus, I needed to dig through boxes to find the dress I would wear. If I knew anything about this game, I knew Alicia would be dressed like a super-model. I didn't know her, but a woman who was calculating and angled toward getting what she wants, would be showing up more than presentable. Javier is strikingly good looking, so it didn't take a genius to assume his wife would be as well. While I was lacking in height and overall body composition for supermodel status, I could look fucking good too. And I fully intended to.

Every New Year's Eve when Sascha and I would take the train to the coast, I would say something along the lines of, "I will not do this again unless I am dressed in warm leggings and boots." And every year, Sascha convinced me to wear something even more revealing. One of those dresses was what I was going to fish from the boxes. I knew just the one.

For security reasons, Javier and I walked together through town to get to Club EX on the opposite side of the city center. I didn't want it to feel like a date and confuse everything even more, but reality is reality. I knew to open my coat so the bouncer could see my dress, but it was too cold to take it off until we were inside. I hadn't been properly clubbing in ages, and the press of bodies around us was disorienting. Low lighting and thumping EDM found a pulse within me. Javier grabbed my hand and led me to the bar, where he ordered us a gin and tonic each, and we headed upstairs to the private rooms.

"At least by getting this in," he said into my ear as we waited for the bartender, "we can have an excuse to not drink whatever they offer us up there."

My hands clenched at my sides feeling his mouth against my ear. His very closeness made my need skyrocket. His breath against my ear was artillery fire to my nerve endings.

He squeezed my coat-covered shoulder once. "We can go whenever you want."

I nodded and grabbed my drink, following him up past the mezzanine. Another bouncer stood outside the entrance to the private rooms, checking our IDs, then one more stood outside the room we had been invited to. This seemed like a far bigger operation than my small university city was used to. I'd always thought of Club EX as a student club. The clientele we were passing up here, however, looked as though they were London transplants. Very strange as nothing ever happened in Exeter. I guzzled the rest of my G&T and slipped my heavy coat from my shoulders before we walked in the room.

"Christ," I heard Javier mutter behind me.

That's why I had chosen this dress. Once past the smoked glass door, he moved beside me, a hand splayed across my bare back, seeming rather possessive. Behind the sofas and seating where Pete and Connor sat, flanked on either side by Sascha, and who I only assumed was Alicia, was a wall of mirrors. It showed Javier in his black suit next to me in my silver chain-mail halter dress. Behind us, through some trick of light and one-way mirrors—as I knew the outside of this room was all mirror—was a view out into the chaos of the club below.

Alicia seemed to be saying something, but the pulse of music drowned it out. She got up and walked to us, slinking across the floor like a cat in a black jumpsuit that was cutdown past her belly button and bare to her ass crack in the back, just like my dress. Her hair was a riot of reds and blondes, almost as though it didn't follow the rules of nature. It swayed with her walk, moving in glossy waves.

"Ciao, Lily," she said with a musical accent similar to Javier's. She kissed me three times. "Husband," she said to Javier. Her lips brushed his, and she laughed, registering how he stiffened. "Come sit."

The four of them were taking up the sofa, leaving a loveseat for Javier and me and a rather purgatorial looking metal chair I was not about to sit on in a dress this short. When Alicia sat, her hand went to Sascha's knee, just as Pete's was on Connor's.

"Do you remember, Javi," Alicia began, "I had a silver dress. When we were in Venezia before the war started."

"I am not here to reminisce, Alicia Geralda Fernandez Montebello," Javier said, sitting forward and pushing his knee against mine.

She laughed and squeezed Sascha's thigh hard enough that it was either a promise of violence or passion. Sascha moaned, drinking whatever was in her glass.

"Ja, Sascha," Alicia said. "Come here." She lifted my best friend onto her lap, keeping an arm around Sascha's bare midriff.

"Lily," Sascha said, nuzzling into Alicia's neck. "This might be strange for you. You've never seen me like this." Like this? I'd seen her in every manner of drunk. I'd seen her high, making out with men and women. Never with a vampire's hand inching up her skirt and under her cropped satin bustier.

"I always wanted to see you two go at it," Connor said, leaning across Pete. His eyes were glazed, and I couldn't tell if he was looking at Sascha or me. Pete laughed and put a hand on Connor's crotch. I felt my miniscule dinner rise in my stomach. Nothing about Connor was attractive to me anymore, so Pete's willingness to touch him like that was nauseating.

"Oh, shut up you troglodyte," I snapped at him. "Are you truly every cliché known to man?"

Pete unzipped his trousers and pushed Connor's head into his lap. I was so stunned, I sat back hard, bumping into Javier.

"We are leaving. Now." I started to stand, but Alicia's fangs shot out, aimed at Sascha's throat.

"You might want to wait a second, mi amore," she said, puncturing my friend's alabaster skin. Sascha grabbed her hand and moved it all the way up under her skirt. Alicia's fingers curled in, stroking Sascha.

I looked away, only to see Connor's cheeks hollowing over Pete's crotch. There was nowhere safe to look. Had it been anyone else, the scene before me might have been a voyeuristic turn on. A sort of burlesque danse macabre to devour the senses. But not as it was with Connor.

"Javier has something I want," Alicia continued. "Something that is rightfully mine under the terms of the sanctity of our marriage."

"Our marriage is over based on your death certificate signed over a century ago. Had it not been, then it would be annulled due to the fact that by every law, we should both be dead and gone, mi *amore*," Javier said, his own fangs descending.

Those fucking teeth were like a bell to my groin. How perverted was I, sitting here? I was disgusted watching my ex give a vampire a blow job and my best friend get finger fucked by Javier's estranged wife, and I felt a gush of wet in my pants seeing Javier ready to fight. Or feed. His eyes shot to mine and looked down at my lap. Alicia and Pete chuckled.

"She smells like desperation and cheap gin," Pete said, raising his hips to deep throat Connor.

"I smell like Tom Ford Fucking Fabulous, which I bought duty free at Gatwick and have been paying off for six months," I said, laying a hand on Javier's thigh. From the corner of my eye, I saw his cheek rise. His arm went around my back, pulling me in.

"What do you want, Alicia?" he asked her. His thumb brushed my side where no bra strap interrupted the exposed skin on the sides of my breasts. His body straightened a bit, as though he hadn't meant that to be quite so sexual of a contact. Alicia pulled a mouthful of blood from Sascha who was tugging Alicia's head closer while she rode her knee and fingers.

"The deed to the estate in Tuscany, to start," Alicia said, wiping a dribble of blood from her mouth.

Javier sat back and pushed at his dimpled chin. His other hand made feather light passes up and down my sides, making my nipples peak through the thin silver chain mail of my dress. The gratuitous sounds coming from Connor and Pete kept my eyes trained on Javier's profile, my thighs fighting for their life as they pressed together. Sascha seemed nearly asleep, and I refused to think about that. Javier looked at me and raised an eyebrow. I scooted closer to him as though our minds were linked.

"Let me get this straight," he said to Alicia, keeping his eyes on me. "You have come to my town after over one hundred years, having never indicated you were alive." His accent became more and more pronounced. He grabbed the bottle from the ice bucket on the glass-topped table in front of us and poured two shots, handing one to me. "After I watched a body, which I believed was yours, set aflame and pushed out to sea, you have reemerged, taken people in my— in Ophelia's life—and held them as collateral in order to get my crumbling vineyard estate in Tuscany? Correct me if I am wrong, but this doesn't add up. Ophelia, as you have done a fair amount of research on properties fit for hotels and such, does this level of manipulation seem worth it for an estate worth maybe three million and in need of an overhaul?"

"Not at all," I answered. "When do we get to the part where she releases my friend?"

"My beautiful Sascha?" Alicia asked, kissing her. "She is not unhappy, I assure you."

"Maybe if you'd let Javi fuck you, Lily," Sascha slurred, "you might not find this so repulsive. You're not any less of a whore not taking dick."

I stood so quickly my head spun. Javi stood with me, angling himself between me and the shit show before us. I made the mistake of looking at them. Pete grabbing Connor's ears as he climaxed into the other man's mouth, and Sascha with her hand pushing Alicia's further into her wanny. I was going to be sick. I was not a prude, nor did I have anything against erotic voyeurism. Voltaire and I had enjoyed our fill. But this? They may have been enjoying themselves. Maybe it wasn't all compulsion and just freed inhibitions, but neither scene would ever leave my mind unscathed.

Javier's claws flashed from his fingers, one accidentally nicking me. All three vampires in the room looked up and Javier snarled, locking me in his arms, possessively.

"You come near Ophelia again, in any way," he said, a low fire in his words, "I will rip you both apart alive and set you on fire. Are we clear?"

"The estate, Javi," Alicia trilled. "I want it. Almost as much as I want you right now. You know how much it turned me on when your monster showed up." She patted Sascha's knee. "Send the wilting flower home, and join us. Pietro was only just getting started, and you know I can go all night long."

Javier's claws sheathed. "I will find out why you want that estate, and you will be lucky if it's not where I bury your ashes." He turned us to leave, and I pushed from his arms, annoyed. "Our marriage was over the day you faked your death. We have no ties to bind us. But Ophelia?" he said prowling toward Alicia. He leaned over her and Sascha, slashed his own wrist and fed Sascha his blood, which she took greedily. "Ophelia is mine. And Sascha is under my protection." Sascha slapped his wrist away in disgust and jumped from Alicia's knee. Her eyes went from glassed over to clear in an instant. They looked at me in horror. Alicia pouted.

"Such a shame. It was just getting good. Pietro, come here."

Javier held his hand for Sascha, and she refused it, storming past me and out into the club. I ran after her, following down the stairs.

"Sasch, wait!"

She paused halfway down the crescent shaped staircase. I touched her elbow. It wasn't the best place for any kind of discussion, with people flowing around us.

"Lily, you must know I'm sorry." She wouldn't look at me. People were going up and down the stairs, drinks sloshing. The music was a second heartbeat, moving through me. Any other night, I would have wanted to dance. To get pissed and dance with Sascha and not let any sweaty guys near us. My best friend. My sister.

"I know," I said, stepping toward her. "I know. I do." I was yelling over the music.

"Listen. I need to be alone tonight. Are you safe? Staying with Javi?" she asked, and I nodded. "I'll call tomorrow, Lil." She kissed my cheek and darted away, getting lost in the crowd.

I pulled my phone and immediately texted her to let me know when she got home. My shoulders slumped. Everything felt wrong. Standing here on this staircase, in this dress that left so little to the imagination, wearing these skyscraper heels, having seen Sascha and Connor so compromised. I had no love for Connor. In fact, I could see him acting like that without compulsion. But I just didn't need to witness it. I needed to go home and like, read Jane Austen or something. Cleanse my palate of this awful evening. Even if Javier did look fucking hot when he got angry.

The icy wall of air that hit me when I stepped out was sobering. I swore to myself.

"I picked it up." Javier draped my coat over my shoulders, careful not to touch me more than necessary since I shrugged him off moments ago. "Home?"

I nodded, my teeth chattering. He pulled me in close for warmth. He was surprisingly warm for one of the undead. I must have said that aloud because he laughed and kissed the side of my head.

"I have my moments," he said. "What do you need? I know that was beyond what anyone should have had to witness. And by the way, I sent a contact to make sure Sascha gets home and stays safe."

I exhaled, a puff of white clouding the night before me. "I don't know. To be honest, it's all a weird blur. I wish..." The lights around the Christmas market were half lit.

"What do you wish?"

"I wish my parents were alive. I wish I could go home. Have Mum bake a yule log, mucking it up, and Dad read me old poetry. Have them tell me it's all going to be okay." Tears were rolling down my face. I was so very alone and lost.

Javier was quiet, and I felt I'd over shared. We turned up his street.

"I cannot tell you it will all be okay. Life is not one to agree so readily. What I can tell you is that with those memories, with Sascha, whom you will have back, you aren't alone. And if you want me around too"—he cleared his throat and keyed in the code for his front door—"I'll be here." The lights turned on when we stepped inside. I hung my coat on a walnut coat tree. "You're not alone."

My head bobbed with the force of my nodding. I couldn't seem to find coherent words. He walked past me and disappeared upstairs. There was no sense in my standing on ceremony in the sitting room, so I made my way to my room, eager to get out of this outfit. Well, mainly the shoes. Javier stood in my bathroom, pouring what looked to be Epsom salts in my tub. He dried his hands on his suit pants.

"I hope you can get some sleep. The past few nights have been messy."

"Javi," I called. Oh, this would be awkward. His face was soft, eyes a warm hazel. "Would it be weird if I asked you to kiss me?"

He blinked several times. I stepped out of my shoes,

mostly because I was super embarrassed and needed to do something other than wait for his answer. His hand cupped my chin, gently bringing my face up. I could feel the heat of his skin on me.

"You never need to ask." His full bottom lip took mine. It was a light kiss, his tongue a soft point, tracing my lips. He held my face, thumb stroking my cheekbone. I wanted to be in his arms. I just wasn't ready for that loss when it happened. As gentle and almost chaste as the kiss was, my nipples peaked against the chain mail.

"Would you touch me here?" I asked, bringing his hand to my chest. "Honestly, I've always wondered what it would feel like to have my breasts touched through the dress."

He chuckled, lips meeting mine again. His thumb flicked over my nipple, teasing me through the soft metal material. I could see why he did not consider Alicia his wife any longer. Now that I had met her and seen her with Sascha, I knew there was no love left between them. Romantic love anyway. Yet, I was in no place this evening to give in to my desire for the man in front of me.

"How's that?" he asked. His thumb swirled round my nipple, bunching the metal dress over my chest.

"Quite lovely, actually."

He laughed openly then, kissing the tip of my nose.

"Enjoy your bath, Ophelia. Just shout if you need me to test the fabric of any other articles of clothing you own. I'd be happy to oblige." He bowed at the waist, black hair falling over his forehead.

"I'll put together a spread sheet and see what needs evaluating."

He chuckled and closed the door behind him. I sighed, thinking the night at least ended well.

CHAPTER THIRTEEN

JAVIER

The only reason I was able to leave that room without sinking myself into Ophelia, was that I knew how traumatic this night had been. I knew, despite her ease with me these moments past, what she had to witness in that godawful club was more than a human should have to process. Granted it was not death, but the threat was imminent to her best mate. The threat still was imminent to that ex-partner of hers. That was doubled because I would snap his neck and toss him off a bridge without a second thought if I didn't think it might upset Ophelia. A few more visits from that boy, and I thought she'd be glad of his demise. Though I'd not been human and encumbered by mixed emotions over rage and death for many years.

In my time, I had been privy to open sexual relations in numerous circumstances. Some I'd been involved in and not entirely proud of. Some, I'd stumbled upon. Some, like tonight, I had to watch in order to gain something. What went on in that club, from Pietro deep throating Connor— who was not even doing it under compulsion, but of his own exhibitionist volition—to Alicia fondling Sascha, barely touched the surface of what I had seen in the past.

Venice, just prior to the turn of the twentieth century,

Pietro, Alicia, and I belonged to a sort of society dedicated to amorous meet ups and bloodletting. It typically did not get so out of hand that partners were killed, but I couldn't say it was rare. Vampirism was an aberration of human genetics. We were predators within our DNA and the beast could so easily take over the human side of us. I could recall many nights in that Venetian underbelly of society, where I was between two or three partners, fluids running along all of our skin, throats bared, fangs and cocks filling orifices. They were decadent, hedonistic times. There was no law nor church strong enough to stop us. We owned the night and took full advantage. My strength was at its fullest in those years. I fed from vein and cunt, cock, and breast, two to three times a night. We were unstoppable, and while perhaps not ever truly in love, Alicia and I were a force. It was then I purchased that vineyard in Tuscany, hoping to hide out the war within the catacombs built under the fields of vines.

Why would Alicia want that property now? I tapped my fingers on the edge of my desk while idly stroking myself with my other hand, needing more release than my sorry hand gave me in the shower last night. With Ophelia in the other room, flushed from her bath, and the memory of touching her pebbled nipple through the silken metal of her dress, I was on the knife point of losing my mind. I needed to feed. I was down to one bag of blood in the fridge, and as much as I hated the mere thought of drinking it, my demon would be insufferable if I didn't have at least a bit of nourishment. Perhaps Ophelia would be well enough for a feeding tomorrow. I rushed to the kitchen so I would be able to make it that long without pinning her to her bed and taking without asking.

CHAPTER FOURTEEN

OPHELIA

Tea. Tea might help calm me down. I was exhausted, yes. Utterly knackered. Yet, I knew sleep was a white elephant I'd never find tonight without some way to wind down. The way Javi's thumb felt against my chainmail covered nipple was maddening. Like I wanted to smash things against a wall to feel more. To feel it all. I wanted his thumb pushed in me. I wanted it in my ass as I rode him. Jesus, I knew I was sexually awakened, but the fire I felt for him was so new and foreign to me. It was well past three in the morning, the only sounds outside were the pelting of winter rain against the townhouse. I whipped the duvet from myself and left my room in the sweatpants and T-shirt I'd worn as pajamas for years.

There was a tang in the air I didn't recognize. Not altogether unpleasant, but something I would have investigated had it been my house. I'd have lit a candle or something. The kitchen light was off, but a small sound made me stop just short of entering. I made out Javi standing over the counter, sucking on a bag of blood. No, tearing it apart with his teeth, letting his tongue wipe clean the inside of the plastic.

I froze. He had needed to feed. I'd known it. His head turned to me, eyes glowing green in the dark. Every hair on my arms raised, yet my feet were planted on the ground. I'd felt this before. He had me enthralled. And it made me hellishly angry.

"Javier," I said, so deadpan, my mum would have been proud. "Get your glamour off of me, or I will walk out of this fucking house and take my chances with a stroll to Premier Inn."

His hands ripped the remains of the bag into two and flung it into the sink. Blood dripped over the webbing between his fingers. He licked it clean, one at a time, the glowing irises not moving from me. I tried to make my legs work but I was still stuck. "You are going to hate yourself in the morning. Maybe for the rest of your miserable, immortal existence. Because I will fight you. The suppliant, drink me and fuck me, Ophelia?" I asked, putting every bit of energy into my anger. "She is gone if you do not release me this bloody instant."

Javier's fingers drummed the edge of the countertop, his skin so pale and luminous, it reflected in the black cabinetry. He pushed off and stalked toward me. What the hell had I been thinking, rooming with a vampire? My knees buckled, and I stumbled backward, having obviously been let out of the glamour. My arm shot out to grab the door frame, but Javier caught it and pinned me to the kitchen wall. His eyes were blazing, whole body shaking as though there were a live wire going through him.

"Javier," I said, realizing he was not himself at all. "Javier. Javi." I grabbed his chin with my free hand. He snarled, teeth so close to my face, I couldn't focus on him. Spittle flew with another snarl. "Javi, that is just disgusting. You need to feed, you big idiot. Get control of yourself and stop this."

His head cocked to the side, like he was deciding if I was worth listening to or if he would tear my throat out before hearing me say another word. I knew my heart was running rampant and that he could hear it. I knew it, but the body understood when it was in check even if the mind still wanted to play the cheeky monkey.

"While I appreciate the gallant attitude," he said to me, voice how I would imagine a talking serpent's to be. His odd accent of Spanish and Italian, a rough edge of German, pushed out the English he always tried to affect. "You are in no position to make demands." His hand came around my throat. I felt a gush in my underwear as my body reacted to the slight pressure on my neck. He hissed and pressed a knee between my legs.

"Perhaps not. Maybe you will kill me right now, in your home, after making such an effort to protect me." I turned my head a bit though his hand tightened a smidge. It annoyed me that he knew I was turned on by the inference of violence. Not that I was okay with bullying or abuse. Not at all. But a bit of pain with my pleasure? A little fright in my foreplay? He could bend me over and rail me right now. Yet I held my ground, even if it was a second away from becoming a ground puddled in my wetness.

"I am very good at cleaning up my messes and accidents," he said, teeth clamping on my collarbone, which was definitely more painful than pleasurable.

I punched him in the stomach and immediately elbowed him in the rib. He let go and snarled, tearing his own wrist open like he simply had to destroy flesh. I gaped at the mess of tendons and open muscle. There was no where I could run. I wouldn't make it a step out of this kitchen, and even if I did, no door would hold a blood-mad vampire lost to his demon. The question was whether I could get him to calm the fuck down long enough to take some of my blood. I had to try.

"Javi," I said, moving my hands up over my paper-thin T-shirt and kneading my own breasts. His growl rumbled the dishes in the cabinets. It also shook lose my inhibitions. I surrendered to my horny self as I had no better options. Maybe I would die whilst having an orgasm. He growled again, watching my hands squeeze my breasts through the white top.

"What is it you need, Javi?" I asked, leaning back against the wall and sliding my hand into my sweatpants. "Or what is it you want?"

His wrist was knitting itself back together but there was still blood all over the floor. I pulled my fingers from my pants, showing him how wet I was. He stepped closer.

"Stay where you are, vampire," I said with far more command in my tone than I felt. I pushed my trousers off my hips more, letting the bones of my hips stick out, then inserted my fingers into my throbbing cunt and pumped, knowing it was just making me more frustrated. "You need to feed, don't you? You should have told me earlier today. I can forgive you if you stop acting like a trampy spaniel."

Amusement flashed over his face, but his eyes were still that caustic green, and his body still trembled. I rode my own fingers and ripped the T-shirt from my torso, exposing my breasts. His breath came out in an animalistic snarl.

"You are playing a dangerous game, my little queen," he said.

I had to force myself to not clamp my thighs together. That ancient predator's voice and the words, "my little queen," had my wanny hot and not at all happy it was being seen to by my fingers alone. I squatted down and ran my hands through his puddle of blood, then stood, drawing trails of his own lifeforce, over my nipples and stomach. I could have sworn he whimpered.

I dared a step in retreat. He watched and smiled but did not move. I dared another, then once more. On the third, I didn't even have time to register that he was in my space in the hallway. My hand shot out to the light switch. He could see too well in the dark, and I struggled.

"What do you think you're doing?" he asked, walking a semicircle around me. I continued to paint his blood on my naked chest.

"I have realized that the need you have for my blood—or rather for human blood—and the way sex increases that need, is also tempered by the presence of your own blood." He staggered back. I gave him a slow half smile, pinching my nipple and coating it in blood. "So, I am attempting to drive some sense into you, Javi."

"And how did you come to this hypothesis?" he asked, leaning in, and nipping at my neck. My hand shot to my core. I hesitated a moment, then moved my hand to the front of his trousers. I rubbed him before answering. His eyes closed.

"Something you had said about the blood in your veins being your humanity and your humanity was what kept your demons in check." I squeezed him light and quick.

"And you thought this would keep me from needing to feed from you? Or from killing you?" His hands came to my breasts and massaged them. It felt much like when he massaged my thighs to get the blood moving.

"I thought it was a card, and I had to play a card of some sort."

"To keep me from feeding?"

"I want you to feed, Javi. I only want you to be fully in control of your faculties when you do it."

His mouth snapped onto my breast, and I felt fangs puncture under my areola. I yelped and grabbed at his hair. He worked the blood from me, teasing the nipple as he pulled and pulled. His hand moved between my legs and flicked my clit. My legs couldn't take much more. I was losing my ability to stand. The tug of his mouth on my breast put me into a sort of trance. Like I was floating above us and watching him feed on me. The way his neck craned over my blood smeared body. The way my body bucked against him. He pulled off, eyes bright, fangs gleaming.

"I will tell you a secret." The words slurred in my ear, the wet whispering touch of his mouth on my cheekbone had a buzzing undercurrent of need. "I am never fully in control with you." He knelt before me and looked up while fastening his mouth between my legs then came away with a sigh. "I just don't know yet who is in more danger because of that."

I pushed the back of his head into me and rode his mouth, feeling the serpent's tongue swirl in me. Each swirl brought with it a psychotropic effect. Light trails danced in my vision. Javi was a drug I could not come down from. He was drinking. I could feel it as he swallowed all of my cum. That tongue tickled my inside walls. My hands slammed on the wall behind me while my hips reared up, as though I could get him closer. Deeper. I felt his thirst for me in the desert of my throat. I could anticipate the feel of his cum soothing my parched throat. My mouth that was sand before a storm surge. His serpentine tongue flickered up in me and slowly licked down the inside of my pussy, curling forward until it slid out and flitted over my throbbing clit.

"Take more," I begged. "Take more. Bite me. Fuck me, Javi. Everywhere. Fucking fill me and empty me."

He tore from me, panting and plunging his fingers in rough and demanding. He licked his finger, reached back, and edged it in my bum while pumping my cunt and rubbing my clit. I didn't know which way to move or how to encourage it. I felt everything all at once.

"Bite me, vampire."

And he did. Hard. On the inside of my thigh while still working every hole. I wanted to feel this forever and wanted it to end now in the climax that was creeping on me. He pushed deeper in the back. My whole body was turbulent.

"Let me"—I panted. "Let me taste you." He stopped. Stopped sucking. Stopped moving his fingers. "I want to taste you."

"Taste me how?" he asked with a note of caution.

"Pull off your trousers. I want your cock in my mouth."

When he did as I asked, the cock that sprang free was glorious. Long and silken with smooth, light-brown skin stretched impossibly tight. It was my turn to kneel. I wiped a hand through my own wet and pumped his shaft before spitting over his tip. He moaned and touched the side of my face. I let the spit drip over him as I grabbed his ass and had him fuck my mouth as deep as he could go. My eyes watered. He slowed and pulled out a bit. I licked a drop of precum before descending on him again.

"I want you to promise something," I said, licking his tip and stroking his balls. He mumbled something that sounded a lot like "anything". "Promise me that you won't let yourself get this out of control again. Not if it's remedied by asking me to feed you." I sucked and took him deeper, once again letting him fuck my mouth.

"Oh, Christ," he said, grabbing my hair and pulling it. I wished Voltaire was in me too. "Am I going to fuck you, or do you plan to do that any longer? Because I am about to cum in that pretty mouth of yours."

He held my hair like the reins of a horse and thrust harder. I wrapped my hands around his cock and worked it as I let him pound into me. I might cum just pleasuring him!

"Tell me now, Ophelia. Am I fucking you or fucking your face?" His voice was raised, words rushed. I knew he was losing control, and I wanted to be the total cause of it, even if it meant not orgasming myself. I wanted to feel him explode in my mouth or all over my face. I wanted to be messy and hot. I tightened my lips around his crown ever so little.

"Fuck!" he yelled and gave a couple sloppy thrusts, bumping the back of my throat before coming in my mouth.

I swallowed and swallowed, taking it all in and wishing I could feed this way too. I loved the taste of him and could suck him off every day. So much cum flooded my mouth and ran down my throat. I backed off him, letting my teeth slide over his shaft and head.

"You never promised."

"I promise," he said, laying on the hallway floor. "Now sit on my face and let me hear you scream my name."

It was over far too quickly, but I was ready to blow when I was taking his length a minute ago. I tipped back and forth, his tongue in me, his lips, over my lips. And we hadn't even fully fucked. I was definitely in check.

"Next time," he said, leaning over me, "we fuck." His words were dirty compared to the gentle kiss he gave me, opening my mouth. "My clever little queen."

His little queen was definitely in check.

CHAPTER FIFTEEN

OPHELIA

Sascha wasn't answering my calls, and her text responses were basically monosyllabic. The rational part of me knew she was assessing what she had been through. If I knew my best friend, I would put money on the fact that she was accepting the likely fact that she wasn't opposed to whatever transpired between her and Alicia or Pete or whomever. She was only opposed to any part of her behavior that had been out of her control. And maybe she thought I would judge her for any part she may have enjoyed. The rational part of me understood her so well, I wanted to give her time.

The less rational, though not completely irrational side of me, resented her chilliness. She knew how hard this time of year was for me and knew I needed her around. I needed to see her family and do the things that made me shut one eye on how my heart rebroke in a thousand pieces every passing holiday season.

It had only been a day since that night in the club, yet it was almost Christmas. I didn't even have the distraction of going to work as everyone working on my hotel had given the "let's circle back in the New Year" bit, which was ever so unhelpful when I was at the tail end of this marathon.

Everyone was done but me. The only good news with my mind on Sascha and Alicia and Javi and whatever the bloody hell had tumble dried my world lately, was that I couldn't dwell on the what ifs with my business venture.

I wandered up the high street, hands shoved deep into the pockets of my puffer coat, deliberately putting off my yearly pilgrimage to my mum's favorite shop. The carrier bag of mince pies and elderflower tonic knocked against my knee as I trudged up the slick sidewalk and into a bookshop. Somehow, picking out a new volume of poetry for my dad didn't hurt as much as picking out Mum's present. I could curl up with the book on Christmas evening, mulled wine in hand, and read the poems aloud and mark up the pages with lines and selections I loved, just as Dad would have done. It was catharsis. Whereas Mum's present made me feel emptier. Like I was trying to fill the void she left with a cashmere blanket or paperwhite tealight. Whichever I could afford depending on the year. I dodged shoppers in the queue so I could make my way back to the poetry section, tucked between the children's section and fantasy shelves. An afterthought of verse in a world of solid prose. That's where my dad existed for me now. I came up short, rounding the table of scores of *Zog* dragons. Javi stood against the wooden shelf, thumbing through a special edition of Keats. His head snapped up when he saw me. Or smelled me. Or however he always knew I was around.

"Oh, hiya," I said, swatting away my scarf. I hadn't seen him today. Or at all after last night's tryst in his hallway. My cheeks heated remembering begging him to let me take him in my mouth. His mouth kicked up in a knowing grin.

"Ophelia." He slid the Keats back onto the shelf without looking. I bet he knew exactly where it went. I shifted from one leg to the other. "Are you nervous around me?" he asked.

I was. "No."

He stepped closer. I wanted to step back and give myself room to breathe, but my feet were locked on the high traffic carpeting like I'd been glamoured. Yet, I hadn't. My body, my heart, my skin, wanted to be close to him. My head? My head told me to run. Not because he was a vampire. Not because of his vampire ex-wife and vampire ex-lover or whatever Pete was to him. Not because knowing him and working for him had put me and Sascha in danger and brought bloody Connor back into my life—a gift I needed like a festering wound. My head wanted me to run from Javier because despite his being undead, he made me feel alive. For the first time since my parents died, and most of my heart died in that crash with them, I felt there was a reason to keep going. Not that I was contemplating ending my life. But my life structure and whole world went up in smoke on the motorway. Ophelia going through the motions of life was a child moving wooden dolls in a doll house. A game of hide-n-seek with friends in a Wendy house until all the friends went home to their real lives. I lived apart from others who didn't have my loss. I lived because that was what you did. You went through the motions. I chased the hope of love with Connor, which killed me more bit by bit. Javi, though, brought out all the things in me I'd thought were long gone. I moved closer to him, but side stepped, reaching for the shelf. Tucked between the romantics was a poet I'd found on social media whose words resonated with me. I pulled out the small book and turned around.

"For yourself?" Javi asked me, pointing to the book. I moved from the back of the store toward the till, Javi falling into step with me.

"For my dad," I answered. His face went blank. "I buy one every year and read the poems like he always did."

We stood in the queue together, and I barely noticed he wasn't buying anything for himself. He seemed content to stand with me. Connor would have been up the pub before I said "bookshop". I wondered again what I had been thinking for all those years.

"What do you get for your mum?" Javi asked with a careful note to his voice.

I waited a beat before I answered. "Her favorite store was the White Shoppe, just across the street."

The queue moved quickly. I was rung up and paid up, pushing out the doors and onto the street. Javi seemed to be happy with waiting for me to finish.

"Depending on my finances, I pick up something from there that she would love. Would have loved, I mean." I scrubbed my hand over my face, knowing it sounded dumb.

"What do you do with the items after Christmas?" he asked, placing a hand on my back to guide us across the high street, where buses and bicycles drove without a care for the pedestrians.

"Depends. I have a box of some of them. The cashmere blanket and socks. The silver locket. The Highland cow cuddly toy."

"Highland cow?" he asked with a smile.

"She loved things like that." I shrugged, pausing at the entrance to the shop. "She loved beautiful things. Soft things. Anything that was bright and looked like it belonged inside a white cottage on the shore. She was a light."

I looked at Javier, somehow knowing he didn't think me childish for saying these things. For buying my long-dead parents Christmas presents. He looked up at the weather-heavy sky and closed his eyes as though seeing something behind the lids.

"Perhaps you should use the items. And feel like a piece of

her is with you then. Though I don't know how one might use a cuddly Highland cow. That is a mystery to me."

I let out a laugh and grabbed his hand, making him come inside with me. Once we crossed the threshold, the idyllic family trees and plush duvets surrounded by matching gray and white family PJs, gave me a pang. I pulled my hand from Javi's, but he held on, lacing his fingers through mine.

"So, what are we looking to get her this year?" he asked, leading me toward the middle of the shop. Deep in my heart, there was a little thump of something unrecognizable.

"I haven't heard from Sascha," I answered, not letting on how the phrasing of his question affected me. "I don't really know how to get through the holidays without her. I will, of course. But—"

He leaned over and kissed me. Once, on my lips. Not a heated, sexual kiss. Not a friendly peck. But the kind I don't think I'd ever received. A kiss that said he understood. And maybe, just maybe, he felt something for me beyond the blood. It confused me. The comfort it gave me. Before I had a chance to say anything, he spoke.

"What if you purchased a candle? One of these enormous ones." He picked up a white ceramic tub with three wooden wicks. The scent was a memory, reminiscent of one of the tropical isles people with loads of money go to escape English winters. "You could burn it and read your dad's poetry. Or burn it before bed each night. Something ritualistic to offer remembrance but also benefits you." I lifted the candle to my nose. "Just a suggestion," he said, giving my hand a squeeze.

"Okay," I whispered. And maybe, it would be.

I finished wrapping the gifts I had bought then placed them under the tiny tree I'd been surprised to find in Javi's sitting room. He stood in the doorway, holding a strand of fairy lights. Without speaking, we both strung the lights. The last bulb topped the spear of the uppermost bough, illuminating Javier's hazel eyes. He pressed his lips together, which I didn't understand how to interpret. Our fingertips touched, pulling out of the pine needles.

"Even without ornaments, it looks magical," I commented. Javi crossed to the opposite side of the room and pulled an enamel box from under the leucite desk. In the glow of fairy lights, the contents of the box looked like a pirate's hidden treasure.

"I used to make stained glass," he began. "Windows mostly. Lamps, chandeliers, things like that. It fell out of fashion some years ago, so my workshop is long since gone." I touched the glass within the box. "I always liked the droplets of liquid that cooled into these gems. Many of them I added holes to and have made jewelry and such. I thought, perhaps, they might suit your tree."

"My tree?" I asked him, pivoting to the object. He reached around me and hung a red glass bubble, no bigger than a thumbprint, on the bough close to my hip. It weighed the branch slightly, swaying from a tiny black ribbon. One of the many ribbons he must have spent time threading through the ornaments. He handed me another.

"I haven't put up a Christmas tree in a very, very long time. And I do not think I ever did it out of anything but irony or acquiescence."

I looked at him, standing and holding another glass bubble, this one a shade of green so similar to his eyes.

"Isn't this out of acquiescence?" I asked, pulling a bauble from the box he'd placed on a lacquered side table. He sniffed in a sound that could have been amusement, could have been resignation, though I wasn't sure how either fit the question.

"This is understanding the pull of the season. For you. For

others. For me, apparently." He looked down at his bare feet. I didn't recall ever seeing his bare feet before and thought it oddly intimate the way his toes sunk into the pile of the rug before the fireplace. "It is your tree. And I hope it gives you a bit of that magic you need over the next few days." He handed me the hazel glass. I wrapped my fingers around his, holding the ornament between shared palms.

"Thank you," I whispered, pushing onto tiptoes to press my lips to his cheek. I could ignore how his skin on mine made me feel. I could ignore the way this gesture of his had me feel like my belly was full of brandy, warm and content. I could ignore it because, sure, I could drop to my knees again for him, or ride him the way my body always begged, but there was something far deeper in this moment between the two of us than the fireworks of sex we were on a path toward. My heels touched the carpet again, and I noticed the scent of spices coming from the kitchen.

Javi left and came back, holding out a cup of mulled wine to me, sipping one himself as we stood hanging his salvaged glass beads on the Christmas tree, which only *he* had thought to gift me. No one, not Sascha, certainly not Connor, had ever thought to go out of their way to make Christmas this special for me. When each bead had been hung, the tree glittered in colored glass and black silk ribbon. I sighed, stepping back, and bumping into the solid mass of Javier. A knee-jerk reaction told me to move away, but Javi brought his arms around me, holding me close. We stood for what felt like hours, me sipping the mulled wine, he holding me as no one had ever done.

I set the cup down, its contents long since empty. Javier's thumb swept across my midsection and that small touch awakened my entire body. As I leaned back against him, his lips pressed to the base of my skull. The small hollow between neck and head had never seemed an erogenous zone until that meeting of his lips and my spine. By the line of tension I now felt against my lower back, I was certain he felt it too. I didn't know if I should lean into it or break the tension with words. Each fairy light twinkled through the glass beads and reflected on the rain smattered window, mesmerizing me. With Javi, I felt transported. Existing somewhere outside of my body yet so fully alive inside of it. The thought that he might not—that he likely did not—feel the same, sobered me. I stepped from his arms. He didn't try to hang on. He didn't pull me back. He let me go.

"You must be peckish," he said, picking up our cups. "Shall I get a takeaway for you?"

I wasn't hungry. I probably should have been. Yet, my stomach felt sour. Too much emotion and mulled wine. I stood, facing the window and its revelry of light refractions.

"Ophelia."

I half turned, looking at him over my shoulder, and said I wasn't hungry. He shook his head and set the cups down again, next to the Balmain trunk.

"What are you thinking?" he asked, standing beside me. Not touching me.

Well, I obviously couldn't say I was thinking he made me feel ethereal. That nothing has made me feel more alive than the undead man beside me, but that he probably didn't feel like that for me. How awkward would that be? I opened and shut my mouth twice, rubbing my arms for warmth. The tatty old jumper I wore needed to be thrown out. I held on to it because it had been my mum's. It was hideous, and I was rather embarrassed I had worn it in front of Javi. I was just about to make a joke of it when he turned me to him and claimed my mouth in one move. My arms were pinned to my chest between us, feeling his heartbeat against them.

"Whatever you're thinking," he said, uncrossing my arms and holding my hands, "stop thinking it."

What had I been thinking? Once his lips met mine, there was nothing in my head but the feel of him. I released his hand and grabbed the back of his neck, forcing him back to my lips. He made a low noise deep in his throat. I let my tongue explore, tracing his lips and teeth. He stiffened when I touched his incisor with my tongue, letting a drop of blood flow into his mouth. Every part of him stiffened at that. Which was exactly what I had wanted. That's when it changed. When his tongue forked into the serpentine muscle and his eyes shone green.

"Reckless, Ophelia," he said, hissing through the teeth I craved. "So very reckless." His teeth scraped along my jaw and neck as he let his hands roam. "I only wanted to kiss you. Now look at me."

I did just that. I pulled back and took him in. From the poisonous sheen of his eyes to the hollowing of his cheeks where I knew he hungered. My eyes looked at him. This predator before me. This machination of evil. Or so I would have been led to believe. I looked at him. I saw the thick bulge in his trousers. The cock I had sucked until he lost all sense. The man who let me do anything to him. And who seemed to do anything for me. Was I reckless? Surely. I was debris in a wave. And I loved drowning.

"Tell me what you want," he ordered. "My hands?" he asked, cupping my cunt. My hips tipped forward. He unzipped my jeans and put his fingers through, brushing my panties aside. I knew how wet I would feel, yet the first slip of his fingertips along my crease lit me up. "Is this all you want?" he asked, slipping a finger inside me. The angle was making it difficult, yet I was just as happy playing this game as he seemed to be. Memories of his fingers in every part of me sent flashbulbs behind my eyes. All I could do was mumble.

"What was that?" he asked. His accent was so thick. Like

cream rolling over his lips and fangs. "I want to bite that hot flesh," he said, pumping his finger. "Want to make you cum as I feed."

I whimpered, rocking on his single finger. I wanted more. More fingers. More everything. I wanted his cock inside every part of me. I wanted to taste his blood too. My heart sped with that thought. He looked at me in alarm as though he'd heard the thought. His fingers pulled from me and went right into his mouth. I watched him lick my wetness from his finger. The pad pricked on the point of his canine. I saw the blood well. Had he heard me? I grabbed his finger.

"Ophelia," he growled.

I met his eyes with my own. I needed this. His closed in resignation.

"Watch me," I said to him.

I brought the finger to my own mouth as his hand went to my hair. The hold he had on my head was sweet and loving, if that could be a word to describe anything between us. I sucked the droplet of blood. Just one, since he healed so quickly. It tasted of him. Of years in the sun and wine. Of something ancient I knew I would always crave. Then it was over, and he was kissing me again. I fumbled with his trousers, and he pulled my ugly jumper from my body, his hands immediately finding my breasts and kneading them over my bra. And then the doorbell went. And a knock sounded at once.

"Javi, open the fucking door. I'm freezing my tits off out here and need to see Lily!" Sascha called.

Javi put his arm out, keeping me from darting to open it. He shook his head and moved to the door himself, whipping out his phone and looking at video footage.

Right. She had been glamoured. Who was to say she wasn't again and this was a trap? Trap? God, that sounded so dumb. He opened the door and a slightly disheveled, damp

Sascha barreled in. She took sight of me and Javier, our trousers half done, empty cups on the sideboard. Her smirk was all I needed.

"Come here, you stupid tart," I said, slinging an arm around her for a hug.

CHAPTER SIXTEEN

OPHELIA

"Did you honestly think I would let you alone on Christmas?" Sascha asked as we sat on the sofa, hands clasped. "Sorry, Javi. No offense."

He made a waving motion and left us alone. I watched him walk from the room, then shook my head. Sascha looked at me with twinkling eyes.

"Don't start."

"Oh, I'm going to start," she said, holding in a laugh. "But first I need to get this out, yeah?"

I nodded. She removed her hand from mine and pulled on a point of her black fringe. Javi came back in and handed us more mulled wine and said he would take a walk outside so we had more privacy. Sascha waited until the front door snicked closed and we heard the alarm set. Javi was taking no chances with our safety it seemed.

"Before you say anything, Sasch," I said. "You and me? We're okay. Yeah?"

She nodded but still looked worried. We took long sips from the warm spiced red.

"You know I would never make you watch me with someone, right?" she asked. I said of course I knew. "Fuck. I thought I knew how to start this."

I made to take her hand again, but she pulled away, and I understood. She couldn't be touched right now. She needed to step back and tell me journalistically. So, I finished my wine too quickly, feeling it go to my head.

"Lily, I almost fucked Connor."

I stood up too quickly. The room went a bit spinny, so I grabbed the arm of the sofa, righting myself. I felt hot and cold all over.

"To be clear, it was not my choice. I was glamoured. It was the night we were at the private club. Pete called him after you left—or before. I don't know. You left, he showed up—no I am not blaming you, for fuck's sake, Lil."

I stood picking at the button in the tufting on the sofa.

"Connor was not glamoured." It was all I could get out of my mouth. Javier had told me Connor was not glamoured, and I'd had my suspicions at the time anyway. Sascha looked sick. Her pallor was morphing into the shade of gray green she wore.

"Ah. That's...that's rather upsetting. I know you know this. But he's the slimiest piece of cockwad I've ever come across in my life."

"Apart from Pete? And Alicia?" I asked. I sounded venomous. I knew I did. But I had a spore of hate in my belly, and it needed to leech onto someone else.

"They are vampires," Sascha countered.

"Javi is a vampire!" I screamed it at her. "He's not like *them*!"

"You don't know the half of who he is and what he's done," Sascha said matter of fact.

I spun and balled my hands into fists. I wanted to strike something.

"How about you shut your fucking mouth about Javi for now and finish what you had been saying. Fucking my ex? Go on."

"Not fair, Lil. I didn't fuck him." She pointed at me, raising a thick, curved brow. "That night I found myself on the table in that club restaurant, with Connor looking at me one way and Pete watching. You don't know what it feels like being glamoured. It's like you're there, inside yourself, seeing someone else acting as you. I wanted to scream at me to get away from Fuckface. I wanted to tell myself to rip his dick off and feed it to Pete. But I couldn't, of course. What I saw instead, was my face—this face"—she made a box around her face with her hands—"smiling at Fuckface while Pete fed from me."

"Yeah, Pete's a real treat," I spat. "I bet he and Alicia have partners all over the world feeling like you did."

"I don't know that they do."

"Why are you defending them, Sascha?" I yelled.

She stood and faced me. "Because I am in love with Alicia." The sound of rain outside was drowned out by the roaring in my ears. "I met her before I was glamoured. I fell in love with her."

I walked to the window, almost hoping Javi would come back in. I did not want to hate my best friend. For either matter she could have controlled and that which she could not have controlled.

"Let me get this straight." I spoke to the glass, my back turned on my best mate. "You fell in love with Javi's ex-wife, who is trying to extort him, before you were glamoured by her or Pete. Or both. Then, whilst glamoured by your new girlfriend or her maybe partner, maybe not, you also almost fucked my ex and Pete. And you agree my ex, who you almost fucked, albeit unwillingly is a waste of skin, yet you are defending the man who watched you nearly fuck him, and defending his partner, who is now maybe your girl-friend. But still Javi's supposedly dead ex-wife? Am I all caught up?"

She started walking over. I saw her in the reflection and held up a hand.

"Lily. I'm not defending Pete. I don't like him. This is all a mess. You know my morals are questionable and I would kill for you. I will happily end Connor and even Pete if you ask. I just cannot help how I feel about Alicia. And I need you to understand that I will give her up if you ask it."

"I ask it." She looked stricken but nodded. Immediately, I regretted saying that. "Sascha, no. I don't mean that. I'm not going to ask you to give her up. I will caution you though. She's very manipulative. Javi thought she was dead for a century. She only showed face when she wanted something from him. And believe me, he will find out what she really wants."

"I'll find out."

"What?" I asked, turning around.

"I'll find out what she wants. You're right. Regardless of my feelings, she's pulling one over on"—she gestured with a wild swirl of her hand—"probably all of us. So, I'll find out, and if it's not good, I'll give her up. Gladly. Because no matter who I may fall for, Lil, you're my sister from another mister. I love you more than anyone else." She crossed her heart and pressed two fingers to her lips to kiss, then split them and wiggled her tongue between the digits, making me laugh. I put my arm around her shoulders.

"Love you too, tart," I said. "I'm sorry you went through all of that."

"Pshaw. That's what meds are for."

"Pretty sure it's 'that's what friends are for'," I said, narrowing my eyes at her.

"That too." She went up onto tip toes and kissed my cheek. "Now, I want to hear all about Javi's abilities with his fangs, what his cock looks like, and when you started having bloody passionate sex with him."

The front door opened then, and a red-faced and very wet Javier walked in, pressing his lips into a tight line. I covered my face with my hands and shook it.

"Oh," Sascha said. "That's a shame. Listen, tomorrow is Christmas Eve. Obviously. And I will see you back here for our traditional get pissed and eat curry, then dance until we toss up, yeah? Javi, you're invited too."

"Thank you. I thought perhaps you were planning to sequester me to my private quarters."

"Nah. The more the merrier, Daddy Sharp Teeth," she said, gnashing her own teeth at him. "Call me later, Lil, and tell me all about Javi's cock and your bloody sex. Ta, darling."

With that, she swept her compact self from the townhouse, leaving Javi and me standing in a one-meter gulf of awkward distance in the sitting room.

Javi closed the distance and took my hand, gently pulling me from the room and into the kitchen. He then lifted me by the hips and sat me on the marble counter before turning around.

"What are you doing?" I asked, half hoping the plan was to lay me back and feel his tongue in me. He stood up holding a pot.

"Making you dinner." He switched on the tap and filled the pot before calling over his shoulder. "Then, I was thinking we might have bloody passionate sex." My gut clenched. "If it suits," he added.

"That water had better boil quickly," I answered. "Otherwise only one of us is eating tonight."

He folded his arms over his chest and smirked, eyes raking over me. "Oh no. We must give you content for your conversation with Sascha tomorrow."

I crooked my finger at him. He stepped between my legs.

"Just a kiss for now then?" I leaned over and met his lips with mine, realizing it was probably the first real kiss between us. Without anything else going on. He must have noted that too as he kept it soft and sweet. Fluttering in my belly told me I was so far gone with Javi, I might never find my way back. His forehead pressed to mine as I took his face in both my hands, content to just be near him for this stolen moment.

Penne swam in olive oil and chili I'd watched Javi chop into fine confetti. His hands made quick work of shaving parmesan over the dish and placing two bowls on the table with goblets of a deep red with an aroma of butter and roses.

"Yes, I can eat," he said, forking the pasta into his bowl with more grace than I had ever managed whilst eating. "I don't need it to survive, of course. So, I save it for when it's something I truly enjoy."

"And pasta is something you truly enjoy? Not, like steak tartar or lamb?"

He smiled at me with his eyes as he took another bite.

"There's something you should know about me, Ophelia," he said, and I set my fork on the side of the shallow bowl. "My love and adoration of simple carbohydrates has carried over from my previous life."

I snorted, taking a sip of wine and reaching my glass to him for a clink. "I knew I liked you for a reason."

I felt his toe touch mine under the table. As I finished my last bite, wishing there was more, as I always did at the end of a bowl of pasta, the table buzzed. Javi's eyes darted to his phone. He unlocked it and opened up the camera footage before I could process his movement. He muttered a string of curses that sounded like they were a mix of three different languages and all teaming with some combination of God, fuck, someone is going to die, and quite possibly, sucking his cock. Which, of course, I was hoping I would be privy to in the next few minutes. He watched the footage and pushed the phone over to me to see.

Alicia stood on the stoop outside the townhouse, holding Connor by the scruff of his neck, blood dripping into his leather bomber jacket. A jacket I'd seen in Selfridges for over 1700 pounds. The fact that I was more disgusted by Connor wearing a jacket I knew he couldn't afford on his own than the fact that he was bleeding out in what seemed to be some sort of blackmail scheme, told me a bit about myself. I couldn't care less what became of Connor. Maybe that made me awful. But he was a black thumb on my life. Decay bloomed where he touched. So, it was not my duty at this point in time to step in to help him. I picked up my bowl, rinsed it, and slid it in the dishwasher.

"It's your home and your ex-wife. I want no part of what she is scheming with Connor. He is dead to me." I kissed Javi's cheek so he would know I felt no animosity toward him, then I went to my room.

CHAPTER SEVENTEEN

JAVIER

I was rarely unhinged. In the past century, I had honed my emotional responses, resurrecting my humanity and refining it with the objective skill that is intrinsic to vampires. At least I thought I had. Until this curvy, dark-haired siren entered my life. Now, all my responses and decisions spun in orbit around three things only: Feeding from Ophelia, protecting Ophelia, and wanting to fuck Ophelia. I needed each as much as the other. When I fed, I wanted to bury my cock to the hilt inside her, taste her cum and the way it mingles with her rose-scented blood. When I protected her, I wanted to feed from her in front of everyone and let them all know she was mine. Wanted them to see me make her scream my name with my fingers and teeth in her skin. I also wanted to kill anyone who did see her compromised, which was a bit of a conflict of need. I was aware. And when I was near her, the need for her was so great, I couldn't tell if I had forgone any sense of my own preservation and sanity.

I had wanted to make the evening special for her. Of course, I always wanted it to be her cunt strangling my cock, with its hot, wet heaven. However, she was so obviously hurting. Beyond the club scene and having to see that horrid boy, Connor. Beyond worrying for Sascha. She was hurting from missing her parents. She needed just a night of someone else taking care of her. I would wager she's not had that feeling since before the accident that claimed her family. That is why I brought in the tree. I wanted to see her light up as the tree lit. I wanted to show her a bit of my past and decorate the blasted tree together. I wanted to *feel* alongside her. To allow her the safe haven of relaxing here with me. I bear no grudge on Sascha intruding on us. That was, from what I gathered, a positive thing. Though, there was a shroud of worry lingering over Ophelia since Sascha left. She would tell me when it was time. When we finally finished our meal and I was beyond ready to tease every tendon of stress from Ophelia's being before sinking into her again and again, and then Alicia showed up? I realized how far gone I truly was with my donor.

I took my time rinsing my bowl and washing the pot and colander. None of us really cared if Connor bled out, but it would be an inconvenience if Alicia left him on my stoop. I loathe cleaning blood from pavement. It was ten minutes or so later when I answered the door.

"You are not bringing in that riffraff," I said, holding the door a fist's width ajar. "Say what you came to say."

She dropped Connor on the ground. His arm hit the iron garden chair which sat outside my front door, the elbow popping at an alarming angle. He didn't so much as wince, so I knew he had been glamoured. Finally.

"Where is our wilting Lily?" Alicia asked, reaching over and touching my hand. I twisted hers until it cracked. She hissed, her fangs descending. "You are mad for her, aren't you, husband?"

I smiled, allowing my own fangs to drop. "I am just mad, Alicia."

"Javi, what I want is so very simple. As you said, it is more work for you to retain the property than it is to turn it over to me. Give me the estate in Tuscany, and I will be out of your miserable, cunt-whipped existence, forever."

"I will find out why you want the property, Alicia. Even you are not so mad as to go to these lengths to simply want property. Your funds are healthy. You can easily buy your own vineyard." I crossed my arms over my chest. I could hear Ophelia in the bath. Each lift and splash of her limbs in the water rang through me. I heard the bar of soap slip over her skin. My cock hardened knowing how slippery she would be. Alicia noticed and laughed.

"She is pretty, I suppose. If you like them tall with hips you can grab on to. You know I prefer petite females. Ones with elfin features and tight cunts just wide enough for my tongue." I rolled my eyes. "Plus, Ophelia's hair is so long and thick. Not like Sascha's. I prefer the pixie cut, myself. Less mess sticking to me when we get sweaty and bloody, no?"

I leveled my eyes at her. Alicia was always a puzzle and she had just handed me clues. Sascha was a part of this, but why? I sighed, pushing at the swell in my trousers, letting her see how aroused I was by the woman down the hall.

"You are right, Alicia. I am cunt-whipped. In fact, your timing is rubbish. I was a breath away from my fangs and cock taking all of her. So, I will tell you what." Her eyes lit up, knowing she had cornered me. "Take that piece of trash out of here and make sure Ophelia and I never see him again. And give me through Christmas to see about transferring the title, with a blood agreement that once transferred, I will never have to see your face as long as we both exist." She did a little dance with her shoulders and kicked Connor, telling him to get up. "Deal?" I made a show of turning to look over my shoulder and adjust my crotch again, squeezing my own balls for good measure. It was half theater, half necessity.

"Deal. My God, Javier. I wonder if you were ever this taken by me."

"What you and I had was a very different animal. Agree to my terms."

"I will see you on the twenty-seventh. No sooner. And I shall keep this pet away from you both. I agree. Go fuck your desperate little slut and give yourself some relief. You're quite pathetic now, Javier."

I grabbed her by the throat. I was always the fastest of us all. Her feet dangled several inches off the ground, her eyes glazed and furious.

"I have been generous with my terms Alicia. If you call her a whore or any such names again, I shall tear your head from your body and worry about disposing of you later. Clear?"

She tried to nod, and I dropped her, knowing she would catch her balance as gracefully as a feral cat. I shut the door and watched the footage until she and Connor had cleared the two blocks I had covered with cameras. It was only then I let myself slump against the foyer wall.

"Javi?"

I looked up at the sound of her voice. I had gotten so used to her sounds and scents, I didn't notice her leave the bathroom.

"Are you all right?"

I must have looked just as pathetic as Alicia said I was. Sitting on the floor in my foyer, rubbing my hand through my hair. Still, as I looked at the woman standing in my hallway, a towel wrapped under her arms, I couldn't answer her. I couldn't breathe. She took a step toward me, and I could see the concern pinching her features.

"Everything is fine," I said as I rose to standing. I gave her the thirty-second synopsis of what occurred moments before, preferring to keep mention of Sascha to myself until I could give her best friend a proper sketch of my puzzled thoughts. She smoothed her thumb down the side of my face, tilting her head to the side like she knew I was hiding something. "If I know Alicia, there are pieces to fit together here, and if it's all the same to you, I would rather not do that right now. I think we both need to forget about the pestilence of my past. At least for tonight."

She gave me a small smile. One that told me there were secrets within her, waiting to be found and unwrapped. In the fairy-lit dimness of the room, her warm skin glistened with water droplets and her eyes caught the reflections of so many different colored beads.

"I don't know if I've said this to you," I began, rushed and if I were being honest, nervous, "you are the most beautiful creature I have known. In all my years."

She stepped back like she had been given bad news. I was confused by the reaction.

"Did I say something wrong?" I asked her, wishing I had just kissed her. She shook her wet head profusely. "Then what?"

Her fingers scraped the sides of her cuticles until she wrapped them in the top hem of her towel.

"I haven't..." She cleared her throat. "No one has ever said that to me." That made no sense to me. "I've had the 'you're so fine' and 'I'd smash that ass'."

"You are beautiful. Not pretty. Not just 'hot'," I said to her, allowing my conviction to shine through. "The only thing I can say about what you have heard in the past is that all those boys—or girls if the case is as such—are sewer rats. And," I said, knowing I was getting angry and aroused at the same time, so my accent was likely all over the place, "quite frankly, those sewer rats should be exterminated. Lucky for them, I am otherwise occupied at the moment."

She still stood in shock.

"You would kill for me?" she asked. I probably already had, though she didn't need to know that tonight.

"I would maim for you. Torture." I stepped closer to her, gauging her mood and knowing I was close to my demon. My demon knew she didn't altogether dislike when I gave way to it. "I would destroy for you. So, yes, Ophelia. I would kill for you. Without question nor regret."

Her mouth popped open in an "o" I wanted to do wonders to. The rise and fall of her chest became rapid, the push of her breasts straining the towel. She hooked her thumb between her cleavage and pulled the towel off. I had seen her nude before. I had touched her and fed from the hidden parts of her. She had been on my face, riding my mouth, filling me with her every essence. Yet, the body before me, flushed and shimmering in the dim lights, *changed* me. Had her eyes strayed from my face, she would have seen the solid mass in my trousers. She needed worshipping. I knelt before her, threading my fingers through hers and kissing the soft point of her hip. Alicia was right. I have never felt about another person nor vampire the way I was begin-ning to feel for Ophelia. I took our joined hands and kissed them, feeling her shiver against me. Her inner thighs shone with wetness. That scent of her rose blood and something calling me home beckoned. I turned and ran my tongue up her seam. As I was fully aroused and allowing my demon to guide me, my tongue forked out, eliciting a moan from her.

"Let me see it," she whispered. "That tongue." She yanked my head back. It slithered out, the forked ends wavering toward her. Wanting her blood. Her cum. "It's so beautiful, Javi."

That was all I could take. I dived forward, sending my tongue into her, letting it lick the inside of her passage, pressing forward where her G-spot sat. Her knees buckled, and I pressed her against the wall for support.

"May I?" I asked, letting her see my fangs drop. "It's okay to say no."

"Yes. Feed."

My face moved in again, fangs stretched to their longest length. I suckled a spot to the side of her lips, then as I pierced the skin, so very slowly, I slipped two fingers into her. The intrusion of fingers and teeth matched pace. She whimpered, digging her long nails into my scalp. How I wanted her to draw blood. Instead, with the final push, I was able to drink from her. My face was covered in her cum as her blood ran down my throat. I drank. This creature I needed for my very existence stood and let me take her life force. Her body tightened and I knew she was close. With one last swallow, I extracted my teeth and placed my mouth completely over her sex. Her climax rocked me to the point of almost coming in my trousers. I would happily die right here with her blood and cum filling me. But tonight, I was making it last.

CHAPTER EIGHTEEN

OPHELIA

A sound like the rimming of a finger atop a crystal glass had called my attention in the bath. Javi was still with Alicia and Connor, and I simply couldn't deal with that tonight. When I heard the sound, my core began pounding. It all seemed so off the wall. Vampires and feedings. Bloody sex I couldn't wait to have. The way that something about Javi called to me. Like he had said or felt something out there, whilst speaking with Alicia, that pinged my body. A chemical text message that might have been checking in on me, might have been a rush of desire. Either way, it was why I rose from the bath.

The look on Javier's face when I saw him was haunting. He was exhausted. I hadn't noticed before. He hadn't let me see. But seeing him slumped against the wall of his foyer, I could never have seen that and said it was a powerful vampire. His dark brows were drawn in, creasing his forehead and eyes. I wanted to push my hands onto his shoulders to get them away from his ears. I wanted to make it better. To protect him. A feeling I have never had outside of Sascha. And his explanation of what transpired with those at the door was washed over with him saying he would kill for me. Maybe it was sick of me, but I wanted that. I wanted to be held high enough for someone—no, not just someone, Javier

—to kill for. It was no shock what happened next. I needed him on me. Inside of me with fingers and cock and that fucking tongue. And he obliged. That forked muscle of his made me erupt every time, and he drank it all.

I knew that look in his eye he had as he licked the last of me from his lips. The look that said he was teetering on the edge of something disastrous. Each cut and cord of muscle, from his jaw to the lines under his jumper, were so tight it looked painful. A pressurized explosive in the slice of a second before it blows.

"Javi," I breathed, letting my head hit the wall behind me. "This is where we fuck." I had never heard my voice so low and thick. As though I myself had a demon ready to pounce. His fangs flashed with the wicked grin he gave me.

"Ah, but this is only where it begins." He stood, helping me up as well, then leaned in to whisper in my ear, "Run."

All thought drained from my head. Where? Run where? Outside? I was naked, and it was December. Our eyes were locked, and I knew as soon as I dropped mine, he would give me a couple of breaths to get a head start. I darted left and sprinted down the hall, careening around the doorframe into a room. Not my room. *Shit*, I thought. I didn't know his room at all. Just as I tried to slam the door shut, it flew open, narrowly missing me. He grabbed my arms and hauled me to him. Those hazel eyes I loved were blazing a toxic green telling me he was lost to his demon. Or letting the demon out to play. And I was ready to play.

"Hello, demon," I said. He lifted me clean off the ground and up against a metal bedpost. I wrapped my legs around his waist, my naked flesh soaking through his trousers. I didn't know how those hadn't split open with the press of his cock against them. "Is this a threesome or am I playing with one or the other?" I pushed into him eliciting a growl and his mouth latching onto my wrist.

"I am my demon, Ophelia. We are one in the same." His tongue swirled on the inside of my wrist.

"Bite," I commanded.

He chuckled, unzipping his trousers with his free hand. They dropped to the ground. His length was hot and so hard it looked painful.

"Bite me, Javi."

"No." He squeezed my breast, making my eyes roll back. "I have taken enough. And plan to take more later." That had me at attention. I covered his hand with mine, encouraging him to massage my breasts. "Once you have fed from me."

Every nerve ending in me stood at the ready. Those words barreled into me, a call to action I had been waiting for. I reached between us and took him in my hand, sliding my thumb over the top of his cock. He rested his forehead on my shoulder, breathing heavily and working a rhythm with my hand.

"Where?" I asked. "And how?"

He held my gaze as he drew fangs across his wrist. Each nerve in my stomach clenched. A cat's cradle of need I'd never known. It dawned on me then what he had wanted that night in the kitchen. Not to simply tear flesh. He wanted me to feed from him. Human, fangless, had braces for four years, me. Blood welled at the gash. I snatched his wrist and brought it to my mouth and sucked. His hips pumped against my hand holding his cock. Each sip of his blood ran down my throat like wine. The thought of ever drinking someone's blood had never crossed my mind before Javi. Humans couldn't digest human blood. I had been wanting this. *Craving* this, probably just as much as he had. Yet, I wasn't a vampire. Merely a human woman. So why did I need Javier's blood in me? Why could I not concentrate but for the desire to let him fuck my mouth until I could swallow his cream? I dreamt about it. About licking his head and making him drip with want. I dreamt of doing what I was doing right now. Lapping his slowing blood and drinking.

His hand went into my hair.

"You have no idea what you are doing to me," he said, voice wavering as though it were moving through petrol fumes. I had an idea. He felt vulnerable in my hands and mouth. My own prey, caught in a welcome trap. And I knew what I was doing to him, because every time he touched me, he was doing it to me as well. I wanted this. All of this. I wanted to consume him in every possible way. The depth of that frightened me a bit. I pulled my mouth from his wrist as the wound closed. He wiped a drop of blood from my chin, placing his thumb in my mouth. That single last drop of his garnet blood sent images to my mind. His blood tasted like him. Like his kisses and cum. Sunbaked tiles and iced wine. Sea salt and greenery. He tasted of eons and summer. Unbridled passion, violence, and freedom. He tasted the way I wanted the world to taste from here on out. I couldn't make myself look away from the unchecked demon in his eyes. The green nearly neon in the darkened room in which I was beginning to see better.

"What do you taste?" he asked me. I continued to slide my hand over him yet inched closer. His tip pressed into my stomach.

"You taste of..." How could I tell him? Clearly, he wanted me. Clearly, he was open to being vulnerable with me. Yet, what tasting him made me feel, also felt so damning.

"Allow me to tell you what I taste when I feed from you," he said, apparently sensing my apprehension. "The taste which haunts me when you aren't flowing through my veins and throat."

He took my hand from him, his cock still at full attention. I wanted to drop down and suck. He lifted my chin with a knowing smile. We walked backward to the four-postered bed. His hand came around my back, urging me to lie back.

"Before we go any further," he said, eyes on me. He looked professional. The Javier I shook hands with the first day I showed up for this new job. "Do you want this?"

The fact that he was asking me for consent, when we had both been covered in every fluid from each other, was almost comical. If it weren't exactly what I needed to be asked. I laid my palm against his stubbled cheek.

"I want this, Javi." His eyes closed briefly. "I want you. In every way."

A shudder ran through him. His cock was laying on me, the feel dizzying where it hit my clit. He rubbed along me.

"You taste of roses. The scent of rose under a summer storm sky. Your cum," he said, reaching between us and pulling a finger through my wet crease, before bringing it to his mouth. He groaned, his cock twitching against my clit. My shoulders shook from pleasure. "Your cum is what the creamy nose of champagne leaves on the tongue. It makes my spine weak, Ophelia. I have never tasted another like you. I have never been so very affected by another. I want to consume you, over and over again, draining you," he said. Our bodies rocked together. My own spine was leaden. His mouth grazed my nipples. I was building again. "Filling you with myself." He pulled away. I wanted to slap him and claw into him to come back. He smirked, leaning to kiss me. His kiss went deep, tongue circling mine. When he moved away again, I did grab his hair, yanking him to me.

"You taste like forever," I whispered. "The past and present painted as one. Like I could drink from you and know the secrets of the world. You taste like summer heat and sweating glasses of wine." With a violent tug, I kissed him, biting his lips until his blood dripped on my tongue. He snarled into me, eyes blazing. "I don't know why this is, Javi, but I want to taste you forever."

He shot back in an abrupt whirl. I pushed onto my elbows, knowing I had said something wrong. His chest rose and fell, beating the air around him. The faint moonlight glinted on his fine dark chest hair and the sleek skin of his thick, erect cock. Was there ever someone so perfect? It seemed he was attempting to say something. The words looked poised to come out, yet he rubbed a hand over his face instead.

"Come back," I said. "We don't have to talk. Just come inside me. I can't wait any longer." He stepped between my legs. I looked down at us. His length so close to my opening. "I need you inside me. I've had you in my mouth, Javier. I need you in my cunt."

That must have been the last straw. He very slowly grabbed himself. The smile that started small and shy, stretched, showing fangs. He watched my face as he ran the head of his cock over my clit. Spots blew in my vision. Javi's tall frame leaned over, sliding a hand under my bum and scooting me back. Still, he stood between my legs, cock at my threshold.

"What are you waiting for, vampire?" I asked, raising a brow at him. I scooted further back on his bed and dropped my knees open in final invitation. He crawled over the mattress and slipped into me. I felt every ridge as he pushed to the hilt and paused.

"This will be the first of many times I fuck you, Ophelia." He thrust in, harder this time. I wanted it rough. I wanted to be pounded. "There may be times I am full demon." His eyes took me in and there was black swirling in the green. "There may be times I am almost human." He stroked my chest and jaw with soft fingertips. Then the thrusting grew more fervent. I raised my legs, wrapping them around his back so I could feel his balls smacking my ass. "Each time I fuck you, my little queen," he said, our bodies slamming in tandem, so hard my teeth sang, "I will make sure you know what forever feels like." His lips met mine but broke away as he started to shake.

"Show me then," I said, raising my hips to rub every sticky part of me on him. "Show me how forever will feel."

Heat rose from my toes to my core, a hand pressing into my stomach. The heat was a cresting wave, ready to swallow me. I cried out, turning my head and tearing my blunt teeth across his chest. He roared, pistoning into me a final time. His hot cum coated me as his cock pulled out. It pooled on my stomach. I sucked at the bite I made on his pectoral. He kept spewing more and more onto me. In me, much like the ping of a bell earlier, something altered. I felt changed. Awakened. I knew I wanted more. More of this. All of it. He looked at me, cupping my face as though readying for an apology.

"You are my undoing," he said simply.

I lay on his bed, his cum on my body, his sheets soaked in mine, his blood in my mouth, and I felt for the first time, I was where I should be.

SASCHA

No one knew Lily better than I did. No one had seen her at her worst. Not her parents, nor Fuckface Connor, and not Javier. Though, it was becoming increasingly obvious that he was worming his way into her trust and heart. My Lily. I wanted her happy. I wanted her to let go and be able to trust someone. To allow someone in, both physically and emotionally. No one needed to be worshipped and straight up fucked more than my girl. I just wasn't so sure Javi was the right one to fill that role. Who was I though? I was one poor choice after the next, saved only by the fact that I had the money to wash it all away, and nine times out of ten, I really couldn't give a fuck. But I gave more than a fuck about Lily. And unfortunately, for all of us, I gave more than a fuck about Alicia.

I wasn't simple. I understood the position this put all of us in. I understood the animosity. I understood why Javi didn't trust her. I would throw a wobbler had I been married to her, thought she'd died, and then have her turn up a century later looking for our marriage settlement. It's complicated.

I left Javi's place, knowing that he and Lil would be slick as eels within no time. Truth be told, I'd never seen her so starry eyed over anyone. She kept that heart of hers locked down tight. Not that I ever wanted to get in my best mate's pants before, as she was my sister in all but blood, but seeing the electricity between her and vamp boy made me wet. I wish I had someone to get slick with myself, yet I walked away from Alicia that night at the club. I had to. Regardless of my feelings for her, she put me in the position to be enthralled by Pete. She sold me out. Pimped me out. And I was not a happy Sascha. When I got home tonight, I was ready to hate fuck my vibrator and send a video of it to Alicia just to rile her up. I knew she wanted me too. And while I was not forgiving her any time soon, I knew I'd let her back into my life at some point. But oh, if I wasn't going to make her beg for it. On her knees. With her tongue.

I stopped at Tesco to pick up a bottle of gin, cranberry juice, and some biscuits before coming home. The thought of making my vampire bitch beg fogged my mind as I unlocked my door and switched on the lights in my flat. Then I nearly dropped the shopping bag.

"Ciao, Sascha." Alicia sat with one leg over the other, haloed in the glow from the chandelier in my foyer. I hadn't thought about it before, but I could see her ancientness then. The way her small features were the epitome of beauty centuries ago. Her face was a collection of softness. So at odds with the killer she was. The slope of her nose and dimpled cheeks looked more the youngest daughter in an aristocratic family than the vampire she was.

I walked to the kitchen to unload my groceries, pulling a glass for my gin.

"I know you are unhappy with me, no?" she asked.

I glanced across the kitchen island and out to the velvet chair where she sat. Her legs uncrossed, giving me the briefest glimpse of the black lace covering her cunt.

"Hello, vamp bitch," I said, glugging gin into my glass. I

didn't really want the gin anymore, but it was fairly awkward, and I was half trying to not throw the bottle at her. "Unhappy is a euphemism for wanting to burn you alive for pimping me out and putting Lily at risk."

She waved me off and leaned forward, her knees opening again, though her elbows came between them, blocking my view. Not that I should be looking, as I was angry.

"Lily will be fine. Javier has gotten—what is the word? Possessive of her."

I tossed back the gin I'd poured, not bothering with the proper drink I had planned to make. The alcohol set my throat on fire. I didn't like it.

"I apologize, however, for 'pimping' you as you say. Though, we see things differently, you and I."

"How so?" My voice sounded like a teenager, and I made a saccharine face at her. She scoffed. "No, really, Alicia," I said, leaning onto the counter and looking her in the eyes. Her eyes dipped to my chest where I knew my small breasts touched the stone. "Tell me how we see things differently. I see it like this: You and I met. We fucked. We kept meeting up. Fucking. Then we started becoming—" I waved my hand and slammed it back down on the counter, denting my gold bangle. Bloody hell, that was Cartier. "Anyway. At some point, you indicated you knew the architect on the hotel Lil and I are opening. We all met for drinks. It was a blur from then on. Someone staged Pete attacking me and Lil up the street. You knew he was enthralling me. You knew I wasn't myself when he was around. You knew it wasn't my choice—"

She interrupted me. "I gutted him for it." She stood.

"What?" She took a step. "Stay there." My command was in a stronger voice than I thought I'd muster in the moment. She stopped.

"I gutted him."

"For glamouring me?" I asked.

"No. That had been the plan. I am sorry, my love. I can tell you truthfully now." I threw the glass, aiming for her face. She caught it and set it on the side table. "It was not the plan for him to try to fuck you. No one's cock but mine was supposed to be in you."

"You don't have a cock, Alicia. You are one big cunt."

She laughed. "I have a strappy one."

"Strap on."

"Sí."

I rolled my eyes, diligently avoiding pushing at my crotch.

"And yet you stood by, knowing he was trying to have a go with me. And all this in front of Fuckface Connor. Knowing I could have been made to fuck Connor." I started shaking. It was a trauma response which started as soon as Javier released me from the glamour. I would forever be grateful to him for that.

"I stood by, yes. But I gutted him. I took my dagger," she said, the lisp of her speech speeding up with the heat in her answer. She was angry too, it seemed. Good. I was angrier. "I took the dagger and stabbed him in the balls." I felt queasy. "He heals. Then I stabbed him in the belly as he was distracted by the attempted castration. I pulled the knife up his stomach. I gutted him. He did not try to fuck you after that. Nor did the fuck faced boy."

She sat back down. It seemed like a subservient action. An apology.

"Why?" I asked her, as I walked into the living room. She looked up at me, big brown eyes pleading.

"As I said. No one touches you but me. No one." I saw her fangs slip over her lips. Whether it was rage or possessiveness or she was turned on, I didn't know. I kicked her high heeled foot, splaying her legs where she sat in the chair.

"You lied to me," I said and kicked the other. Her legs

were fully open. I was too close to see that slash of black lace again, but I knew it was there.

"I did." Her response was somber. She started to stand, and I shoved her back down. She allowed it, of course, as I was as tall as a bar stool, and she was a vampire. I saw her tongue dart out, licking her lips between razor sharp canines.

"You let him trick me," I said, leaning over her. "Let him do some carnival trick on me so he could get to Lily, Alicia. So he could get off with Fuckface in front of me and Lily. My best mate's ex!"

"And I have apologized. I cannot change the past, my Sascha. But I can tell you," she said raising up slightly so we were close enough to kiss, "I regret I was weak enough to not see he would do that. Though, I understand his desire to."

"I hate you," I said.

"And you love me. So very tedious how they balance, no?"

I growled in frustration and kneeled on her lap. I hoped it hurt. Hoped my knee was bruising her pelvis.

"I want to make you hurt. I want to fuck you up the way you fucked me up." I dug my knee down. She grabbed my hand, unclenching my fingers one by one.

"Do it," she said, placing my open fingers on her chest, under her shirt. I yanked my hand back, but she was quicker. Fucking vampires. Her shirt was off, her full breasts on display, my hand back between them. "Make me bleed, my Sascha. Use these," she said tapping my black acrylics nails. "And hurt me. Hit me. Bite me. You want to. I want you to."

But I didn't. Instead, I sunk my nails into her soft skin, groaning at the feel of her breasts in my hands. Her fangs fully descended. My knees slipped to either side of her hips, our pelvis bones pressed against each other. She reached behind me and lifted my ass so I was seated fully on her. Both our skirts rucked up, allowing the wet heat of her cunt to mingle with mine, through the thin gauze of our underwear. I continued massaging her breasts, stopping only to take one nipple in my mouth. Her hands went under my top, unhooking my bra, and pinching my nipples. I bucked against her.

"Ah," she hissed, kissing me. "If you want to walk away, my Sascha. Do it now. My demon is about to cross her line of no return."

"Your demon," I said, reaching between us and ripping her underwear to the side to stick my finger in her, "can go to hell."

"My demon will bring you to hell as well," she said, her eyes going a poisonous shade of amber. She rode my finger.

"When do we leave?" I asked.

She lifted me from her, laying me across the side of the sofa and spreading my legs. The face looking at me was not the same as it had been a moment earlier. The tiger's eyes and sculpted jaw were pure predator. Pure demon. And I was hitchhiking to hell.

Her mouth worked the inside of my thighs, the side of her face becoming slick with my wetness as she suckled the sensitive flesh.

"Bite," I said. Her fangs pierced, sending me into a startled jump. Her hand came down on my stomach, then she walked her fingers down my pussy pleat, rubbing my clit.

"Jesus," I said.

"No." She pulled her teeth from me, blood sluicing off the ivory. "There is no one here but us. You pay deference to me, Sascha." She licked me from my arse to clit. "And I worship you in return. No false god."

I grabbed her head and shoved it back to my cunt, riding her face. The moment her fangs sunk into me, I howled, then bit my own arm to shut myself up. Her hair was in a matted fist as I tore her head back and forth over my swollen cunt. She drank from me in every possible way. Large swallows of blood and cum. I went over the edge, still not letting go of her hair. She came away smiling, her face a gored mess of me. I started to rise but found her on top of me.

"We have time. And I have plenty of apologies in me," she said. My rucked skirt and hers were discarded, naked bodies finally in line with one another.

"Beg for my forgiveness." My directive was a plea from my mouth. Her wet folds moved over mine. I felt the nub of her clit teasing mine. *Fuuuuuck*.

"I am." Her cowgirl style laptop dance nearly brought us both over the edge. I couldn't get enough of seeing her soft curves writhing on me. "But I have to put a cock in you. Baptize this cunt and bring it to my church."

I grabbed her hips, begging her to not stop. I was so close. I knew she was so close. She stood from me.

"Fuck!" I yelled. "Bottom drawer of my closet. Hurry, you fucking vampire."

I kept touching myself when she left, reveling in the mix of blood and arousal. I wanted to taste hers too. She came back, and I stood. She was wearing my strap on. Her naked curves were pinched with the black belt, a matching cock, locked in place between her pubic bones. She stalked to me. I laid back down watching every second as she coated the cock in lube and angled herself over me. Her knees clamped my hips as the strap on impaled me. I moaned. Normally I wasn't the biggest fan of dildos. They were a means to an end. I preferred the pliancy and soft steel of a real dick. However, with Alicia I did not mind the dildo. I wanted it. I did not want nor need a real dick. She was all I would ever need. I felt her wet cunt against mine as she stabbed the cock in over and over again. I sat up, taking a mouthful of her tits, biting them to make her squeal. We came together in a hot messy rush.

CHAPTER TWENTY

JAVIER

Ophelia slipped from my bed and left my room, giving me only a slight nod and a smile I took for half regret. *You taste like forever*, she'd told me. How long had forever been? A stretch of time I did not care to go through again without someone by my side. Not someone. This human cohabitating with me. The human from whom I fed and who sipped from my own blood as though it fed her as well. The look on her face as she sucked my fingers and the gash in my chest she made was enough for me to turn this city to dust. It was too much. She was too much. And I wanted more.

I found myself rubbing the healed wound on my chest, nearly erect again knowing she was actively consuming me. More than the cum I fed her last night as I lost myself so completely fucking her face in my hallway. She was near to demon drinking from me. Yet, I didn't know which move to play next. Was she meant to stay human? Could I bear altering this perfect specimen who encompassed my soul? I shook my head, realizing what I'd admitted to myself. It was probably best she left the room. I didn't know if I should leave her. Keep her safe from this world of mine. Had she still been in here with me, her warm curves against me, smelling of the mess I had made on her chest and belly, I didn't know if I could entertain the humane notion of walking away. At least now, with a wall between us, I could pretend I didn't hear her soft breathing. The songs she hummed when she washed herself. The sound of her turning in her sheets. I could pretend these were sounds of another house. Another life. One I wasn't privy to. And in that fantasy, I could make arrangements to flee.

It was hours and several travel documents later when I heard her stumble from her bed. It was a rush, the toilet door hitting the wall and shaking the house. I moved quickly and stopped in shock when I saw her on the washroom floor. Her mouth had blood caked in the corners, her eyes blazed in an orange fury I had not seen in centuries. Eyes that belonged to someone I knew very briefly around the time I had left Florence en route to Venice.

"Javi?" she asked. Her body shook, a fine rash broken all over her pearlescent skin. She retched, coughing on a dry heave. I dropped to my knees and wiped at her bloody mouth with the cuff of my jumper sleeve.

"What's happening?" she asked.

I saw her stomach lurch under the tatty old T-shirt she slept in. Nothing came out of her mouth, but a line of saliva tinted red.

"I don't know," I admitted, feeling desperate. Was this because she drank from me? No human ever had. "Did you cut yourself?"

More bloody saliva dripped over her lips. I had an unnerving desire to lick it.

She shook her head, wiping her chin.

"I'm dizzy. And hungry. Almost like"—she tried to raise herself on the toilet seat but sat back down. I pulled her to me—"like I have a migraine but no pain."

"Do you think you will need to vomit?" I asked her.

"No. I think I'm nauseous because I'm so hungry."

I thought back to our dinner a few hours ago. She had two large bowls of pasta, and it made me so happy to have been able to feed her. She leaned into my chest. I held her and carried her to her bed, where I wrapped my arms around her, keeping her shaking body next to mine. She nuzzled my neck, murmuring. Her stomach buckled again. I felt her whole body stiffen. Her eyes flashed up at me, and I knew, with a heaviness in my heart, what was happening. I just didn't understand why.

Ophelia pressed in and held my wrist close to her nose like a child with a security blanket. Her heartbeat sped up then calmed. My own ancient heart gave a great thump.

"So hungry," she whispered, her tongue tracing the veins on the inside of my wrist.

I shifted. My body was reacting to her more than I wanted to admit. Whether it was my cock or my demon, I didn't know. She was changing. How, I did not understand. As a rule, the human must have had her last heartbeat as her system is flooded with the blood of a vampire. Only then can her life be rewritten. Her DNA altered.

I had always been so careful about how much I took from Ophelia. She was never remotely close to the brink of death. So how was she changing simply from tasting me while we had sex? Cold prickles ran up my spine, and I wondered if she would transition completely. I had only seen a failed transition a few times. All in those with too many immune or chemical issues within them. Ophelia was healthy. Unmedicated. She was perfect. And somehow, I had ruined her.

I left her bed in a blur to get my phone. As quick as I was, shooting off a text to the last person I wanted to talk to, Ophelia was just as quick. An impossibility my mind rebelled against. She stood in the doorway to my room, her eyes locked on my computer screen.

"You are leaving?" Her voice was gravelly. As though she

hadn't had a drink in ages. I glanced at the screen, the airline site blaring my flight details. "For how long?"

I ran a hand over my face. "I'm not."

She hissed, which drew me up short. Her facial expression shifted around, not settling on what she was.

"That," she said and pointed at my computer, "begs to differ." I walked to it and shut the lid. "What's in Florence?"

"One of my partners. Business partners," I clarified.

"Were you going to tell me?" She moved to me like a leopard. Her thigh muscles contracted with each step. "I can smell your nerves," she said. Her eyes were on fire. "How can I smell that, Javi? It smells odd. Like something delicious that's not quite ripe enough."

I coughed. The precursor to fear. The taste of fear was intoxicating. Absinth to vampires. The taste of nerves was frustrating. As she said, like a perfect harmony of flavors, not quite ripe.

"Were you leaving me, Javi?" she asked, running a long fingernail down my chest.

"I was."

She snatched her finger back, eyes flashing from anger to hurt.

I grabbed her hand, keeping it in mine. "I was afraid for you. I was afraid of my world and what it was doing to you. I was afraid," I explained, trying to force her eyes on me. "I was afraid of this happening." I gestured to her.

"I'm not desirable like this?" she asked. Her voice was dangerous. She was a predator. Yet her face was human Ophelia. The Ophelia I was falling for. Had fallen for.

"Believe me, my little queen. Desire is not the issue. I only wanted to keep you from harm. I did not want you to change because you were perfect as you were."

She lunged and tore my throat, my arterial blood spraying across the room and over her flawless skin. She drank more and more from me. Manic sucking preceded her tearing from my neck and growling because I had started to heal before she was sated. I imagined in her early vampire state, fangs not yet dropped, she would not have been sated until I was drained. Until the last beat of my heart.

"I was not perfect!" she screeched, falling to the ground and scratching at the shirt on her. "I had no one left. I had nothing. I was always a stone overweight and a paycheck short of comfortable. I was stagnant. Never enough. Until you. Until I felt enough with you. And now you are telling me I'm too much? Like this?"

I sat next to her.

"You would never be too much for me." My fictitious English accent was gone. My speech regressed to some sort of accent I had acquired between the Mediterranean states of pre–Great War Europe. "You have always been perfect. Your mind, your body, your drive. All of it. I never felt you *needed* to change. Not for me nor anyone. Now that you have—now that you are changing, you are perfect in a different way. Whatever you are or become, you are still perfection to me. For me. For my demon."

She laid her head on the side of her forearm where it rested on her knees. She watched me speak, her eyes a fluid tide, moving from brown to amber and back again. The front door clicked, and Ophelia's attention snapped up.

"It's only—" But I didn't finish. Alicia came round the door and Ophelia had her pinned to the doorframe, her blunt teeth buried in the cleavage on my former wife's chest. Alicia laughed in a maniacal giggle as she yanked Ophelia by the hair and held her just in front of her own face. Ophelia gnashed and hissed at Alicia.

CHAPTER TWENTY ONE

OPHELIA

"Enough," Javi said, coming behind me and putting a calming hand around my middle, resting on my belly.

"You are positively feral, little flower," Alicia crooned. "I want to keep you as a pet."

"Why is she here, Javi?" I managed to ask, feeling murderous and embarrassed at the same time.

"He texted me to come deal with you, vampiricita," the vampire bitch answered. I turned in Javi's arm.

"Do you trust me?" he asked me.

No. Yes. I wasn't sure anymore.

I felt like one moment we were having world-breaking sex, the following moment I felt like I needed to throw up, so I left the room. Next thing I knew, I was starving and hissing and tearing out Javi's throat. My eyes darted to the healed mess of his neck where blood was smeared and soaked into his cream jumper. Would blood come out of cashmere? I doubted it.

"Fela," Javi said. He'd never called me anything but Ophelia before, yet the look on his face told me that Fela was meant for me. It was soft. The "e" a whisper on the wind between the kiss of sound from the "f" and the song of "la" at the end. It was beautiful. My shoulders dropped. Tears pricked behind my eyes.

"Yes," I said. "I trust you."

He leaned forward and kissed the tip of my nose. It felt hard, like blood was crusted. It occurred to me I was probably a horror show of a sight. Alicia sighed behind me, and I fought the urge to show her how feral this flower could be. My gums ached. I wanted to feed more. I wanted to gnaw on something. Suck on something.

Javi said into my ear, "You can do whatever you want to do to me later. You have my word. But now I need you to let Alicia help us." He stepped back, still keeping a hand on me. "Can you do that, Fela?"

"Javi, you owe me," Alicia said. "I was in bed with Sascha when you texted."

Javi and I both cringed. I guess Sascha really forgave her then. I wasn't sure how I felt about that. There was a pounding in my head; it echoed through my gums.

"Ja. Let's see what is wrong with you."

"Nothing is wrong with her," Javi said through clenched teeth.

Alicia waved him off and motioned for us to follow her into the sitting room. I hesitated as I'd already made a bloody mess of both of our bedrooms. I didn't want to gore up the sitting room too. Javi steered the two of us to the large armchair, where we barely fit. Alicia perched on the arm of the sofa. I looked between them.

"What?" I asked, seeing them both at a loss for words.

"You should not have transitioned," Javi said. I sort of knew that. "I have not heard, in all my years, of this happening."

"Well," Alicia cut in, "I have." Her words were more careful than I'd heard before. "Only once, but she told me of her lineage." I scooted further back into Javi.

"Yes, but that doesn't account for Ophelia," Javi said. "Her lineage would be mine and no vampire I have known in my line has transitioned without having died first. Myself included."

Alicia swallowed. She was so smug and obnoxious most of the time, her earlier cautious words and this hesitation seemed quite uncharacteristic.

"Alicia." The word had her narrow her eyes at him.

"Not her vampire lineage, Javier," she said and looked over at the tree. "How quaint. A Christmas baubly tree. Reminds me of Venice."

"Don't," Javi cautioned. "I do not want nor need your memories and their flawed, agenda-filled falsities. If you are here to help, now is the time, Alicia."

She stood and walked to the console, unplugged a decanter, and poured a measure of what looked like brandy or cognac into a tumbler.

"The ability or, I should say, predisposition to transition to vampire from human without having to first die, is through the human blood line. Human genetic code. Not vampire line."

"That makes little sense," Javier argued. "It is when a human dies that the vampire DNA overrides the system and rewrites the genetic code. It wouldn't matter what was in the human line unless they were so sick their body shut down before it actually dies. Which was not the case with Ophelia."

Alicia poured another drink. Then two more which she handed to us.

"Are your eyes orange, little flower?" She directed the question to me. "When you were feral. I did not get a chance to see as you were feeding at my breast."

"I don't know," I admitted. Javi was still beside me. I touched the top of his thigh. He looked at me and nodded once. Alicia fondled a bead on the tree.

"Like this. The way the light shines through this orange glass. That was how Isabel's eyes looked when her demon was showing."

"What exactly are you saying? What is she saying, Javi?"

He knocked back the brandy. I sipped mine and held it in my mouth as I awaited an answer. The heat of it felt good on my sore gums.

"I am saying that you—your human family—is a direct line of what could possibly be the original vampire. The oldest being on earth. They fed off each other and nearly killed themselves in the process until they learned to procreate the human way and make their line stronger."

"They learned to…"

I had barely formed the question when Javi was out of our seat and pinning Alicia to the wall. The tree swayed. I got up and steadied it. I would be very angry if this vampire skirmish destroyed my Christmas tree. Alicia's face was turning blue. Javi's hands were around her neck, his fingers piercing her skin.

"Javier," she wheezed.

I touched his arm. He snarled at me to step back.

"Isabel?" he growled at her. "Isabel, whom you stabbed in the heart with top of the fence post? The same fucking Isabel you brought into our bed and is now buried under the vineyard at my estate in Tuscany? Is that the Isabel of whom you speak, you bruja?"

"Yes," she said through a wheeze. Javi dropped her. She caught herself like a cat and was rubbing her throat.

"I am trying very hard right now to not kill you, Alicia. The reasons not to are rapidly becoming outnumbered."

"Javi," I said.

He spun to me and took my face in his hands, kissing me hard and fast. I held his forearms. He took a shuddering breath like kissing me had been the only thing tethering him to sanity.

"Oh, Javi," Alicia said. "I am sorry."

I looked over at her.

"What are you sorry for? What have you done?" My question was logical. Clearly Javi knew something I didn't. The only thing that rang a bell was that the estate in Tuscany was what Alicia was trying to get out of Javier.

"I am going to ask this just once, Alicia. I expect the truth. If I find your answer to be untrue at any time, I will cut your head from your body and set you on fire so that not even your soul remains. Are we clear?"

She nodded at him, cowed, as I never would have expected her to be.

"Is the reason you wanted the Tuscany estate because of Isabel's body?"

"Sí."

Javi stroked my face as though soothing himself with my skin. My gums were throbbing, and the feel of his fingers on my cheeks both hurt and felt good. Like pressing a bruise.

"Is the reason you wanted Isabel's body because you knew she could create vampires without having to first kill?" Javi asked. His eyes were only on me. It was unnerving.

"Sí. Yes."

"Here is the biggest question, Alicia," Javi said. "Do not lie to me. Did you know Ophelia was a descendent of Isabel's human line? Is that what this has all been about?"

"Javier," she tried. He turned to her. She took a step back. "Yes."

His hands clenched at his sides. I reached for one, keeping it pressed against my heart.

"I didn't know she was yours, Javier. I swear to you. It was becoming obvious. Especially in the club. Your scents were mingled." Alicia kept backing up, one step at a time. "I thought she was simply your donor."

"What were you going to do to her?" he asked, far too calmly.

"Javier, Isabel was pregnant when she died."

"Impossible," he barked.

"Yes. Impossible. Yet it was so."

"You know this how?" he asked.

His hand squeezed mine like he was reassuring me. I knew at this point, my hand in his was soothing him. The room was becoming spinny again. My gums ached. They burned like hellfire, and I felt parched. Yet, I knew it was more important to hear what was between them than to call out I was thirsty and uncomfortable like a whinging child.

"She shared my bed yes, as she did with so many others at the time. She also shared with Pietro. You know at the time I did not find him so weak. He had agency back then. Before he was everyone's leech." She waved a hand and made a disgusted face. "He was dashing. He was mine."

"I was yours," Javi said. My stomach dropped. "It is neither here nor there now, but in the interest of historical integrity, I was yours. Pietro was a plaything."

"Yes. Javier, I was volatile then. Ruthless. I found Isa and Pietro rutting like pigs in the guest house. She chased me outside where I grabbed the fencepost. She begged me not to hurt her because she was pregnant."

"Yet you killed her anyway?" I couldn't help but ask the question, and I let the venom in it show.

"I was angry. And anyway, she was a vampire, so I thought she was lying."

I felt I was going to be sick.

"How or when did you figure out she was not lying?" Javier asked.

Alicia chewed her bottom lip. Javi seemed to soften

seeing that. A detail in the nuance between them I was uncomfortable with and decided to file away for later.

"I raised the fence pike above my hand, and she tore her gown from her body. It had been a fluffy one. The gown hit the gravel as I pierced her heart. I tried to fix her. When I saw the belly. I did. I tried. But I shattered her heart. Pietro came out then. He tried to cut her open. Save the child."

"I take it he was unsuccessful?" Javi asked.

The room was silent. Dawn had to be close at hand as there was a soft keen of gulls in the distance. I must have been awake all night. And now I was so very tired.

"I didn't think you would want it, Javier," she said. "The child. You hated children. You were playing at the verge of war."

"Alicia," he said. Javi's eyes were wide. He pulled his hand from mine. I felt my heart starting to break. A pain I was not used to. "Please tell me what you did." He stalked to her and grabbed her shoulders. She looked to me, then back at him before putting her arms around him.

"We took the child, Javi. That is when I faked my death. Or shortly after. You sealed the body under the estate and had the mage seal it with your blood for as long as you owned the estate. And that is why Pietro is beholden to me. He was part of the whole scheme."

"You raised a child? A vampire child?" Javi's shoulders squared. His hands clasped behind his back. Dark edges crept into my vision. My head felt as though it was filled with cottonwool. I just needed a drink. Just needed some water.

"No, Javi. Allegra was a human child. She grew and thrived and died as a human."

Lances of gray light peeked around the curtains in the sitting room. Dawn was not far. It was Christmas Eve and it seemed I would be celebrating with sore gums and a need to suck off Javi in a very different sort of way. The thought pushed a flush of heat to my core and more dryness to my mouth. Neither vampire in the room seemed to notice or care. Both stared at each other in a duel of silence. I felt there should be a question for me to ask. The dark fog moved over my eyes more. I was feeling really quite poorly. A quick wipe with the back of my hand revealed a sheen of cold sweat over my brow.

"She never married, but decades ago, I found evidence that she herself birthed a child. I searched for the child, but it seemed Allegra covered her tracks well. Until I heard of a car accident a decade ago. Annabella Rose Montebello James." Alicia's focus switched to me. I knew I was swaying.

"Mum?" I asked. The room fell to black.

CHAPTER TWENTY TWO

JAVIER

I reached for Ophelia, catching her before she hit the ground. I wouldn't have blamed her if she had fainted from the shock of it all. However, I knew Ophelia, and simply being overwhelmed was not enough to make her pass out. Looking at her as I carried her to her bed, her face was clammy, skin a sickly color. Her lips were shriveled as though she were severely dehydrated.

"She needs to feed, Javi," Alicia said from two steps behind me.

"Yes. I am aware." I touched the tip of my finger to my incisor, drawing a droplet of blood, which I wiped across Ophelia's lips. They absorbed it instantly. I repricked my finger, as the wound had already healed, and put the blood back to her lips. She mewled at it this time.

"Ja, Javi. I'll clean this up." Alicia left and brought back supplies to clean. I held my finger in Ophelia's mouth. The force of her suckling kept the wound open. Her lips started becoming moist once again.

"Fela," I said, my face close to hers. "I want to wake you and have you feed properly."

Her eyes fluttered. I stroked her face. Her cheeks had red blossoms on either side of her jaw and above her top lip. I touched it and she hissed. The blossomed skin felt hot. She kept suckling my finger, but I slipped another finger in and felt her gums. The flesh was inflamed, a fever running throughout her body. Right where they should be, tiny points of fangs poked through the fiery skin. She had two on either side of her top teeth, in front of her molars.

"Is she teething?" Alicia asked.

I looked over. She had the blood wiped from the floors and several towels and articles of clothing binned in a laundry basket. I thought she must have been feeling guilty. Alicia never raised a hand to help with anything domestic. If cleaning arterial spray from a transitioning vampire could be called domesticity.

"Yes. The teeth should be fully through in a few hours. Until then, she will likely need to keep suckling."

"I can let her have mine too," Alicia suggested.

I snarled. "Stay away from her!"

She backed up. Ophelia's eyes opened to look at me, before closing again, her mouth still latched onto my finger.

"I would kill you right here before I'd let her suckle at your breast the way you are used to transitioning vampires."

She held up her hands in surrender. "I meant, she could take my blood from my finger or wrist as she is doing from you. I know better than to suggest anything further from her now. I am aware of what she means to you, Javier." I felt my shoulders drop. "You will weaken that way and when her fangs fully descend, she will need a full feeding from you. A full *everything* from you, Javi. You may want to rest a bit."

She was correct. I needed to clean myself up anyway. I whispered to Ophelia that I would be right back. She hissed when I pulled my finger out, but Alicia's took its place imme-diately. Ophelia looked at the other woman with a question in her eyes but gladly kept suckling. Alicia slipped a second finger in too, massaging the gums. Ophelia moaned. I growled low in warning.

"Relax, Javi. I will not ravage her in the time it takes you to wash. Go."

I had seen my share of injuries. I had been attacked by friends, enemies, lovers. I had been to war. Several times. Alicia in our early days had a wicked temper and often left me bloody. I had felt pain. Of course, I had. I still did. What I felt when Ophelia tore my throat was pain for her. Pain for the loss of her humanity. The beautiful broken and healing parts of her that are so different to who she would become as a vampire. My long dead heart hurt that I never told her as a human what I felt for her.

The hot water ran over me, the bottom of the shower turning brown with the dried blood I washed away. In the steamy heat of the Christmas Eve morning, rage built in me. Anger caused by her bloodline. By Alicia. By the parts of Ophelia she believed to be imperfect and needing altering. Rage for the lover I lost when she drank from me. Would we be the same? Not likely. Would she even want me, or was it time now for her to explore this new, lethal, multifaceted side of herself? And would I truly be able to watch her feed, fuck, enjoy someone else? Or would this thing between us become a new history of blood and revenge I could never control? I roared and slammed my fist against the black tiles, splitting open my knuckles.

The fact was that I no longer knew who I was, needed to be, or what I was capable of. I supposed I should get out of the damned shower and start figuring that out.

I had been running low for days on the blood supply I kept for extenuating circumstances, yet there never seemed to be a moment I was able to replenish it. It wasn't as though I could run into Sainsburys and grab a sack of O-negative. I'd drained three bags the night I was trying to keep myself from feed-fucking Ophelia. The blacked-out wine fridge in my pantry held a few extras, and I stood drinking under sufferance in my unlit kitchen. I imagined this was how humans felt having protein shakes and meal replacement bars instead of real meals like pasta Bolognese.

It was chilly in the house, I realized. Typically, I kept it warm for my house guest, but her body was flushed enough now. After my shower, I peeked my head in to see that she and Alicia were still huddled on the bed, Alicia finger fucking Fela's mouth. My cock twitched seeing it and I knew I needed to feed before I was able to give myself over to Fela as completely as she would soon require.

I was never the type of man to salivate over seeing two women together. It is a natural thing and simply the way of the world. No sexier than a man and woman or two men. I have had centuries to partake and watch in every combina-tion of sexual act one could imagine. Yet, the simplicity of Ophelia sucking on my former wife's fingers, as I knew, blood dropped from the tip, had me hard. I drank the bagged blood, standing in the darkened kitchen, and stroked my shaft, careful to not make a sound. I was a lost man. Fela's soft features and dark eyes swam before me, as I tugged my skin, trying to release some of the hunger and rage I felt. A click from the other room made me tear my hand from my trousers and quickly finish my meal.

"Javi," Alicia said from the doorway. Even from across the room, I could see her smirking. She could scent arousal from ten kilometers. "Once upon a time, this would have been fun, no?" she asked and walked toward me.

I was somehow comforted by her presence here. Likely why I had called her in the first place. We shared a long history, however sordid and unreliable in its narrative. Her hand splayed on my bare chest. It smelled of Ophelia's saliva and blood. I groaned. Her nails curled in and marked my skin.

"Please," I begged her. I never begged Alicia. "I'm—"

"You are not so different now as you were so many years ago, lover," she said. Her fingers curled and uncurled, nails chipping at my skin. Her body pressed in closer. I knew she could feel my erection where it was pinned against her stomach. Closer now, I smelled Sascha on her. A mix of blood and cum. My senses were overloaded. I felt my demon pushing me out. If I lost control, Ophelia would be gone from my life for good. This I knew.

"Please," I begged again, grabbing her fingers. She dropped them to my crotch and cupped me. I hissed, fangs bared.

"You need to feed, lover," she said, massaging my balls.

My acid-green eyes reflected in the cabinetry behind Alicia. I grabbed her throat and wrenched her neck sideways. I could smell her arousal now, and it made me see more clearly.

"I do need to feed," I said low as I skimmed my teeth over her tight skin. "So take your hands off my balls and be a good girl."

She whimpered but dropped her hand. I did not wait for permission. I opened my mouth to its fullest and clamped on. The wound was wide, allowing her artery to gush directly down my burning throat. Alicia pushed her hips into me, but I held them back. So long as I was eating, I was able to keep my cock in line. Until I walked back into that room with Ophelia. I knew that would be game over. The mere thought made me latch on tighter to the female in front of me. I drank and drank. She became languid in my grasp, indicating I had taken enough. Perhaps a bit too much. Call it payment for what she had done.

I helped wipe her and stand her upright, giving her my last bag of surplus, and a glass of wine to fortify her system. She was quiet in a way I didn't remember.

"Are you well?" I asked.

She touched her healing wound with two shaking fingers and smiled.

"There were times," she began, "after I left you. Nights I sat up late with Allegra and I was alone. Of course, I had servants. Donors. But those nights I was alone because I did not have you. All things heal with time, no? But I want you to know that leaving you was not easy for me. Not in the beginning nor for years after."

"You had decades to rectify your mistake," I said to her, wiping my wet hands on a tea towel.

"No, Javier," she said in Italian. "Because I knew I left you for you."

"You left because your proclivities got the better of you, and you wanted to raise a child you knew I would be patently against."

"I left because you hated me." It was an anvil falling. "It has been a century, lover. Part of me knew it then and all of me knows it now. Had I gone back to you, you would not have taken me back, Javier. I never loved you the way you deserved to be loved. The way I see the Little Flower love you. And you her."

My back hit the edge of the countertop.

"And because of you, she may leave me. She will be different and want different things. Different people. So, it's all a bit full circle, then. Grazi, Alicia."

She got up to leave the kitchen.

"I will be in the sitting room downstairs. She should be waking soon and will want you. Do not sell yourself short, Javier. Ophelia is not me. She is not damaged as I have always been. She would be a fool to give you up."

I stared at the empty doorway, barely hearing her walk downstairs. I didn't know if hearing all of that would have made a difference a hundred years ago. Fifty years ago. Ten even. I don't know if I needed to find Ophelia to understand how poorly I had been treated. There was a soft creak in the mattress a level above, so I made my way back to the bedroom where I found Fela sitting on the edge of the mattress. She looked as though her eyes wavered between lucidity and confusion. I didn't want another uncontrolled bloodbath like earlier, so I approached her with caution. I remember turning vampires. I even remember when I turned. What it felt like. How I needed a strong hand and guidance. I knew I needed to be that and more for this specimen before me.

"That was not your finger in me earlier," she said by way of greeting.

I huffed, running a hand through my hair. She growled. The sound had me at attention.

"It was Alicia's, but believe me, Fela," I said, taking a step forward, "it will be my finger from now on. In your mouth." I took another step. "In your cunt." Another step. "Your ass."

Her eyes glowed amber. Mine prickled in response, alerting me to my demon wanting to play. I took another step. The T-shirt Alicia had put on Ophelia was tented by peaked nipples.

"No one else's fingers will be in you again. No one's teeth will be on those nipples."

Her hands shot to her breasts automatically. I saw her thumbs brush over the cotton covered buds. My cock was in full salute, pulling my joggers from my hips like a divining rod to Ophelia. A hiss escaped her.

"You smell like *her*," she said, and I saw the tip of a fang poke into her bottom lip. It was my turn to snarl. My demon was in full cooperation with my cock. I was starting to feel blinded with want, even though I knew she had to feed first. Actually, she had to be tamed first.

"I do," I answered, standing touching distance from her. She sniffed and looked at my groin. "I had to feed, Fela. We knew you would need me at full strength."

"She *touched* you, Javi," she hissed.

"Are those baby fangs, Fela?" I asked, amused by her jealousy. "Let me see." I reached to touch her mouth and she snapped at me, breaking the skin on the side of my hand. My demon groaned, ready to move.

"Why did she touch your cock and chest, Javi?"

She stood, and I took my chance. I dived forward and grabbed her with one arm snaking between her legs and the other over her shoulder, then flipped her onto her back. I had her pinned under me. My full weight pressed her into the mattress as she bucked and snarled, showing me more of those baby fangs. Razor sharp and ready to tear me to pieces.

"You can feed, my little queen," I told her, nipping at her neck and jaw. Her breathing was rapid with her inhuman heart now ticking double time. "But first you learn the rules."

She slammed her head into mine and while it made me see stars, I ground my groin into her. She moaned at the press of me, hard as steel, against her softest parts, laying just under me, with no panties between us. I used my teeth and tore the T-shirt from her body in one go. I felt her cunt soak through my trousers. I couldn't keep her pinned and remove those, so I just let her grind her wetness into me.

"You do not feed from unwilling people unless you have been attacked or compromised." I rode along her crease once like a small treat. "Understood?"

She nodded. "Please, Javi."

I took her nipple in my mouth, sucking hard but not breaking skin. Not yet. The soft tissue filled my mouth as I rolled my tongue over the tip.

"You do not go public in any manner with your nature. Stay out of the public eye. Yes?" She whimpered yes, gnashing teeth at me. My demon tongue snuck out and penetrated her mouth. Her moans were beastly. I ground harder against her. The sheets were soaked with her cum.

"I'm going to sink my baby fangs into you so deep, you won't know where they begin or end," she said in a voice like nightmares. I lived in the dark and wanted her nightmares in me.

"Such promises," I cooed as though she wasn't utterly destroying me. "And while you are with me, no one so much as tucks a strand of hair behind your ear. Are we clear?"

"Yes," she breathed.

"Are we clear, Fela? Speak up. Because if someone touches what is mine, there will be a massacre. And breaks rule number two."

"You would kill for me, vampire?" she asked. She was slipping back into herself, though her eyes still shone like a Gaslamp.

"We have been over this." I freed one of her hands to remove my trousers. Her hand came down on me, grabbing the back of my neck. "I will burn the world for you. If you are mine."

She yanked my head down and bit me.

The flood of chemicals in my system made me shake. Her legs wiggled free of where mine were now half-heartedly keeping her down. She wrapped hers around my waist, slamming her cunt against my groin as she swallowed my blood. I needed to feed from her. I needed to be inside her with my cock and fingers. My tongue. This...this wasn't enough. I couldn't see straight.

She pulled from me and dived back in, teeth piercing above my heart. I held her face to my chest, rubbing my cock along her soaking folds. It was too much. I snarled and ripped her face from me watching as my blood sprayed between us. I claimed her mouth, my own fangs sinking into her lips. I tasted us both together. My hands found her ass and squeezed, knowing that yesterday, I would have left marks. She moaned, pushing into me before flipping me over with the absurd strength of a new vampire. Her breasts hung heavy over my face, framed by her wild hair. I smiled at her in challenge, laying my arm behind my head. She answered by sliding down and holding my balls while she sunk her fangs into my inner thigh. I cried out, grabbing her hair and holding her tight to me as she fed more. Her hand moved, wrapping around my cock, and stroking in time to her sucking. I was leaking precum and she came off my thigh with a pop and smear of blood to lick my head clean.

"All I've wanted since I first tasted you," she said in that midnight voice, her hands playing with my balls as she licked me from head to base, "is to feed from your cum."

I groaned, fucking her mouth. I would not feed her that way that day. No, I would make her wait for that. Temper the little beast. Mainly because I needed to fuck her so very hard, she would be at the edge of breaking in two. Her tongue dipped into my hole, a sensation of pain and pleasure rolling into one. I tightened my hand in her hair and raised my hips, railing my cock at the back of her throat. She groaned but pulled off, moving like lightning, back to my neck.

"How could you not want this for me, Javi?" she asked.

Her eyes lit a fire in me. I tore my neck from her mouth, feeling my skin giveaway, and kissed her with all I had in me. "I have wanted to feed from you as you feed from me, for so long now." She pinched my nipple and bent to bite it.

"I never wanted you to be something you weren't," I told her.

She stopped sucking and moved on top of me. Her eyes shifted from lamplight to brown and back again. The curves of her body balanced over me while she notched my tip at her entrance. My whole body shook with need. We locked eyes as she slowly slid over me, seating me to the edge.

"I am who I was meant to be, apparently. And I was meant to be yours." With that she rode me harder, our two bodies making obscene noises I could not be bothered to care that Alicia could hear. "And when you cum inside me today, I want you to know that every drop you give me—" She leaned over me, edging more with her position. I reached behind and slid a finger in her ass. She moaned and caught my lip, sliding back and forth over my cock. "You are feeding me."

I dug my nails into her waist, leveraging myself to impale her with my cock, moving us slowly until we were both sitting upright. I latched on to her neck as she did the same. The force of energy between us blew the bulbs from the bedside lamp. The warm flood of her rose blood rushed down my throat and there was nothing I could do to stop the release. I nearly choked as I gave her one last thrust and emptied myself into her. Ancient growling began from her stomach and echoed from her mouth as she took in one more mouthful before shattering with her own orgasm.

CHAPTER TWENTY THREE

JAVIER

Beyond the click of the heating and ever-present cry of gulls outside in our quayside city, there was silence. The opaque, marbleized lack of noise I had once come to expect in my world. A dearth of human sound as though entombed in the years lived and those inevitably to follow. The poured concrete hush of loneliness. Of vampirism.

Few of us had families or packs. Most were too leery of one another or too competitive. Most of us stood out too much in accord. It was an existence synonymous with being alone. Humanity was not always a niggling factor, making the solitary nature of us not a thing of loneliness. I was not wistful for companionship in my century without Alicia. In fact, I cherished my quiet life. Until Ophelia's blood trickled down my throat, and it was clear, I would forever after be desolate without her. Her warmth and sounds. The shallow wheeze of her breath, the click of her right knee when she stood, the erratic beat of her human heart, were all sounds I became accustomed to having in my still home. And now they were muted. A curtain pulled down over the world I was readying to reenter.

Ophelia's fingers kept a clawed grip on my back, locking me against her, barely inside her still. She fell into a heavy sleep after we made love. Her muffled words as she drifted off were a plea to not move. To keep my body pressed to hers. And I would do anything she asked. I felt the tips of dagger-point nails poking out and retracting from her fingers while she slept. The sharp tips breaking my skin each time. Was she meant to be a vampire? Meant for this life simply by fate of her bloodline? I supposed that was how it all worked. Genetics and bloodlines. Vampirism was the anomaly. Once it set in, there was no hope for any other genetic code to rewrite itself. As I lay with this woman I would go to my final death for, I finally admitted to myself I did not wish for her genetics to be rewritten. I wanted her this way. This extended version of Ophelia, who would be alive as long as I lived. Who I could love and fight for and worship. Forever. Because in her, I tasted forever. And like any drug, forever was the high I refused to give up.

Footsteps kitten-footed up the stairs and down the hall. Alicia had been in the sitting room the whole time. The bitter part of me wanted to think it was so she could hear me having sex with Ophelia. So she could relish in having a hand in turning her. However bitter I was, I did know Alicia, and I knew she stayed for two reasons. One, to talk to me and possibly Ophelia after I fed my newly made vampire. And two, she stayed to be a safety net. To protect me or Ophelia or both of us. Perhaps I never loved her as I find myself loving Ophelia. Perhaps she never loved me in the way I needed. Perhaps she was ruthless, violent, and self-serving. She was all those things, yet under it all was a heart I recognized eons ago. Beneath the blunt sword of her personality was the woman who left me to raise a child.

My naked arse was exposed to the room when Alicia pushed the door open.

"Javi?" she whispered.

I turned my head toward her, popping Fela's claws from

my flank. She hissed in her sleep, gnashing her teeth. I smiled and brushed my lips on her chest as I rose. The sound of Alicia backing into the hall let me know I could rise without my former wife seeing me not only naked but coated in Ophelia's and my blood and pleasure. I pulled up my trousers just as I came into the hall and motioned for Alicia to follow me back downstairs. The idea of being farther from Fela while she was still in a transitory state left me twitchy, yet she needed sleep and I needed to speak with my ex.

"You always did look beautiful naked," Alicia said with a pout. I chuckled. "Ja, Javi. I'm sorry."

"I know."

I sat on the settee and crossed one leg over the other. The Christmas tree was still glittering. I had wanted so much to make it a special Christmas for Ophelia. Instead, she became undead. Or something of the sort I couldn't quite process yet.

"You know?" she asked, sitting on the settee beside me.

I sighed. "Yes, Alicia. I know you came to get what you wanted, thinking it was at any cost. I know you organized the grandiose plan to blackmail me. But I also know you aren't as awful as I make you out to be, and you feel bad about what has transpired."

She opened her mouth to speak but I held up my hand.

"I know all this, yet I am still angry. I am still angry, yet I also realize perhaps Ophelia was supposed to turn at some point."

"Love is complex, no? she asked. I sniffed a laugh. "Lily will be fine. She fed from me. She fed from you." Her eyebrow raised along with the corners of her mouth. "I wish you had known Allegra, Javi. I wish I had done things differently."

"I would not have wanted a child, Alicia."

"Yes, I know. But we could have been civil. I understand now I did not have to disappear completely."

"Divorce?" I asked with a laugh and a hand to the heart. "You are a catholic." She laughed and swatted my knee. "No, I think you may have done the right thing. Maybe not for a century," I said and rolled my eyes. "Díos, Alicia. But I don't know how I would have responded, and the world was at war. Things happen for a reason."

She was nodding at me. We were silent for a few moments, both entranced by the tree.

"Javi," she started as I said, "Alicia."

I motioned for her to go on.

"The reason I wanted Ophelia—"

"You want a child again." That had to be why. The reason she would risk everything and everyone. She tucked her head once in agreement. "Is it possible?" Before she could answer I was horror-struck. "Please tell me, Alicia, you do not think Ophelia is going to carry a child for you."

"Javier Eneide." She rose to her knees and leaned in my face. She smelled the same. Like the rocky shores where the top of Spain met France. Her scent was as though the rosemary and bramble kissed the sea salt and clung to her throughout all her lives and travels, never leaving her without a sense of her home, centuries ago. "I was going to use her DNA. Maybe even have her give me an egg."

"An egg?!"

She shrugged.

"It's just one," she said, drawing out the numerical. "Women have loads. Not me, of course. Because I'm dead." She fell back and rolled her eyes into her head, mimicking a cat that had been hit by a car.

"So, you were going to harass and then blackmail Ophelia into giving you one of her ova?" I said, switching into a mix of Italian and Spanish I doubted anyone but Alicia could comprehend. "I'm honestly in a bit of shock. This is rich, even for you."

She picked a bit of dried blood from her long nails.

"Well," she said waving her hand, "it's all different now anyway." I was looking her dead in the eyes, waiting for it. "Because I have hurt you enough for many lifetimes. And I want to make it right."

That hadn't been what I was expecting. A smug look crossed her face as she knew she had surprised me.

"Not because you are involved with Ophelia's best mate?"

"That too, yes." I stood and checked the time, seeing faint washes of sunlight bleed through the curtains. The bed moved upstairs, and Alicia and I both looked upwards as though we could see through the ceiling. The sound of two feet touching wood was followed by measured walking and the door opening. Nothing uncontrolled or ravenous sounded.

"We are in the sitting room, Fela," I called to her. I figured why not feign some sense of normalcy. There was a grunt.

"She doesn't sound normal, Javi," Alicia said.

"She hasn't had her tea yet."

"She is vampire," Alicia countered. "She should not need tea."

"She is Ophelia, and you have no idea what she should need." There was a growl lacing my tone.

"I'm showering," Ophelia called down with annoyance. "Then having tea. And possibly blood. I've not decided yet."

I covered my face and looked at my ex sideways, laughing. She smirked and shook her head.

"She is as moody as you, Javi. Good luck."

CHAPTER TWENTY FOUR

OPHELIA

It was hours before Sascha would be up, and it wasn't like we ever had Christmas dinner at a typical early afternoon hour. Sascha was usually too hungover from drinks on Christmas Eve to roll out of bed earlier than noon. I was under no illusions that this year would be any different despite the fact that literally everything was different this year.

Truly I was knackered from the days that had passed. I mean, I knew I had every bloody right to be since I finally had mind blowing sex with my vampire boss and then oops, inadvertently turned into a vampire myself. I guess one could say Javi slays in the bedroom. I also had every bloody right to keep making absolutely trash jokes to lighten the magnitude of what had happened. What was still happening. God. Every Christmas, I wished Mum and Dad were still here, but this year, I was pulled between wanting them here even more to help me through this colossal mind fuck and being glad they were gone and couldn't see what I'd become. Maybe it was better they didn't see their only daughter whoring her blood for money and then fucking her boss only to become the thing she fed.

I blew out a long breath and squatted down in front of the Christmas tree.

The gems on each bough threw light in every direction of Javier's sitting room. I never asked for a proper Christmas. Sure, I had verbal diarrhea to him outside The White Shoppe, admitting to him my cache of gifts for my dead parents I had stashed in bins. But I never told him how important Christmas was to me and how scared I was to not see Sascha. Despite what I'd left unsaid, he did this. My vampire boss, lover, self-described demon, surprised me with a fresh Christmas tree and made a show of decorating it with me using his antique glass beads. Maybe Mum and Dad wouldn't hate him for me that much. I mean, it was an obvious improvement over Connor. No, it wasn't Javier I worried they would disapprove of. It was me. Me, who let my relationship with Connor dictate living in and leaving London. Me, who couldn't find my footing for a few years and decided to sell my blood for money to fund my hotel.

Through the mostly pulled curtains, the morning brightened. It looked cold and as though the pavement would be covered in ice. I set the two wrapped parcels under the tree and stood, pulling the sides of my dressing gown closed. My stomach gave a great lurch, sending my blood lust to a momentary level ten.

"I heard your stomach rumble from the hall," Javi said with a smile. He stood behind me, holding a tea towel and steaming cuppa. "I think the warring instincts of needing blood and needing bread will calm as you settle into your new self."

He handed me the cup and I inhaled, knowing he was right. Tea was exactly the right start and immediately following, I wanted pastries.

"Your eyes are glowing," he said, sitting and pointing to me.

I widened them at him and flashed a smile I knew had a bit of fang in it. His laugh warmed every part of me.

"It's bizarre," I said. "I've always been a need to eat now or someone dies kind of girl, but now it's a bit more spot on than before."

Javi must have realized he was still holding the tea towel, which seemed a little off character for him, since he rarely made an uncalculated move. I narrowed my eyes at him and kept sipping my tea. My stomach groused more. Pastries probably needed to happen straight away lest I wind up drinking from Javi again, which would undoubtedly turn to more sex. My ass was slightly sore and noting that made a throb of pleasure announce itself in my core. I drained the tea.

"It's going to take a bit of getting used to distinguishing whether I am hungry for food or if I need blood. Or if I'm just horny and want to have sex while we feed from each other. Really, it's all a bit of a headache," I told him.

Javi jumped up and left the room, taking my cup with him. I sat wondering why he seemed nervous. Music began streaming in from some unseen speakers. Classical Christmas music like Mum used to play. We didn't have family around, but when Mum and Dad were alive, Christmas was always spent with friends. Parties and brunches with family friends who seemed a constant fixture in our lives, but who simply disappeared once my parents' bodies were lost to the frigid Bristol Channel. I wasn't a child when they died, of course. But I was their child, and I was certainly not yet adult enough at age eighteen to sort through life on my own whilst still harboring the acute grief of losing my entire world. I was broken once by the loss of my family and broken again when I found I had no one to turn to. No one to hold me and say they would have me for Sunday supper or help me figure out finding a flat to let or tell me under no circumstances should I date nor marry anyone like Connor.

Javi came back in, his very own Carol of the Bells soundtrack preceding him like the ancient art piece he was. He was dressed for the day in a black jumper and trousers and was holding a tray of biscuits and scones that looked freshly baked.

"Sascha said you loved currant scones and preferred them with orange marmalade to strawberry jam." He set the tray down. "But she added, and I quote, 'as long as there's enough cream to cover even the most well-endowed' you would be happy."

My eyes pricked with tears. My Sascha. The only person who had ever sworn to stand beside me and actually did. The one Connor could have asked a hundred times which scones I preferred. I blinked the tears away, not wanting to soak this moment in any amount of sadness. Javi was someone else entirely. A man, for all his demon self-talk. The kind of man who not only found out which type of scones I liked and how but made them. Himself. At God only knows what time of the morning. Sometime between the early dawn when he was buried farther in me than anyone ever had been, and now. I had fallen asleep for possibly a couple hours. My body was spent. Emotionally and physically. Javi's must be as well. Yet, instead of napping with me, he made me scones.

"She is one hundred percent correct. Now, lay down and undo your trousers so we can see if you've brought enough cream." I motioned for him to lay back and he laughed, reaching for my hand and pulling me down next to him on the sofa. "Thank you, Javi. There's more I want to say. More I know I should and need to say, but nothing is coming to mind apart from thank you."

"You are so very welcome, Ophelia." His accent rolled my name as elegantly as the cream I was spreading on the scone.

"You were calling me Fela last night," I said, taking a bite and sighing. The scone crumbled in my mouth, warm currants oozing onto my lips. Javi handed me a serviette.

"It is a very old diminutive of Ophelia. It came naturally to me to call you Fela, though I wonder if it is okay with you." His face fell slightly. I placed a hand on his cheek.

"Of course, it's okay. It surprised me. I had never heard it before. But I love that it felt right for you to call me that. Along with Little Demon."

"Yes, well, Little Demon is for when we are otherwise engaged. And perhaps when I hear your veins singing to mine and both our fangs answering the song."

Honestly, I needed to eat about five scones and drink more tea, but when his voice dropped like that, and there was talk of our demons at open mic night, I was beginning to need more than just breakfast. Or at least breakfast with a bit more iron.

"Javi, I might need to feed," I told him, my breasts feeling heavy and aching with want of his hands and lips and fangs.

"My scones are so good, it makes you need blood and sex?" he asked with a raised dark brow. Those liquid hazel eyes reflected the light of the tree gems. I leaned in to kiss him softly. "Come here, Fela. Let me give you a full brunch experience."

"Like a boozy brunch?" I asked, my voice raspy with thirst and hunger.

"Something like that." He moved the far side of the sofa and lifted his legs so they were stretched across the length. "Come."

There was an ember of command in that one word. I shifted and sat in front of him, nestled between his legs, with my own stretched out between his. After tugging off his jumper, he picked up the glass dish of cream and spread a thick dollop over his wrist. I smiled and looked back at him. Amusement shone on his face. He handed me a piece of scone to eat and held my throat as I swallowed, the piece making a long journey down my throat.

"It's more of a bloody brunch," he whispered and put his creamed wrist to my mouth.

I licked it off slowly as his arousal pressed into my backside. Bloody brunch was everything. I laughed, sucking on his wrist, and felt him rock with amusement while he idly stroked my hair. I fell back against him, brushing crumbs from my body. I spun on him.

"You haven't fed!" It had been what? A day? And all we had been doing. All the violence and sex and feeding me, he must be starved.

"I fed from you a bit as you fed from me. And from Alicia last."

I stilled, knowing if I let the distress signal take over my body, bad things would happen.

"I told you last night, but of course, you were in no state. I apologize for not bringing it back up sooner."

"I knew I smelled her on you." My fangs came out again. That was a reaction I needed to curb because I couldn't have demon Ophelia popping in for a chat every time I was angry.

"I needed blood, Fela. I was drained and needed to be at my best as you transitioned. We were in the kitchen, not anywhere private."

I slumped. Of course, he would need to feed. It couldn't always be me and I couldn't always feed from him now. We would need donors. Oh God.

"I suppose we need to find a donor?" I asked, covering his hand with mine and laying my head on his chest. The tree lights twinkled at us, and I could see a hazy reflection of our forms in the slice of windowpane.

"Perhaps soon. No need to rush at the moment." His fingers tightened on mine.

"Javi."

"Ophelia."

"I love you."

He put both arms around me and held me tightly, tucking his head over mine so that there was nothing at all between us.

"I do not understand how I can be loved by someone like you. But Díos, do I love you, Fela. With every drop of blood in my body."

We dozed on the sofa for a bit, waking only moments before I heard the distinct clomp of Sascha's heels on the front porch and a sort of hiss from who I could only imagine was Alicia.

"Javi, no one is out on the streets for the little flower to eat. You don't have to guard her. Open."

Javi shut his eyes briefly and stood, shifting me from his warm body. I slipped to the toilet to see what I was looking like now, fully expecting to see that post stomach flu look. There was a slight sheen to my skin, but not in the poorly way I'd thought. It was almost as though I had finally gotten good at contouring and highlighting my face. Seeing no remnants of blood or scones around my mouth, I dashed to my room to switch into a red slip dress and gold heels. Was I overdressed? Possibly. Was I willing to risk wearing a fuzzy jumper and jeans and have Alicia looking like she was spat from the mouth of Milan? Not a chance. And the dress matched my lipstick so perfectly, all I could think about was seeing it later on Javier's cock.

"Take a deep breath, Ophelia," I said to myself out loud, knowing full well, two out of three people downstairs could hear me. "New is your wheelhouse. New is where you thrive." I spritzed my favorite perfume on and nearly choked from the strength of the scent. I felt like I had a funeral bouquet shoved down my throat. It might take a bit to get used to the heightened sense of smell.

"Lil!" Sascha jumped from the settee and reached for me. "Ohmygod I was going to ask how you were feeling since

Daddy Sharp Teeth made you a creature of the night, but holy fuck you look so hot I think I'm wet."

"Daddy Sharp Teeth?" Javi and Alicia said at the same time.

"I'm feeling...odd," I said honestly. No one in this room wanted to hear me lie.

"Of course you are," Alicia said, sipping her champagne. The bottle in the Murano glass chiller on the coffee table told me it was a Laurent Perrier Ultra Brut. "You are vampire now. But not really. You are a half dead creature. Like a dog in a shelter you adopt and don't know if it will love you or tear your head off because you said something triggering."

"Alicia Geralda Fernandez Montebello," Javi barked. He shot off a string of what sounded like a reprimand in three languages. She shrugged and drank more champagne.

"Well, I clearly need to go to the shelter more, because I'd take a chance on any dog that looks like you do tonight." Sascha jabbed me in the ribs. "Seriously, Lil. How do you mean, odd?" My best mate led me to the settee and sat us down. "Not like sick?"

"No," I said. "No. Like I'm me, and I know I'm changed. But like, I still feel like me. You know when it's like three days before your period and you want to kill everyone and you're crying over the John Lewis Christmas advert, and then you realize why you're being such a nob?"

"Yeah, 'course. But I generally want to kill everyone. Especially when they're walking so slow and I'm trying to get somewhere."

"Yeah, you get road rage walking."

"Oh, does she?" Alicia asked and took a step toward us.

"Down, girl," Sascha said, waving her talons at her date.

"Well, anyway, like that. Like I'm having hardcore PMS, and I'm hungry like all the time and I can't figure out if I need to eat or if I need to *eat*."

"Or fuck," Alicia chimed in. Javi shot her a look.

"Yes." I looked to Javi, all those feelings of rage and emotion and wanting Yorkshires and wanting Javi's cock hitting the back of my throat, were a tempest inside me.

"Ah, sí. Javi, she's doing fine. Can you smell how turned on she is?"

"What the fuck, Alicia?" I said, finally standing up for myself with her. I knew she was just a strange personality, but it needed an off switch. "Play nice or leave."

The corners of Alicia's mouth poked up like two devil's horns.

"Happy Christmas!" Sascha said, voice overly cheery. She raised her glass, and we all echoed the happy Christmas with a snort.

"Now that that's done, I want to open presents." Sascha pulled two small parcels from her large quilted leather designer tote and handed them to me.

I inhaled through my nose, dreading opening it. Sascha had exceptional taste in her style and home décor. She had more money than I ever hoped to have. Yet, she was the worst gift giver despite her best efforts. She handed another parcel, about the same size, to Alicia.

"Didn't get you anything, Daddy," she said to Javi. "A man can only have so many cashmere jumpers."

Javi smirked and inclined his head. My fingers plucked the paper wrapping and I saw a bow from a local jeweler who was well respected. I had a small spark of hope. Maybe this would be something like silver hoop earrings, or one of those gold friendship bracelets I keep seeing online. I opened it. Javi and Alicia leaned in, heads tilted in question. Hanging from a thin gold box link chain, was a long object.

"Is this—"

"A vibrator, yes," she answered.

Not at all what I was going to ask.

"I was asking if it's a...stake." I lifted the necklace from the box. I could hear Javier snicker behind me. Sascha sighed.

"Turn around." She moved my hair to the side and clasped the chain, then motioned for me to turn back. "See!" She jabbed me in the breastbone. "I had it made weeks ago. Of course, I didn't know then that you were actually fucking his brains out. So, I thought it would be funny. Like, you know, because it's a stake. And you can put it in your wanny and have a lovely little orgasm and feel connected to Javi because it's a stake. And he's a vampire. But I suppose it's less funny now because you're a vampire. I'll process this later and find out if I fucked up."

"Quod me nutruit me destruit'" Javi muttered with his glass pressed to lips. *What nourishes me destroys me.* My dad had that Marlowe line tattooed on his back.

"Open yours," Sascha commanded Alicia.

Javi sat on my other side and fingered the golden stake hanging between my breasts. He touched a tiny lever, and it began a soft hum against my sternum. The thought of what it's for hit its own lever down in my core. Javi switched it off and coughed.

"Ah, Sascha," Alicia said. She held up a pair of wanton red silk knickers with a diamante "A" on them.

"They're an ouvert. The crotch is open. So, I've got easy access—"

"Isn't that maybe the kind of gift you would want her to open in private?" I cut her off. She waved at me and made a "pshaw" sound.

"Oh please, Lil. Open your other one." I untied the ribbon and pulled out essentially the same pair of knickers, except mine were an emerald green with an "L" on them. Festive.

"You do know that my name isn't actually Lily, right?" It was all I could think to say.

"You're my Lily. And you usually don't wear red, so I got you the green. I got myself a pair too. In black, of course." Of course. Because why get yourself the Christmas cracker colors? I mumbled a thank you, feeling my cheeks heating. Sascha opened the box I passed her and pulled out a pair of YSL booties.

"An old client of mine told me she had a sample sale, and these were not selling since they are so tiny. Perfect for my sprite of a bestie who has teeny feet and expensive taste." I winked at her. She was already switching out of her platforms and into the booties, admiring the designer monogrammed heel that sort of looked like someone's mum got a 3D printer and decided to become a cobbler. Or maybe I was just jealous that my feet were bigger. I hadn't noticed Javi slide a box onto my lap. I looked up to see a shy smile on his face and had to kiss him, which made my fangs pop.

"Ah!" I grabbed at my face, hoping I hadn't smeared my double decker red lipstick. Javi pierced the tip of his finger with his own fang and inserted it into my mouth. I was sure there would be a wet stain on the silk of my dress when I stood. Javi rubbed the finger over my gums, around the sore tissue where the teeth had protruded. I moaned. His blood had a numbing effect. His finger in my mouth had a completely different effect.

"Better," I said around his finger. There was a ring of red around it and I smirked at him when he noticed it. "I should open the gift."

"Yes, please do. The smell of sex is worse in here than the club the other night," Alicia said, pouring more champagne.

In the black linen box lay a necklace. Tear drop sized gems in a rainbow of colors were bezel set in gold, looping the necklace. A gold tag hung from the clasp. It was no bigger than my pinky nail and stamped into the metal were my initials: ORJ and the year. A sloshing feeling moved around in my gut. I felt heat press against the back of my eyes. I couldn't look up because I didn't want to cry. And I didn't know what to say. Alicia and Sascha were being uncharacteristically quiet.

"You don't have to wear it," Javier said. His accent rolled through the statement, thicker than I'd heard it. I whipped my head toward him. "Jewelry is personal, and I understand if it isn't your style."

"No, Javi. It's brilliant. Really. I'm overwhelmed. The inscription. All of it. Thank you."

"It's yours, Javi, No?" Alicia asked. She crept closer to get a better view.

"Yes."

"What do you mean?" I asked them both. Javi gave a half laugh and rolled his eyes and made a move to cover his face. I grabbed his hand.

"I made it. For you," he admitted. I dropped his hand and stared at the necklace. Each gem reflected the light and caught on my dress and Javi's white shirt. They shone in a prism of glory around the room. I gasped.

"I didn't know you still blew glass, Javi." Alicia touched the piece and I snarled.

"Sorry," I said, feeling ridiculous. She patted my shoulder.

"I hadn't in a long time," Javi said. "But When Ophelia came into my life, I felt myself wanting more and more to create. To be more. Do more. Last month, I started to make this, hoping it would be ready by Christmas. I didn't even think it would be a romantic gift. In her eyes at least." He ran a knuckle over my cheekbone. "It was almost a thank you. For giving me purpose. They are only glass, I'm afraid."

"Only glass?" I waved my hand around the room. "The decorations on the tree are 'only glass'. They are more magical than anything I've ever seen. This is treasure, Javi. I'm speechless."

"So, I am feeling like a bit of a douchebag for getting you a stake necklace when the vampire in question went all renaissance love story, balcony in Verona on you."

"Don't feel bad," Alicia said. "Javi likes it rough." She winked at him, and I found myself standing up and growling in a low rumble. Javier stood behind me and looped an arm around my waist. His mouth met my ear.

"Easy, Fela," he whispered. "You are welcome to attack her, but it would be far more fun if you took it out on me." His thumb smoothed over my belly button.

The last box under the glittering tree was for Javier from me. I didn't know what to get him. Now, after this gift he made me, I was feeling totally under prepared. Sascha passed it over. I saw Javi's nose twitch like he was trying to suss out what was inside.

"No vampire cheating," I said and tapped his nose.

He popped open the wrapping and lifted the lid.

"Handmade pastas," he said, almost to himself. He lifted the two fresh jars of orecchiette and fusilli. At the bottom of the box was a recycled glass jar of smoked sea salt. It was barely a hostess gift, yet it was my Christmas present to the man I had fallen in love with. Who was allowing me to live in his home and was protecting me and helping me, and who had used his God given talents to create for me. He was looking down at the box, head hung. It was a disappointment of a gift.

Fuck's sake, Ophelia, I said to myself. I could have tried harder. Let go of my sad little orphan girl, missing my best mate, pantomime. He put more effort into helping me find a gift for my dead parents than I'd put into finding something for him. Plus, I'd had to order it in the middle of the night with same day dispatching. I downed my sparkling and set the empty glass on the leucite table, trying to look unfazed.

"Thank you," he said, still looking down. My stomach dropped.

"It's not much," I said quickly. "I thought—"

"It's perfect." He cut me off and looked up. His eyes were shining, the light from hundreds of baubles bounced from his irises.

"Why would you get a vampire pasta?" Alicia asked.

"Because he likes it," I answered her simply. Her eyebrows were drawn together.

"Because I told her it was my greatest joy and that which allows me to embrace my remaining humanity." Javi's statement was in retort to Alicia, yet his eyes never left me. "She feeds my humanity and every part of me that may have been good."

"Ah, well. Happy Christmas then."

I giggled. I could see Alicia through the centuries, leading with her instincts and not giving a thought for anything in her rear view. I could see how it would have worked for Javier for a long while. Her wildness and beauty. Her prowess and bloodthirst. A perfect vampire duo, giving each other what they needed to sustain a long, violent existence. And when one of them needed to seek out her own humanity, the other was set on fighting a world war for the sake of humanity itself. The battle of what made them reconsider their existence, pulled them apart, creating a new path for each. A path which led Javier to me and I to him. I found myself grateful to Alicia. For who she was.

"I'm going to go get the dinner ready." I walked to the kitchen leaving them all to chatter. I hummed along to Christmas hits, while I pulled Yorkshires from the oven and made brandy butter. The kitchen door snicked shut. Javi stood against it, arms folded.

"Need help?" he asked. There was a thundercloud in his voice. I stopped whipping the butter and leaned against the counter. He walked to me and picked up the fork, licking the butter from it. "I've not had this in a while." He tugged at the ties on my apron. "I'm hungry, Fela."

"Then get on your knees, vampire."

He dropped to one, and wrapped his hands around my calf, sliding them up my leg and under the silk of my dress. I shook as his hands neared my center.

"Just a taste. An aperitif." The backs of his hands slid through the wetness at the top of my inner thighs. "So wet already." He looked up at me. On his knees, ready to give me what I wanted and take what he wanted. I could have come looking at his expression. "Will you be a good girl and stay quiet?" he asked, accent strong and voice dark. His finger slipped inside of me, circling in impatience. I swallowed hard and pushed into him. "I am going to feed off you, but you are not to orgasm. Understood?" I whimpered. He stuck another two fingers in and pumped. "Understood, Ophelia James?"

"Yes, papi," I answered.

His eyes went bright as a green flame before he dived under my skirt and fastened his mouth to me. I gasped and fell back, hitting the counter and holding on. I felt his fangs pierce my flesh as he drank my blood and my cum. My own fangs dropped, slicing my lip. I was tasting my own blood and it lit me up further. I too needed to feed. I felt myself building.

"Ah, ah," he cooed, pulling from me. "No coming. He slapped my pussy, and I cried out as a gush left me. He ate my pussy again, lapping at the wetness. My body shook as I tried to come, but every time I was about to release, he pulled away. He drank all of me. I felt his Adam's apple bob against my thigh as he swallowed again and again. The wave of pleasure crested, and I was about to break. He pulled off again and stood, lightning fast.

"Ja. Much better. May I carry the dinner out?"

My legs were slack as I stood there, fangs out and crazed. Javier gave me his wrist, and I tore it open without a thought.

"Enough," he commanded me to stop. I hissed. He was edging me?

"I need more." The voice that came out of me was not my own.

"Of course you do, Fela." His body pressed against mine, caging me. He put his mouth to my ear. "But I am in charge, and you won't be getting more until our Christmas company has left." He squeezed my breast through the dress.

"So, you get what you want and leave me unfulfilled?" I whined. He grabbed my hand and thrust it against his trousers. I could feel him strained against them.

"Does it feel like I got all of what I want?" His fangs dropped again, and his eyes lit up with green fire. I knew mine must have shone orange. He was rock hard under my hand. He pushed my hand closer and ground against me. "I will never leave you unfulfilled. But I will keep you wanting more. Because," he said, trailing his teeth down my neck, "you need to understand that you deserve more. Not only a quick fuck in the kitchen. You deserve to have me tear you apart and put you back together as you drink from me and reduce me to ashes. Burn yourself with me, Fela. And watch yourself rise." I was burning. Our hands were between us, our hips grinding for purchase. "Now. Is dinner ready?"

CHAPTER TWENTY FIVE

JAVIER

It had been a long, long time since I wanted to edge someone, and it mind fucked me too. As a game, I would do it all the time. I could keep edging a partner for hours just to quell my boredom. I very much like to be in charge. For months, I had been fantasizing about how I could keep Ophelia begging for more. Begging for me. I asked her once if I could keep an extra vial of her blood for emergencies. It was a lie. The emergency was my ancient, decrepit body wanting to sip on her while I got off, spilling myself over my stomach whilst tasting her. I fought to keep myself professional. Hell, I had written legally binding agreements to keep us both professional. Beyond needing the control of our employer-employee relationship, I didn't want to corrupt her. I didn't want to change her. Who would have known she was destined to change anyway.

In that kitchen, with Ophelia standing and looking like a succubus in prowl, I wanted to laugh at her saying I got what I wanted. She may have been feral with bloodied fangs and glowing eyes, her breast spilling over the sanguine silk of her dress, but it was I who was a moment short of combusting. I nearly came in my trousers suckling the cum from her wet, bloody cunt. I needed her more than the blood. More than my humanity. But to keep her...to keep her I must make certain we both held on to our humanity. And right now, that meant getting Yorkshires and roast dinner out to the table. My ex-wife and Sascha lounged at the table, speaking softly and touching hands. Alicia looked calmer with Sascha. She appeared the way I liked to remember her in the rose-tinted memories which were so few and far between. I hoped she could find love.

It was apparent that Ophelia's penchant for topping her scones with glorious amounts of clotted cream was a habit mimicked with butter on her Yorkshires. I liked watching her eyes close momentarily as the grease touched her lips. Yes, I was still hard. Painfully so. I wanted her lips coated in butter and sliding over my cock like a harmonica.

"Are you sure your mother is dead?" Alicia's question was a gong in the serenity of the dinner.

Ophelia dropped the fork and knife she held, carrots splashing in the gravy and staining her Christmas dress. We all looked to Alicia, incredulous.

"What? She had the vampire inside parts like the little flower here. That she died in a car accident seems unlikely. That's all I'm saying."

I could smell the hurt and fury rising in Ophelia. Her cheeks flushed and eyes burned.

"I was their only daughter," she said through clenched teeth. "My dad was the love of her life. They spun round each other like the moon and the sun. Ask anyone. She was his white light, and he was her cool dark reprieve."

"People are not always what they seem, Little Flower."

"Enough." I was about to say it, yet Sascha beat me to it. "Loads of things are not as they seem, but Annabella James was light like Lily said. She was mum to everyone she met."

"And the one thing I have always known in this life. In this horrible fucking life that I wanted so many times to end, was that my parents loved me. My mum loved me. With every bit of her heart and soul. She never, ever let me doubt that. So, for you to sit there, eating the dinner I prepared for you, after all the shit you have pulled lately, and telling me that maybe my mum who died—who died tragically when I was age eighteen and left me alone in this world—may not have really died...that is sick." Ophelia stood, dropping her serviette into the gravy that molested her dress. "That would mean she purposefully stayed out of my life for ten years as I struggled. As I let my ex abuse me and I lost my job and my will to live. Does that sound like something a mother would do to her only child?"

Alicia had a look I could not decipher. One I had never seen before. Or had not recognized. A repentance.

"She may have," Alicia said, making me see red. "If she felt it kept you safe. From her. From her world."

There was a profound silence in my dining room. The crackle of fire was deafening. Ophelia's chest puffed in and out. Sascha walked over and took her hand.

"And my dad?" Ophelia asked. Her voice was over quiet. "Where would that have put him in this fantasy retelling of my life?" She rubbed at her nose. "Murdered? By the love of his life? The one he would write poems for and tattoo them on his back? You think my mum would have killed the man she rushed home to each night, diving in his arms because she couldn't stand being apart from him all day? Just to keep me safe? I'm sorry. But your fan fiction of my life sucks. Happy fucking Christmas. Get out."

Alicia rose and nodded at me. She knew not to ask Sascha to come along. She knew she had over stepped. She had planned it. And for that fact alone, I was worried she was right. And my heart ached for Ophelia. The packages Alicia was given were left by the tree. She gathered her handbag and walked out.

"And what if you're right?" Ophelia called after her. She stood in the dining room still, speaking into the darkened hall. "If what you are considering is true and my vampire mother murdered my father and left me to protect me. What then?"

"I do not know. But when I set out to find you, I was also looking for her. As you both descend from Isabel. As a vampire myself. And a mother—please to God, Javi do not say anything—"

"I would not."

"As a vampire and a mother, I can sympathize with what she may have felt. The choice of leaving the love of your life to save your child or staying and putting them all at risk."

"She was not your child to begin with," Ophelia said, a cold note in her voice I had never heard. "And the difference is that you left Javi. You two had destroyed each other enough. My mother would have *murdered* my father. My beautiful, moody, gentle father."

Alicia's voice was low from the foyer.

"I will see what I can find out. I know I have upset you. I'm sorry." And she was gone.

Ophelia collapsed to the carpet. She was not crying. She was shaking and shivering. Her body was in a human state of shock, with a vampiric force behind it. I lifted her to me and gave her my wrist again.

"Lil, d'ya want me to stay?" Sascha put a throw blanket over Ophelia as she fed from me. Ophelia pulled off.

"No. But thank you. For standing by me. Literally standing by me."

"D'ya get the impression she had been planning to say that all night?" Sascha asked me. I nodded. "What a cunt."

"Indeed." Because, what else could I say. Alicia was a witch of the first degree, yet not a liar. Not a shit stirrer for the sport of it. She was blunt and self-serving. Dangerous.

But it all served a crystalline purpose. She had come looking for Ophelia because she wanted to have another child. Once she realized she would not be using my Ophelia, she switched gears. She started looking for Annabella. An undead Annabella, capable of having a child. What I needed to do now was use this evening. This oddest of Christmases, to get Ophelia calm. She was a newly turned vampire, and she was a rubber band stretched to its max. The city wasn't ready for her to break.

We both trained our ears on the sound of Sascha walking down the road. She had her present with her and had even grabbed Alicia's. I hoped really that Alicia was waiting for her. This sleepy city in the southwest of England had only recently become a dangerous place to be human at night. And I did not like it. The footsteps faded, even enough for our inhuman ears. Ophelia launched herself at me—a bat in flight—from where she was sitting like a mermaid on the ground onto my person. Her mouth found my neck.

"Please," she begged. "Please, Javi."

She did not need to beg. Not for this. Not now.

"Take what you want. Take everything." I had meant it. She owned my soul. She could devour me at will. I exposed my throat to her. And grabbed a fistful of her hair, forcing her head to me. Those eyes of hers bore into mine, asking permission. "Feed." Teeth sunk into my throat, dull and painful. She was too hungry, too upset to regulate, and her fangs hadn't descended. My skin ripped under her, and she didn't notice.

"I'm here," I whispered, stroking her head. I allowed my hand to slip down her back and over her ass. It felt like heaven in this dress. "Take all of me, Fela."

She drank, and through her knickers, where she sat straddling me, I felt her soaking me. My cock pressed against her, hard and ready. Her body moved of its own accord. I groaned and moved my hand under her dress. The heat from her cunt was like sunshine, welcoming me. Effervescent nights in Venice, Bali, Shanghai. Those addled, blood crazed nights when I was buried between cock and cunt, drinking in what I wanted, were but whisps of light between shaded branches. Ophelia was a cloudless sky, no hint of rain. An endless summer, ripe and ready for me, eternally. I wanted to please her. Tease her. Consume her in ways I didn't remember ever wanting and needing. As she fed, grinding on me deliciously, I unhooked her necklace and switched it on. My hand reached between us, holding the tiny golden stake. She paused at the buzzing against her stomach, licking the gnarled wound she created on my neck. The thought of her gore covered mouth made my cock twitch. She licked at me like a cat with cream, humming. The stake in my hand circled her belly button. I pressed it inside, holding there and kneading her breast with my free hand. She mewled, kissing and flicking her tongue at my throat where I knew the wound was closing. She was changing from blood lust to fuck lust. Thank God. I had been hard for hours now, and if I didn't find my cock in one of her holes soon, I would become an animal. Still, I played along. I released her breast long enough to drop the straps of her dress, letting it fall off her and pool at her hips. Jesus, she looked like Venus incarnate. Or Lilith incarnate. I moved the stake up between her ribs, tracing her areola.

"Do you like this, my Fela?" I asked, holding the buzzing weapon to her ruby nipple.

"Yes," she hissed between fangs that had finally come out. They shone with my blood and her saliva. A combination I very much wanted all over me. I wanted to drown in her. She undid my trousers and palmed my cock through my under-wear. My head dropped to her shoulder with a moan.

"Will you let me come this time, Papi?" she asked, grabbing my dick hard. I retaliated with a slap to her round ass. She bit her lip and drew blood. I had it in me before she could blink. I needed her blood. "Again."

"You want me to slap you again?" She nodded. "Say it."

"Slap me, Papi. Harder this time." I did. Had she been human, it would have left welts. As it was, the heat radiated from the handprint. I curled my fingers into it. She moaned so low, I could have sprayed my load into her hand. But I wasn't done with her yet. I moved the stake into her seam, running it up and down through her slick cunt. Her body shook over me, inching closer to my cock. I moved it faster, watching her face bloom with color. Bright pink spots glowed on her cheeks, brightening her whiskey shot eyes. I dragged the point of the stake over her clit, holding it there while I impaled her with my middle and ring fingers, curling them in to hit that spot. She gasped and knocked into me harder. I wanted to tear her throat. Gnash her chest and have a mouthful of her breasts. I shoved my other hand over her rounded ass and squeezed, making her cry out just as I knew it would. She shuddered and screamed, messing all over me, ruining ever piece of clothing I had on. Between us, I held up my hand, dripping like I'd dipped it in liquid, then painted her torso with her cum. One by one, I sucked my fingers clean of her, then leaned forward to lick her chest clean, pausing to indeed put my mouth over her breast, allowing her to see my forked tongue dart out and taste where I'd made a mess of her.

"That was only the finish from earlier," she said. Oh, how that mouth was about to get to work. "Merely a taste. An aperitif if you will."

I let a smile twist my lips before snaking my tongue out

toward her I knew what that did to her. The very first time she saw it, I could smell the gush in her pants. "I have been very sad tonight, vampire. I need loads of tending."

In answer, I stood and dropped my trousers and underwear, stepping from them before wrenching off my jumper. She did away with the dress completely and stood naked in just her heels. I grabbed my own cock and pumped it, watching her watch me. I stepped to her, cock still in hand, and held out the necklace. She clipped it back on and let it fall between her peaked breasts. The glass beads around us and the glass beads surrounding her neck threw prisms across her face. If there was magic in this world, it wasn't creatures like me. It was her. It was this thing between us. It was the light play on her curves, making me rub the tip of my cock, smearing precum.

"Are you going to play with yourself all night?" she asked me.

"Would you like to watch?"

Her eyes flashed to mine. "Yes," she said on a breath.

CHAPTER TWENTY SIX

OPHELIA

Javi leaned back and sat on the settee, legs spread wide, dick in hand. He was a god on his throne, toying with his people. His subjects. Disciples. His forked tongue slithered out, tasting drops of me that shone on his chin. I clamped my thighs together. He smirked, waggling the tongue at me. His hand released his cock, which stood at attention, begging for me to sit and fuck him until we were both raw. I stepped forward, not knowing if he was going to let me watch him get off himself, which I very much wanted to see, or if I would jump on him again.

"Stop," he commanded.

And I did. In the back of my mind, I thought I may have once felt silly listening to him. Might have felt silly begging for him to slap me. But not now. Now I wanted him to slap me. Command me. Choke me and tell me what to do. I wanted to be used then loved. But never loved then used. Never again. I knew Javi loved me. I could taste it. Feel it in the air around us. I could read it on Alicia's face. So, I felt comfortable asking to be used. To be slapped and bitten. I wanted it. And wanted to give it back.

"Show me you finger yourself like you did the other night.

The night you made me feed." His hand was back at his cock, hovering. "Show me you fuck yourself with those long pink nails."

I parted my pussy with two fingers, baring myself for him before touching my own clit. I hummed, watching his hand lazily glide over his cock. He spat in hand and made easier work of the job.

"Cup your balls," I told him.

He stopped and raised an eyebrow.

"Get on your knees, and do it for me."

There was zero room for debate. I got on my hands and knees and crawled to him, my ass high in the air for him to see. And I knew he did. He wanted my ass. I dripped a snail trail as I crawled to him. On my knees, I was directly at level with his groin. One long, slow lick from the spot just next to his asshole, all the way up over his balls. I took one in my mouth and rolled it around, savoring the feel like I was pinpointing flavors in a wine. He dug his fingers into my scalp. I wiggled my ass in the air. He slapped it once.

"Keep working," he ground out, jerking his hips up. I used both of my hands to spread his thighs wider, stroking him with my thumb. His hips were bucking, and I would put money on him not even knowing. He was controlling me, but I was fucking owning him right now. I took another mouthful of ball, humming as I rolled my lips over it.

"Jesus," he said. "Fucking Christ." I smiled around a full mouth. The necklace from Sascha banged against my sternum as I bobbed my head over his base, peppering it with tiny nips and drags of my needy fangs. I lifted a hand from his thigh to switch on the stake and put it in my mouth. Raising myself up higher, I let him see the gold chain swagging over the corners of my mouth as I lowered myself over his impressive cock. The stake vibrated where it sat against my tongue.

"Oh," he said, sinking a bit and grabbing hold of my

breast. "Oh fuck." He twisted my nipple and held on for dear life. "Good girl," he said. "That's my good girl."

I didn't know so much liquid could drip out of my pussy. Truly, it was like a faucet had been turned on inside me as he spoke. I was moving my body, fucking the cold air as he held my head over his huge cock. I felt the buzzing through me as he took the sides of my head and began fucking my mouth in earnest.

"Such a good girl getting dirty for me. Suck harder. Let me feel that dirty fucking mouth."

I hummed on him, massaging his balls. He became erratic, hitting the back of my throat. I gagged and swallowed, trying to breathe through my nose.

"Swallow my cock, Fela. Take me so deep." He bounced his body into me, and his base and balls were at my lips. "Fucking breathe, beautiful. Fucking breathe. You are a vampire. You take me so fucking well. Look at you swallow my cock like it was your Christmas dinner."

I had wanted to taste him. Consume him. Feed off him as he fed off me. I had wanted that before I became what I am now. So, I did take him well. I took more. I swallowed him deeper, loving the desperate moan in his voice. I loved feeling the soft skin of his balls pillow over my lips. I could breathe just fine. I slipped my finger in his ass and felt him slam into me like a sword.

"You," he said on a thrust. "Fucking." Thrust. "Take. "Thrust. "My." Thrust. "Cock." Harder thrust. "Like." Thrust. Oh God I was getting close myself. I wanted to fuck him. I wanted to feel his cock in me. But I wanted to have him blow into my mouth. I wanted to drink it all down and have it nourish me. Like a slut. A vampire. A needy, needy girl. Thrust. "I." Thrust. "Was." Thrust. "Made." Thrust and slap. I cried out around the massive cock in my mouth. "For." Thrust and slap. "You."

He let go and spewed into me. I sucked and drank. His hot, salty cum flooded my mouth and ran down my throat. I kept swallowing as he rode through it. The stake dropped from my mouth, tinkling spit and cum all over me. Before I knew what was happening, Javi had me pinned to the floor, my head under the Christmas tree. My vision was filled with sparkling lights and Javi's poison green eyes. Thank fuck. He clamped on to my breast and drank from me. My legs were around his waist, relishing in his body on mine. I'd had good sex. I had had great sex even. But I had never had anything like sex was with Javier. Even before we actually fucked. The way he made me feel was an addiction. A necessity. Like there was some nutrient in my body that had been missing until he touched me. When he pulled from my flesh, he held my face, gentle and calm. Those eyes were still gleaming with need, and I felt his cock hard again.

"You can have your way with me as you like," he said, placing a kiss at the tip of my nose. "In every possible future, there is you and there is me. And I will always, always love you." His cock speared into me with a fever of emotion. I grabbed hold of his hips, urging him in. I wanted it rough. I wanted to be broken. Split in two.

"Make it hurt," I said, looking into his eyes so he could see how serious I was. "Make me bleed everywhere. I want to need repairing from this." His brows knit together, unsure. I touched his face as gently as he had mine. "It's okay, Javi. I need to feel it all. Do not hold back."

His hands were around my throat, a tentative choke. With that, my pussy became a waterfall he felt rushing around him. He slammed into me, over and over.

"I want to feel your cock in my stomach. Want to swallow you in reverse."

He was groaning. He raised to his knees and pulled my ass

off the ground. That cock I needed like air, rammed so far into me, I saw stars.

"Oh fuck, yes. Javi. I need your cock all day. All fucking day."

His nails were shredding into my thighs, keeping me elevated. I lifted further. He was so deep in me, I swear I could feel him in my chest. He ripped his forearm open with his fangs and dripped his hot blood all over my body and into my mouth. I lapped at it, catching drops like snowflakes on my tongue.

"How good are you taking me, Fela?" he asked, tearing me in two yet looking like he was dancing. "My blood is in your mouth, where you still taste like my seed. My blood is all over your tits and cunt, baptizing you in my demon. I bet it's dripping into your asshole right now. Is it?' I nodded and caught more blood in my mouth. "Yes," he said. "I knew it was. I bet it's hot and making you feel like you're going to burst. I bet you don't know where to look. What to do with yourself."

My eyes were darting around. I had never felt so unhinged. I held onto his hands and pressed them into my throat, cutting off more air.

"You want me to steal your breath, Fela?" he asked, squeezing.

I tried to nod. He placed a hand over my mouth and kept the other on my throat. I couldn't breathe at all. Yet he still impaled me. The world was exploding in fireworks of colors and emotions I never knew existed.

"I want you to scream and bite my hand and I will come in you and on you. You will be bathed in my demons, fresh from the flames of hell. Do you understand?"

I raised my hips in answer, my eyes rolling back in my head.

"Let go."

And so I did. I bit his hand, taking a chunk of flesh and

consuming his blood while our releases mingled together and broke from me. He pulled out and pumped once more letting go a last release of cum that hit my face and neck, soothing where his hand had been. I licked at it as I rode out the orgasm. He rubbed his torn palm over my cunt, soothing his own wounds. And we fell into one another, perfectly sated.

CHAPTER TWENTY SEVEN

OPHELIA

I never thought to ask if Javi had cleaners for his home. I could not picture him having people in to clean his toilets and wipe his fridge. Yet, I couldn't really picture him dusting and scrubbing the shower door. I hated cleaning shower doors. Mine were always foggy and had a layer of soap scum that never came off. Javier's showers were pristine. The sitting room and dining room were currently a tip. It stunk of debauchery and Christmas dinner. We had stained the carpets, but Javi waved it off and said they could be replaced. I showered first, smiling as I scrubbed myself of the crusted layer of Javier's and my various fluids. I was not hungry. Finally. It felt blissful. There was no primeval need to feed on blood or butter. I was completely sated. Finally. Javier came into the room as I was donning a dressing gown. He looked cleaner than I'd last seen him, but he paused to give me a small kiss before heading to the shower himself.

"I've tidied downstairs. Feel free to relax if you'd like. I won't be long."

I took the opportunity to head down and collect my parents' gifts and brought them up to open on my bed. Javi's bed. Our bed? The first was a collection by a poet named Randall, who wrote about finding yourself in dark times. My dad had been passed between homes as a child, since his mum was an addict. His gran died when he was eight, so he stumbled between distant relatives and neighbors until there was simply no one left. He had always loved poetry and literature, so when it came to choosing his own path, he had chosen to blow everyone away with his A Levels. That's how he ended up here. In our sleepy uni city with its ancient catacombs and Roman wall. That's how he met Mum. She, like me, was orphaned at eighteen. Alicia's accusations were beginning to tiptoe up my spine, planting spores of distrust in my own upbringing. I felt even stupider now with my habit of buying my dead parents' Christmas gifts. If Mum were really a murderess, she didn't deserve the fucking highland cow or the million-wick candle that cost me the same as a winter coat from Hennies would. I did not want to believe my mother, who sang to me every night as a child, would have killed my dad. Would he have even fought back? I decided he would have. Not for himself. Had it been just the two of them, he would have given her everything. With love and regret in his eyes. The way he loved my mother was a cosmic blast. A splintering of the universe that pieced itself back together into what was between them. I would have sworn on all that I am, she felt the same. She was quieter with her devotion though. Mum had a careful, hushed way about her, but once you felt the warmth of her sun, you understood what it was to be loved by her. And Daddy flew so near. So, I knew she could have killed him with his blessing. Except it wasn't only him. And for how much he adored her, I was his star. His bright tomorrow in a dark galaxy. He would have fought for me. Fought for himself because of me. And I didn't know where to settle the depth of my despair. For the woman I knew loved with every burning ember of her being, and may have had to destroy us all, or for the father who could never live with either outcome. His daughter being alone, or his wife having to make it hurt.

I lit the candle and said something that wasn't quite a prayer—I didn't do faith. It wasn't quite an incantation either. It may have been a line of a poem, or the lyric of a forgotten song. It voiced that serrated dagger of pain in my chest I felt thinking about my parents. Their empty graves. The wicks crackled next to me while I kept my eyes focused on the wavering flame. I stared as Javi came to rest behind me, pulling my body against his. My eyes fell closed at some point, feeling his lips touch the edge of my jaw. Happy Christmas, Mum and Dad.

CHAPTER TWENTY EIGHT

JAVIER

I did not need as much sleep as Ophelia did. She was, after all, not undead. She was a curious vampire-human. The likes of which I had never seen. I suspected something in her genesis, which I knew without any crumb of doubt would be broadcast to others like me. Other vampires. Ones who were neither trying to pass for human nor wanting to refrain from pillaging the world of our food source. I knew Alicia would not be that disseminator of intelligence. She was too selfish. Too insular. Ophelia slept in my arms, soft snores telling me she felt safe. It made my heart less heavy. I wondered how well she had slept since her parents' deaths. That mystery was one I intended to solve as it was even now beating at my brain in an incessant throb. The scent of blood tickled my nose in those early morning hours whilst I held my lover. Leftovers from the insanity of our love making earlier. I thought I had cleaned it all, but anyone who has ever watched a police procedural knows, there is no surefire way of getting all evidence of blood from carpeting. And vampire senses of smell were more reliable than any blacklight.

Ophelia stirred in my arms, turning and nestling into my bare chest. Part of me wanted to scream to the world how it felt having this magnificent creature cuddled into me. The rest of me wanted only to live quietly alone with her, fenced off from the horrors of this life. Her nose twitched on my collarbone like she was smelling the mess we had made. I should go back down and re-clean before it set in completely. There was very little that would get me to leave this bed with her so keen to have me hold her. Perhaps sleeping a little would do us both some good.

I do not ever remember waking to another's eyes on me. It was in my nature to be alert before anyone else. To never let my guard down. Yet with Ophelia, I had slept through the night, and woken to her smiling down at me.

"I'd like to show you where I grew up. And maybe take you to the seaside." Her words were whispered, as though she wasn't ready to fully wake me. But I was awake. The stiffness of my cock was evidence of that.

"I'd like that," I told her. My voice was gravelly as well. "Perhaps we must both first eat?" Her smile was devilish. She ducked under the duvet and began feasting on me, swallowing what I released, too quick for my liking. I made haste in feeding the same fashion, nipping her inner thigh for a little extra sustenance to get me through the day.

Weather had taken a break for Christmas it had seemed but had no intention of leaving our skies clear for all of Boxing Day. Winds whipped at our scarves as we made our way across the river into the newly redesigned Quayside area. Ophelia led me to a section of rowhouses I knew had once belonged to university faculty. I had a donor once upon a time who taught physics, and though he was well versed in the formula for life in the cosmos, he was very intrigued by my kind and ultimately could not handle our arrangement. It had taken me months to cover up his death. I ended up having to enthrall nearly thirty people he had let something slip to. My life was a constant uphill battle.

"That window," Ophelia said, pointing to the end unit.

"That was Mum and Dad's room. You could see all the way across the river and into the marshlands. Mine was at the back and looked over the shared garden and the marsh behind us. It's rather marshy here, isn't it?" She smiled, though I knew being here was costing her. Wicked winds swirled around us in a scarf dance with our cold tolerance.

"How long since you've been back here?"

"Ten years," she said. I stopped and squeezed her hand. "Once I couldn't make the rent and was officially kicked out, there was no reason to stay. No reason to return to a haunted house. Let someone else feel the emptiness inside." She shrugged and wiped at her nose. I must have been looking at her with a certain intent. "It's okay, Javi. I wanted to come here today. With you. We don't know what we will be facing soon, and I need to have some closure with my past."

That was a fair statement. I admired her tenacity. Only aged twenty-eight yet the weight of centuries sat on her shoulders. She pulled me back to the footbridge so we could take the train out to the coast.

"We have to have an ice cream," Ophelia said, jogging to the stand dusted in wintry sand.

"It's December twenty-sixth and about one breath from snowing," I countered, not helping my smile.

"Oh Jesus," she said.

"What?"

"That smile of yours. When it makes a rare appearance, I swear to God, there's a light from the heavens."

I laughed at her and bent to kiss her before urging her toward the ice cream place.

She groaned. "I'm not even remotely religious, but your smile is my come to Jesus. Honeycomb and..." She looked me up and down like she was deciding.

"Mango, please," I offered.

"Huh. I was going to say coconut. Mango it is."

"I do like coconut," I admitted, licking the tropical ice cream in a swirling, methodical way. "It has to be fresh, though. Not artificial. I can taste chemicals, and false coconut is offensive."

She was watching me eat. I saw her swallow hard. I locked eyes with her and let my demon take over, my tongue becoming the forked abomination I only now accepted because she liked it. It hissed and curved around the cone, lapping at the orange custard. I could hear her teeth crunch on the bits of honeycomb in her vanilla ice cream. She was wet. I could scent it.

"Sometimes I wish I could have footage of past Javi. I want to see what that tongue has done in the past."

"That would be a terrible idea." I leant forward and kissed her with a mouthful of mango and a forked tongue that slid down her throat. She moaned. "There is much you shouldn't see. Things I regret. Things I do not, and perhaps those are the things that haunt me the most. Regardless, I would not wish for you to see me with anyone else but you. Just as I would not wish to see you with anyone else but me. I even have a slight jealousy toward Voltaire."

She giggled. It was a sound I wished to hear more. I wanted to bring out the easier side of Ophelia. The side that she rarely afforded herself the grace to show.

"Would I feel jealous and want to rip off the heads of anyone who touched you?" she asked, taking a long lick of her cone, and swirling her tongue around the tip. I smirked. "Yes. However," she continued speaking with a pause only to plunge her tongue into the top center of the ice cream. Vixen. "I would love to see historical Javier bleeding someone while having his cock sucked. Or taking it from behind while you have your face fucked."

I was not ready for this conversation. I saw spots in my vision. She had me so turned on, there was nothing on this beach nor in this county, but the two of us. I calculated how fast I could pull her into a dark alley and fuck her blind.

"Do you wish to see me with another?" I asked instead, knowing I would never disgrace her or what we have with a quick fuck in public. Our faces were close, heat bouncing from one of us to the other.

"No." The answer was succinct. "I have a filthy mind. I'm horny and mind fucked by how much I want you. And honestly, the idea of your past turns me on. Not because I want to share you. See previous comments about head ripping off. But because I want to squirt in my knickers getting to know you. Every kill and every conquest. Every fuck. I want to have it wrap around me like a tornado and swallow me whole." She took a breath.

I reached into her long coat and touched her crotch. Soaked. I rubbed it, angling us from any prying eyes. Though it was bloody freezing, and there was no one at all about. All the windows of the townhouses across the boulevard were closed for the winter. I rubbed her over her jeans, pushing the unforgiving seam into her clit. "So, when I say, I'd like to see those things, I mean it. Was your hair longer when you spit roasted a victim in Venice with Pietro? Did you have a girl eating your ass while you ate another's cunt? Were you bleeding her dry while a third took your cock?"

This woman would be my death. The ocean beat the rocky shore near us, yet there was a roaring in my ears not unlike a tempest sea.

"And would that turn you on?" I asked. "When I tell you it all happened? I had my mouth and fingers filled with cunt and cock. I had my ass filled and my balls swallowed while I fed from breasts. I drank from a dripping dagger that pierced the heart of a whore who Alicia had killed while I was fucking her. Out of spite.

"None of that turns me on anymore. They were actions of

an ill-guided demon who took what he wanted because there was nothing left and no direction. I do not mind that the thought turns you on. You as Ophelia the human and you as my little queen vampire. But understand that I do not ever wish to partake in such things. I will do anything to you that you ask. But I do not want or need more than you." I had stopped touching her. It felt like what had been a bit of flirtation had turned into a serious conversation.

"I understand, Javi." She placed a hand on my cheek. "I don't want or need more than you either. I simply want to know all of you. The darkest and lightest."

She offered her ice cream to me. I smiled and took a long lick.

"But now," I said, "I'm indecently horny and cannot believe we have to take the train home."

The clouds on the channel were darker than my demon, pushing toward the coast. I guessed we had an hour before that storm came ashore. It was time to head back before we were stuck.

"Should I try to clean the blood from the carpeting more?" she asked me in a low whisper on the train.

"I did already," I said.

"Huh. I keep smelling it. Guess that's these super senses now."

I kissed the side of her head.

The rain was spitting in icy drops as we sprinted for my front door. Through the door, I could smell the damned blood from our night. Ophelia waved a hand in front of her face. I stopped inputting my code and looked around, suddenly on edge.

"What is it?" she asked, voice barely a rustle of leaves.

"It's not our blood." I walked around the side and unlocked the gate leading to the back courtyard. Trees dripped their skeletal branches between my house and the neighbor's house. He was gone for the holiday, I knew. Visiting his mother in Gloucester. There was a box, wilted and soggy by my back door. Ophelia's hands were fisted in my jacket. We both smelled the blood. I recognized the scent and didn't know if I hoped she did or not.

"Will you do me a favor and go inside, Fela?"

"Absolutely not."

Dios. I knew she would say that. She stepped toward the caving box. I shot my arm out and blocked her, probably knocking the wind from her with the force. "Oof."

"Apologies. Please step back and allow me." I pulled my phone and texted Alicia.

In Venice we had stray kittens, I texted her in an odd sort of code I was not sure she would understand, since we had not seen one another for a century. *When the neighbor's cat saw them, she was not happy. Do you remember?*

Sí, she wrote back. *Do you have souvenirs?*

Let's reminisce. I didn't know what else to say, but I was fairly confident she would take that to mean she needed to be here as soon as bleeding possible.

"Javi," Ophelia said. "I know that smell."

She darted ahead and pulled the box open before I could stop her. The speed of a new vampire, filled with every protein source imaginable. Her voice let out a strangled cry. In the box, face up, was Connor, Ophelia's ex. The first thought in my mind was that I was sorry I hadn't been the one to do it. The second was I also knew it hadn't been Alicia. And Pietro did not have the balls. I looked around and noted my cameras still running. There was no one else here. Of that, I was sure. I took Ophelia's coat, a cheap one from a fast fashion store on the high street, and covered the rapidly disintegrating box and its damning contents. I carried it into my professional quarters which hadn't been used in the weeks since I brought my lover home with me. I sat the box in the shower, still draped in the acrylic fabric of Ophelia's winter wear. I would get her a new coat. Something to weather the English winter more than the trash she had in the past. Every instinct to protect her drowned out my logic. The negotiable calm I possessed. Logically, I believed this to be a double-edged blessing. I was glad of the boy's demise. He was a toxin. A toxin that I did not believe should have the privilege of creating hell for Ophelia or anyone else in this world. On the flip side of this sword, was the rusted, dull reminder that we live in a modern world. When people go missing, the world takes notice. Even should he not be missed by actual people, which I was banking on, he would have bills unpaid. A workplace at which he fails to show. Digital pings alerting thirsty do-gooders to the fact that a human has been extradited from the earth. This would be a complication.

CHAPTER TWENTY NINE

OPHELIA

"Who the fuck was it?" Alicia demanded. She stormed into the house, dropping a dripping umbrella, and shucking her rain boots. I wouldn't have entirely put it past her, but Javi was insistent that it wasn't her. She had no motive for it apart from the fact that he knew about us. Sort of. He could easily be enthralled. I felt an odd numbness in my limbs.

Connor was dead. Not just out of my life or two hours away by train. Dead. Forever. I would never have to worry he would show up at the wrong time or try to swindle his way into my life or review bomb my business. This had happened twice. Dead. I was sick. Relieved. Upset. Numb. So fucking numb.

"We don't know." Javi was rolling up his sleeves and sitting down to his laptop. I didn't know how he could be so calm. So clinical it this moment. There was a head. A human head, dropped on his back doorstep. Connor's head.

"Did you tell Sascha?" I managed to get the question out and not tremble. Javier still snapped up his head to look at me.

"You okay, Fela?" he asked me.

I nodded. I wasn't. I didn't know what I was, but there

was nothing for it at the moment. There was no one way of describing what I felt or didn't feel. I was numb.

"No. She was still asleep." It was four in the afternoon. It wasn't atypical of Sascha to sleep in that long. Especially on Boxing Day. "And I wouldn't have told her without asking first."

"Okay," I said. "Okay. Yeah. Right." Maybe Alicia had a moral compass after all. Or at least the black and white version of one. Existing, but not quite resembling reality.

"Javi, I do not think the little flower is okay."

"I'm fine," I said. I sat hard on the settee and grabbed a throw pillow to press into my middle. Javi was scrolling through news articles from local papers and presses. Every once in a while, he would screen shot something. While he scrolled, he began giving orders.

"Alicia, you need to get the head out of here. I want it as far from Ophelia as possible. We need to find the body and figure out how to make it look like a drug deal gone wrong. And take Pietro. Make him grovel and work off his involvement in this."

I started shaking. He couldn't see me, but I knew Alicia could. She grabbed a blanket and covered my shoulders without saying anything. I was always Connor's next of kin. I was his worst enemy because of the breakup. The girls and guys he fucked on the side all knew about me. He kept secrets from me, not them. He got off telling them they were side quests as he called them. His bullshit wannabe gamer personality with a penchant for things he couldn't actually afford, yet still bought. I was the one who had filed a suit against him for fucking up my credit. I was the one who appealed to review sites for his mucking up of my jobs. We had both been seen in two clubs this month. Everything untoward would now point to me.

"He had dealers," I mumbled. "Connor, I mean. Someone

he worked with in the bar. She was in prison for a bit for getting high whilst pregnant. He was there that night, snorting with her, but managed to slip out the fire escape when she overdosed. He told me that. I had asked if he had been seeing some other fuckboy who I'd caught him with three or four times. He swore it wasn't him and pulled up a news story on that girl. The pregnant one. Like that was better because it didn't fully answer my question. It was always talking to a fucking genie." I scrubbed a hand over my face, knowing there was eyeliner likely drawing a fissure up my forehead. "Am I making sense? He showed me that he was with *her*. His alibi for not being with fuckboy, was to show me he had been with the pregnant coke head." I made a choked half laugh sound. In retrospect, I didn't know what in the ever-loving fuck of fucks I was thinking. Why I cared enough to question whom he had been with. I knew he was a loser. Cheating aside. I mean, anyone who cheats is completely lacking integrity. But Connor was a loser on so many levels. And I supposed I was too for allowing it. It takes two to tango and all that. What a thought.

"Did she survive the overdose?" Alicia asked.

"Yeah. Baby did too. Apparently, she stopped doing drugs but still sold. Times are tough, blah blah."

The earlier feeling of being sated was gone. Lightning strikes of hunger and anger fired through my stomach. I pulled my phone and used the camera as a mirror. I knew there would be eyeliner. It had been a perfect wing too. Sigh.

Javi and Alicia were looking at me. Both gave me space to speak when I was ready.

"There was someone else," I continued, using my pinky to attempt to fix my liquid liner wing. "Another fuckboy. Someone he met at work. I'm sure you could find the guy's name in his phone. Another gem. This guy used to sell to his kid's friends behind his wife's back. She found out about it, and called it in. So, he laid domestic violence charges on her for slapping him. He told the police she beat him all the time and threatened their kid. She went to jail. He didn't. Their kids suffered because the guy didn't want to admit to fucking some loser guy behind his wife's back." I gave up on my liner and was simply trying to not cry for being so bloody stupid. "The more I say these things out loud, the more I realize what an absolute idiot I was for staying with him."

The others were quiet, not offering anything. I knew from group therapy, the only support I was able to get from NHS, despite my traumatic history, that there was not much to say to a survivor. I didn't like calling myself that because I had only been hit a couple of times. Mostly in a drunken rage. But the emotional abuse. The gaslighting. The cheating. The putting my life and career in danger. It was all abuse. I knew that now. And I thought, as I sat there, a hybrid vampire human amongst other vampires, that if Connor hadn't been killed, one day I might have killed him myself. I could humanize myself enough to logically know where to draw lines. But Connor hadn't any lines he didn't snort away. And I may have one day been angry enough or hungry enough to do away with him myself.

"I don't have a map here," Javi said. "But it doesn't take a geographical genius to see that there have been killings in and around London." He typed a few things into a search bar.

"How do you equate it to vampires?" I asked. "I keep up with the news and never hear anything that would point toward people drained of blood or any of that old adage."

Alicia stepped next to Javier and placed her hand on the back of his chair. I reigned in a snarl, because I knew she wasn't trying to touch him. My vampy demon didn't care about her intent. Only that she was within touching distance of him.

"Most people who go missing are either too sloppy to

cover their traces, have odd back-office habits, or it's such a high-profile case, there is news coverage of every inch of their life and abduction," Alicia explained.

"So, with vampire involvement?" I looked at some of the media Javi had pulled up on his screen.

"Things get hushed." He looked at me over his shoulder. "Most of us can enthrall humans and use that to our advantage. John Smith stopped showing up to work. He was let go. The wife gives up on him, etc. No big to do. Or, if somehow the case got out and there were too many moving parts to bring to a stop, we can guarantee there is nothing which would point toward vampirism. And our DNA is untraceable. Because we can turn humans, our DNA mingles with theirs, becoming simply a mutation. We are wraiths. Perfect predators."

I thought about his explanation. It made sense, of course. However...

"So, what are you finding?" I looked closer.

Crawley man sells off wife's belongings after she runs in the dead of night, leaving him for lover and heading to Spain. One headline read.

Missing uni student found backpacking across Croatia last month. Another one. Both seemed fairly innocuous to me.

Bristol doctor found dead in bathtub after apparent suicide days before opening private surgery. Leaving pregnant wife. Stress does all sorts of things to people.

Single E. London mum, high on heroin, stabs self in neck. Found by neighbor accused of buying drugs. Blames neighbor missing after buying train ticket to Penzance.

That made me hesitate. Could that have been Connor's neighbor? Javi pointed at the screen.

"There is no record of the missing student having left the UK nor entered the EU at any point. Cross reference shows he was never back at uni, which seems odd if he had been found. Coroner has a listing which matches the boy's description." Javi pulled up more pages. I sat hard on the arm of the settee. "The doctor treated a casualty case of a man who swore his throat was bitten by a human. The man was taken care of, yet the doctor had reported the case to the authorities. The file was officially closed but I can access backlogs. The single mum was in the same building—"

"As Fuckface," Alicia said. We both looked at her. "What? That is what Sascha calls him, is it not?"

"I had a contact tell me last week that someone matching Connor's description was talking up a vampire sex ring. My contact did not know how many people had been told as it was in a club in Bristol, a few days after we saw him in the club here."

Ice ran through my body at Javi's words. Alicia swore under her breath in what sounded like it may have been Catalan. "This is one of many reasons we don't pull the sort of stunts you pulled, Alicia, in bringing someone like Connor into our lives. And Pietro for that matter."

"I was desperate, Javi. I regret it. I do." She sounded convincingly repentant, but I did not know Alicia, and she had centuries to perfect the kicked puppy façade. He made a knife hand at the air before him.

"It's done. We are in clean up mode now. You need to be very careful, Alicia." Javi turned to look at her and there was a whole conversation in his eyes.

I knew it must have been complicated for him having her around so much after so many years. Even if he no longer felt for her how he once did. However, they had a past, and there were bound to be particles of love left.

"I always am. You thought me dead for one hundred years." She made a slicing lotion across her throat.

"Who do you know could be doing these killings?" I asked, uneasy. *Please not my mum*, I thought.

They shared another look. I growled and hopped off the settee and left the room. I could handle the ex-factor between them. I could handle her being in my life because of Sascha. I was not so sure I could handle the unspoken conversation and telepathic communication. It made me uneasy and quite frankly, hungry. I pulled out leftover roast potatoes and chocolate digestives. The scent of salty earth, rosemary, and perhaps musk, entered before Alicia did.

"I do not mean to make you uncomfortable. I believe I have been enough of a nuisance to you."

I snorted at her words.

"I spent a long time in hiding. Hiding in plain sight as the phrase goes." She sat on the counter stool next to me. I poured us both a glass of wine from the open bottle of tempranillo. She seemed thoughtful. Or calculating.

"I am not a child," I said, drinking a large mouthful of red.

"No, you certainly are not. And I hope that I have not treated you as such. My existence, and now yours, is based on the ability to keep secrets. To be seen and unseen within the blink of the eye."

"An eye."

She waved me off. "When I left Javi," she said, "my thought was to protect Allegra. He would not want her, and if he knew how she had been birthed, he would have seen only danger. The world was different for us then. More so, Javier and I were different. I was dangerous. And he would have been right to see Allegra as a ticking bomb."

I had trouble picturing Javi threatening to kill a baby. It occurred to me then, that though I was in love with him and felt as though I have known him forever, I hadn't. He had been many people, and the one at his core is his demon. Demons don't regard half vampire babies as sweet. They see them as a target to eliminate. I shivered. Alicia noticed and nodded.

"For hundreds of years, Javier and I would be in this shadow world together. We worked together. Moved through time and place together. We knew how to cover each other and stay off anyone's radar." She took a small sip of wine and closed her eyes in appreciation. "When I left him, I had faked my own death. So, I had very little time to prepare how to exist in this world without Javi. Beyond that, I had to make sure I could stay out of his sight and not use any of our previous tactics. All whilst being a mother. I do not try to make you uncomfortable with how I speak to him. I am now having to reassess myself because I must still exist in the shadows as do you and Javier. But he was very much a large part of my life. And the switch is a bit unnerving for every-one. He is yours, Ophelia. There is no doubt. I hope one day, we can be friends. As I am essentially your adopted great grandmother." She patted my hand. My glass was held aloft at that little tidbit. So bloody weird.

"Allegra died as a human though," I said.

"She did. She was elderly I am told. I wished I had been there with her. I only found out after the fact. There is no record of what happened to your parents, Ophelia. A death certificate handed out, yet no official record of the accident. No coroner's report. Nothing. I'm sorry." Alicia stood up and left her glass on the black countertop.

"I want to find her," I said.

She paused at the door to the hall. "I know."

The digital beep of the kettle switching off drew me out of my stupor. Javi did not care for proper tea but had kept some in house for me. Before everything went to hell in a handbas-ket. Would I still like tea as this new Ophelia? Regardless, when things went to shit, we put the kettle on, and that was bloody that. The soft gurgle of near-to-boiling water, and the scent of tannic herbs lifting to me brightened my outlook. I fished out the bag and dumped it into a dead tea bag bowl before leaving the kitchen.

Alicia was gone. Javier stood by the front window, watching the storm bluster beyond the panes. I could see his reflection in the dark glass.

"Alicia has taken the object of concern. She will begin erasing his previous steps and help this from becoming a larger problem. I have a plane on standby should we need to extradite you. In the unlikely event fingers start pointing at you."

I sipped my tea, having forgone any milk. It didn't hold any desire over me as it once did. The tea itself was still soothing in this tense time. I had made up my mind.

"I have an idea," I told Javi.

"I have a feeling it has nothing to do with you undressing and letting me pound myself in you until this all goes away."

"Okay, now I have two ideas," I added. "But the original one is that I plan to lure my mother to me. Or whoever is creating this havoc."

Javi looked wary though not surprised. He sighed. "Whoever is doing this decapitated your ex. This isn't a game."

"I'm not stupid, Javier."

"I did not say that, nor do I think it. I am simply saying that though it might be obvious, it is worth saying that luring anyone to you at this moment is a huge risk." He was fully turned to me, palms held open. "And I will be next to you every step."

My shoulders sagged. We needed Pietro to start wagging his tongue around England. Talking up a girl he enthralled who still bought Christmas presents for her dead parents and carried around a highland cow. He was promiscuous and quick and leaned into a paycheck. Within the hour, he had hit up several pubs and clubs and taken the train to Bristol, the site of the last questionable murder. By night's end, he sent us photos of people he'd told whilst in a faux drugged state. I sat with Javi, curled up in his bed, watching the footage Pietro sent.

"He was my architect," I said with my cheek pressed into Javi's chest. He laughed under me.

"He is an architect. A decent one at that. He was as a human too." Javi kissed the side of my head. "I will help in any way to make sure you and Sascha can open the hotel on time."

I snuggled closer. We had seven weeks until opening. The night before Valentine's Day was approaching quickly. Luckily, I had accounted for this time off between Christmas and New Year's. After the first of the year, it was crunch time. And I couldn't be a bloodthirsty vampire stressed out and hissing with dropped fangs every time something went wrong. Because things would go wrong. Repeatedly.

Lil A text came through from Sascha, who presumably had only just awoken on this Boxing Day.

Hiya, Tart I shot back, far more flippant than our entire situation called for. Javi ran a finger across my cheek before leaving the room to give me privacy.

Not that I'm worried about her ffs, but have you heard from my vamp bitch?

I chuckled. Those two were hot and heavy for sure.

Yeah. There's been…a lot today. Listen. I'd feel better if you stayed here with us while Alicia is out of town.

Ellipses blinked on screen for a long while. I thought I needed to say something innocuous that she would understand as meaning things are absolute shit at the moment.

Sasch. Our architect is running some PR in the bigger cities. Alicia is helping.

WHAT THE FUCK HAPPENED, LIL

Was she thick? I obviously couldn't say through text that my ex had been decapitated, his head delivered to Javi's back door, and we needed a team of vampires to clean up the mess, so I wasn't done for murder.

OMG nothing! You know I'm overprotective of you and don't want you alone. Javi and I will come over for a glass of prosecco and then you can come back and have a girly sleepover with me tonight! Be there in a half hour!

I sighed and leaned my head back. Vampires needed less sleep, but I felt like I could sleep for a week with the exhaustion pressing down on me. I didn't want Sascha here when I was still transitioning and when everything was so new with Javi. I didn't want her hearing what would surely be raging sex multiple times a day. But if the person who killed Connor could bypass Javi's cameras and get to his back door, then they could surely get through the seventeenth-century building in which my best mate lived. However refurbed it was.

Sascha opened the door and pushed a splashing glass of prosecco at me.

"M&S finest. Now talk," Sascha said. "What do you want to drink, vampire?" she asked Javi. "That isn't from Lily's veins or cunt."

Javier winced. Sascha was blunt at the best of times, but nervous, on edge Sascha was worse than a pirate.

"Prosecco is fine, thank you," he answered. Javi walked to the expanse of windows that looked over the street below. His gaze flicked like credits on a screen, noting the streetlamps, the cars, the other buildings. The church steeple in the background. He pulled the draperies shut and double checked the latch on the windows. Sascha held out the squared bowl coupe to him, but he was laser focused on inspecting the flat. He sniffed at the drawers of her little used desk, the corners, the lamp in the hall, and the sofa, which made him smirk.

"Don't get cheeky, vampire," Sascha said, knowing exactly why Javi had smirked. "You want to get more from that, I can show you the video. There was as strap on involved."

"Ew, Sasch," I said with a laugh. "But also, I'm very intrigued. But not about you and Alicia."

I saw Javi's eyebrow shoot up as his eyes flashed green. *Oh, he's intrigued too*, I thought. I wondered if he liked the idea of seeing me with a strap on for another woman or to use on him. I'd always liked the idea of pegging a man but had never had someone who was into it. Connor liked to get high and fuck other men and women but was never adventurous with me. Good lord, there was really no reason at all I should have stayed with him. I shook my head.

Javier was still sniffing around, both literally and figuratively. He disappeared into the bedroom. I turned on the kitchen tap and switched on some music. Thumping EDM that would have the neighbors yelling if I didn't hurry.

"Connor's head was delivered in a box to Javi's backdoor. This afternoon. We had been by my parents' old place across the river and then out to Exmouth. Whoever it was skirted the securities Javi had set up. Alicia and Pietro are trying to get control of the situation before I am implicated, as we had only the head, not the body, and someone was bound to find it." My words were rushed and whispered close to her ear. Her almond tipped nails were digging into my skin.

"Fuckface?" she whispered back. I nodded. "Jesus, Lil." She turned the music off. "I'll grab my bag. And I'll pop in the strap so you can introduce Javi to Voltaire."

She winked and left the kitchen, passing Javi. There would be no way I was touching her strap. Ew.

We drove the short distance in near silence. Javier finally pulled up to his spot and turned to us.

"Someone—a few someones have been in your flat, Alicia. I don't know if you are seeing anyone else. The scents were both human and vampire. Neither were Alicia, nor Pietro. Nor Connor for that matter. It indicated to me that we must be ready to deal with three others. One or two of who must be vampire. The other, possibly a donor, or an enthralled." He shut off the car and got out first, scanning the area before motioning for us to exit the vehicle as well.

As a child, I remember the Christmas holidays always going by so fast. It was like Christmas Eve, Day, and Boxing Day were a fleeting magical blur. This year, it felt as though the days had no end. It was a stream of events and atrocities sprinkled in with being in Javi's arms. In these few days I had been fucked beyond recognition, turned into a human vampire hybrid, my ex's head was sent to me, and my best mate and my lover's ex had become a couple. And the part I could swallow about as easily as a lump of coal from Father Christmas, I found out that my mother might have been or might be a vampire and she might have killed my father.

The three of us walked in the front door, quietly, bar the ever present clomp of Sascha's heels. I would have teased her. In another time. On another night. A different Christmas. I would have ribbed her for wearing YSL booties only to come over to have a shelter-in-place sleepover with me and Javier on Boxing Day. But I knew why she wore them. I knew, beyond them being the shoes by her front door (next to at least eight other pairs of mismatched designer shoes and boots and the odd pair of Jordans for which she likely paid twice over MSRP), she wanted them with her. Because someone had been in her flat, and she had known before Javi told her. I could see it in her eyes. And those had been from me, her closest friend in the entire world.

I walked her up to my old room. I say old like it was ages ago, yet it was my room just two nights prior. Prior to my sex with Javi that broke the world. My world. His world. The seismic event of our lovemaking tore open some crack in the universe and allowed its demon to escape, peppering the world I knew with darkness I was not keen to shy away from.

Sascha dumped her quilted tote and Vuitton weekender bag inside the door, where a chair draped in my scarf and coat stood. She sucked on a tooth and tapped the pointed toe of her boot.

"Do you know who was in your flat?" I asked, giving her the opening to just spit it out. I folded my arms across my chest.

"I might." The words were a mumbled rush.

She ran to the loo and emptied her stomach. It was quick. I figured she hadn't had much to eat today. Maybe a hair of the dog or two. She often had a gin and tonic after a night of drinking. She hadn't had much last night, that I was there for. But I knew as soon as Sascha got home, angry and upset over Alicia and my parents, she would have taken to a bit of self-medicating. Her drinking had me increasingly worried about her, but I knew Sascha, and there would be a time I could suggest she slow it down or stop all together, but it wasn't now. It certainly wasn't this night.

The loo light switched off and she walked into the bedroom, unzipping her boots as she entered. She sat on the edge of the bed and tugged on a piece of her black fringe. I envied that cute pixie cut of hers. It was more 1960s model than punk rock, but Sascha always managed to look like she was a new genre of music, ready to inflict itself on heart and mind. She crossed a red satin pajamas clad leg over the other. It took me until that moment to notice she had been in her pajamas. How did I miss that? I had been so dead set on getting to her, getting her informed, and getting her out, that Sascha's outfit of the day simply hadn't been on my radar.

"It took me like an hour to get home last night," she began. I sat next to her on the edge of the mattress. "I called the fucking Pineapple Cab co and unsurprisingly, there were no cabs on Christmas." Not surprising at all. Getting a cab in this city was like winning the bloody lottery. "Tell me again how they have the power to keep Uber out when Pineapple Cab is like the most half assed transportation monopoly in existence?" she said, and I laughed. "Anyway, so I was already halfway to town when I gave up. I just didn't want my boots" —she gestured to the ones I'd given her, discarded near the bathroom wall—"to get messed up on the wet streets. So, I sat on the bus bench and switched to my other heels, but after I got just near Cathedral Yard, I'd torn my fucking heels open." She held out her foot where there was indeed a scab on the back of her ankle. "So, I had to take them off and switch back. It was really a ridiculous thing altogether and ultimately, I was angry I hadn't just stayed. Whatever. Okay, so cut to a million hours later, I was finally at my flat. I smelled perfume as soon as I walked in. But not super strong like when you pass one of the boys who work in Superdry and think 'holy fuck, I would have to hold my breath fucking him'. Not that I would. Because they are usually uni students and way too young."

"Good to see the morals coming out."

"Morals? Oh no. My New Year's resolution two years ago was to not sleep with anyone with less than stellar experience." She waved a hand in the air. I vaguely remembered her making that resolution as I stood on the concrete wall on the shore in Exmouth, freezing half to death. She placed both palms on her knees and took a breath.

"You smelled perfume," I prompted.

"Yeah. It had reminded me of Christmas. But not in like a

Christmassy way, you get?" I shook my head no. "It wasn't a holiday scent, but it was one I always associated with Christmas. Because of you."

"Me?" I asked. "I was here. Well, I was out walking with Javi, then we took the train to the coast and had ice cream, then—"

She grabbed my hand. "Lil. It wasn't you. I'd know your Fucking Fabulous anywhere."

For years when I had done exercise classes, from CrossFit to Spin to hot yoga, I always dreaded that moment when my body started to sweat. The smidgen of a second when it wasn't pouring out, but the threat was there, and one drop appeared from my pores and tiptoed its way down my spinal column. A drop of reticence began its own path down my spine then. An unwillingness to properly accept what I suspected was going to come next.

"I didn't think too much of it. Honestly, I was a little drunk, a little more needing a bath, really knackered, and I was so worried about you. So, I thought it was just kind of my mind. My memory. Scent is the most powerful memory trigger, right?"

I wasn't breathing. I knew I wasn't. I wasn't sure my heart was beating either.

"Then I found the note." She twisted her fingers together, clicking the tips. I hated when she did that. It sounded like pincers on some giant insect. "I thought it was Alicia," she said. "I've never seen her handwriting and she had snuck into my flat before, despite my locks and alarm. Well, you know I always forget to set the alarm anyway."

I turned to face her fully, though she was still facing the opposite side of the room, head hung.

"What note."

"It was really lovely handwriting. Like when we had those calligraphy sets and thought we could do wedding invites for extra money. D'ya remember that? It said 'Please make certain you look after Lily. I hope I can keep you both safe.'" She took a breath.

"Okay. That doesn't seem out of the ordinary," I reasoned. Right? She hopped down and began pacing.

"Alicia has never called you Lily. It's always The Little Flower or Ophelia." She looked at me.

My gums pounded, wanting to let my fangs drop. I tried to breathe in through my nose and out my mouth to control the urge. Mostly because I didn't want to attack Sascha.

"And Alicia wears Chanel Biarritz. It's one of the new collections of Coco Chanel's favorite places. Remember when we had too many shit margaritas upstairs at Gatwick and we were trying all the perfumes?"

I nodded. I did. That's when I bought two hundred fifty quid's worth of Tom Ford I am still paying off. The thoughts were all buzzing around me like I'd had too many shit margaritas tonight, when in fact, I'd had nothing in the way of booze. I never even drank the prosecco at Sascha's.

"Lil, I swear I didn't put two and two together until Javi said he knew someone had been in my flat. It was all a jumble. And I'd had a bottle of prosecco to myself before you lot even arrived." My eyes widened. "Yeah, I know, I'm a goddamned lush." Her hands were erratically waving.

"What didn't you put together Sascha?" My tone told her my patience was gone. My fangs scraping my lips punctuated the aggravation.

"It was Seychelles," she said. "The perfume was Seychelles."

I blinked several times, aware she was stock still looking at me. Seychelles. Where people with money went to spend the holidays away from the cold of England. Seychelles, that smelled of sand and salt and subtle tropical blooms. The scent of the three-wick candle on the nightstand in Javi's room. The whiff of scent clinging to the scarf I still kept of my mum's. The perfume she always wore. The one my dad gave her for every Christmas, and I kept alive when I bought her stupid Christmas pressies at The White Shoppe.

I dashed from the room. There was no way to tell whether my skin was hot or cold or suffering from a hyperactivate mix of both. It was as though I needed to tear my hair from my head. Javi grabbed me by the elbows as I careened around the corner of the doorframe. I gnashed my teeth at him. Logically, my mind was saying to stop it you bloody great idiot. It's neither of their faults. But that demon who took up residence in me was spoiling for a fight. Javi spun me and locked his arms around my middle, attempting to keep me under control.

"Sascha," he called in a calm voice, "lock yourself in there for a bit and please place the dresser against the door."

Distantly I could hear her whimper. I knew it wasn't fear. I hoped it wasn't anyway. The last thing my logical self wanted was for my best friend to be afraid of me. I took the whimper for her being distraught. For me. For all of us and the situation. Alicia was correct. I had known. Deep down. As soon as she said it, I had known. Everything fell in place like puzzle blocks, clearing a line of murky memory. Javier was whispering to me in what sounded like Italian. I had no idea what he was saying and had it been in my native tongue, I still wouldn't have processed it.

"I will let you feed but you must calm down," he said in English at last. The fight was still in me. Live wires snaking under my skin. "When a child throws a tantrum because he wants a cookie, you do not give him the cookie. You realize he is hungry, and once he calms, you invite him over for a snack and perhaps include the cookie." His accent was so strong I had to focus on what he was saying.

"I'm not a child!" I hissed, catching his forearm with my teeth. He squeezed me tighter.

"Ja. You are not. You are currently a terrorist. A dangerous, blood-thirsty vampire terrorist, and I don't negotiate with terrorists." He spoke low against my neck, below my ear. "Even sexy, deadly ones who can take my large cock all the way down their throats." He began to purr. The live wires in me were fusing. Sparking and catching fire. "I wish nothing more than to have you feeding off my hot cum again and feeling your lips kissing my balls. Your fingers in my ass like a dirty little queen."

He pushed his crotch into my ass crack so I could feel his length. If I didn't get to tear open a throat in the next sixty seconds, he would see just how strong this newly made vampire baby could be.

I snarled, and beyond the door, Sascha whimpered again. Javi backed me away from the door. My bare feet kicked at the ground as he did it, scrambling for purchase.

"You are a very strong little vampire, Fela. So strong. I bet you could drink me dry and need more. You might need a room full of throats and cocks to satiate you," he cooed.

I groaned, picturing drinking from another beautiful man as Javi ate me out and someone fucked me from behind. Thoughts I'd never had and likely would never again have.

"Yes, can you see it?" he asked, voice like glazed rust.

He knew I could. The impressions on my mind were crystal clear. I could smell the sweat and nerves of one man, baring his tanned throat to me. I could clamp on it and feed while Javi fed from my pussy. Then, the sensation of having a new cock in my ass filling me. Just as quickly, the vision was yanked away. I did not know how Javi had done that, but I was running at a fever pitch, needing all of it. Immediately.

"But no," he barked. He moved his hand like a whip and slapped my sweatpants covered pussy before locking me against him again. My head spun. "No other cock goes in this pussy. Nor in this ass." He bumped against me again. "No other cock goes in this beautiful mouth." He grabbed my chin and forced my head sideways to kiss me, breaking the skin on my lips with his teeth. The taste of my own blood surged in me. "Once you can be a good girl again, I will give you what you want. It isn't Sascha. It isn't three cocks in a nameless room. You want to feed from *me*." He bit my neck and sucked at the piercings. I went limp. Finally. His teeth dragged from the shallow punctures they'd made. "You want to have my blood running through your system. You want my cum, but right now, you need to feel my cock so deep in you, there is no god nor country. Only me."

CHAPTER THIRTY

JAVIER

She went boneless. At last. I didn't know if she was losing control enough to harm Sascha, but I was not going to take that risk. Every vampire hurts or kills someone close to them. We have all been there. However, Ophelia is different. Her control is different. I have never seen a vampire transition as she has. Though she is not fully vampire. So, if I could prevent her from the heartache of killing a loved one, I would. I wanted her to continue her life. Her promising, beautiful life she deserved to have after all she had been through and worked for. I don't know who of us was more in the throes of bloodlust then though. I needed to drink of her as much as she did of me.

I half dragged her to the office space I had used for our donor sessions months ago. A semblance of privacy away from our guest. Once I closed the door behind me, I dropped her. She landed with a thump and made an indignant sound.

"Thank you," she slurred.

That stopped me. I did not think she was revived enough to realize what I had done for her. Her fangs were still out, eyes still glowing like acid rain. I looked down at her, then unbuckled my belt before rolling up the sleeves of my shirt.

"You will feed," I commanded.

It was partly my sire command, telling her what is expected of her. It was also harkening back to our powerplay last night, which I had very much enjoyed. Ophelia could play both sides. When she subbed to me last night, she didn't even know that I was the one under the whip of her. I may have been giving her direction, but she had me bound just the same. I saw her crumpled mess of a human on the floor, jumper and joggers askew, hair in a tangled mess. It was like watching a selkie coming into its humanoid flesh. I shivered for the first time in a long time. How had I ever thought she was purely human? That selkie wanted out. It wanted to command me. I could see the war in her eyes. See the desire to feed because she needed my blood and cum. But the demon in her slid quietly to the surface, smoothing the angered, flushed lines on her full face, even relaxing the mess of her hair. The transformation was so beautiful it was obscene. My cock strained at my trousers. I took a breath to fully sort which of us would direct this next scene. I feigned indifference, continuing to roll my sleeves and push them past my elbows. Slowly, I undid my trousers and stepped from them, leaving me in my briefs and shirt, cock pointing to its life source. I pricked my thumb on my incisor, locking eyes with Ophelia whilst the blood welled. She straightened her spine, still sitting on the ground.

"Still in a heap where I left you, Fela?" I asked, voice deadly.

Her eyes snapped up. I took my bloodied thumbs and slid it inside my briefs. The tip of my cock peeked out the top where I rubbed the blood over my head. A low growl rumbled through her. Her body was visibly vibrating. I pricked my thumb again and rubbed more blood over my cock head, sliding my thumb and index fingers down over the head, letting her see a bit more if it. She narrowed her eyes at me and hissed. I let my tongue fork from my mouth, vellicating toward her.

Ophelia ripped the clothing from her body, leaving her in the green silk knickers she'd received from Sascha and a matching green silk bra that tied in a bow over her nipples. Jesus Christ. I think I knew who was going to be master here tonight. The little selkie was on her hands and knees, prowling toward me. A mythical cat ready to kill.

"I *will* feed," she said in a voice I had not yet heard. Her shoulder blades stuck up on her back with the held position. "I will feed however I want, vampire. But you will do as I say."

I could have blown then. Instead, I gave her cocky grin and licked my lips.

"Whatever you command, my queen." I bowed at the waist.

"Take off your shirt."

I did as I was told.

"Good boy. Now slice open your pec."

I wanted to groan. Instead, I grabbed the quickdraw knife from the pocket of the trousers at my feet. She clocked the opening of the blade and the slow, deliberate way I drew it across my chest, which allowed the thick blood to drip in an artistic line. She was still in a quadruped position, giving me commands like an alpha she wolf. Her hand drifted to her satin bow covered breast, then down to her knickers. I could smell the wetness. She stuck her finger in and pulled it out to show me, then sucked herself from it.

"Oh, the cut is healing, love," she said, malice in her eyes. I was about to spank her. I wasn't very good at being the sub. "Slice it again."

I did it in a distastefully fast motion, then licked the blade clean.

"I did not say you could lick it," she said. "Just for that, you need to slice the other one."

I was not a fan of pain. I'd truly rather not be in pain. I had known my fair share and generally opted for avoidance. Yet, I found myself drawn toward it on both sides with her. Dark magics spun itself around us, making our demons fast friends. After cutting my other pec, she licked her lips.

"Use the blood to lube your cock." It would dry quickly, but the sentiment was there, and I was never one to shy from a blood-lubed cock. I flexed my pecs as she watched, allowing a bit more blood to surface. Then with both hands I ran the blood down my shaft, pushing my briefs from me.

"Step out of them."

I did.

"Listen carefully, vampire," she said, wolf crawling closer. I kept pumping my shaft. Cum leaked from the tip. "Taste it." She pointed at the cum. "You are going to do whatever I say now. I say when to stop and what to do."

"Yes, my queen." I pumped twice harder, knowing it would make her want to take my cock in her mouth. "Permission to speak."

"Go on."

"There is still a bit of blood coming out." I pointed to my chest. "Perhaps Her Majesty would like a quick taste."

She was latched on before I'd finished then pulled off nearly as fast.

"Slap me," she said.

I didn't like that.

"No." I showed her there were lines I would not cross, however silly they seemed. I would not slap her face. "I will not put a hand to your face like that."

She nodded once.

"Now I have misbehaved," I said. "Punish me."

"Suck." She pulled open the bow on her bra and stood.

I took her nipple in my mouth and rolled it then sucked hard. Her nails went into my shoulders, urging me on. I bit lightly and was rewarded with a cry and savage clawing of her nails on my arms.

"Now, put me over your knee," she said.

I sat on the chair where it had all begun and whipped her curved figure over my lap. My blood-encrusted, steel cock was digging into her lower stomach.

"Spank me hard like I need to be punished."

I was slightly off balance. There was an odd power exchange here. Our desires and need for dominance were dancing in the bars of rhyme, which existed only because there was so much love and trust between us. I had never known this. Her hand snaked around me and poked into my ass.

"Spank. Me."

Before she got both words out, my hand came down on her round ass cheek. Then again. Ripples of reddened flesh quaked under my hand.

"Spank me harder."

I did. Each time, when I lifted my hands from her, I let it glide over the sore skin and trail through her crack. Her legs widened a bit. I saw the slickness between her divine thighs. I wanted to touch her. To ask her if I could touch her. I wanted to bury my face in her glorious ass. But this was her time. So, I kept spanking her, changing the rhythm, and alternating cheeks. Her hips were bucking against me, begging for release. I would do only what I was told, though if she kept dry humping me, I would release. Her naked belly was heaven on my swollen cock. I pushed her legs further apart before she could protest and slapped lower on her bum, cupping the underside as I released her. She moaned, mouth latching on to my waist where she had curled over.

"Spit on me," she said. "I want to feel it dripping in my ass."

I did and watched it slide onto that path I wished my mouth, fingers, and cock were on. I spit again and used my fingers to slide it into her ass, pushing where I knew she liked it. Her hips were moving more. My fingers strayed to her pink, soaked cunt. I slapped her there. Her belly moved on my cock. The soft skin pillowed around it.

"Fela," I growled. She sat up like a match had been lit under her. "Keep doing that if you wish for me to come all over your belly and between your breasts."

She turned on my lap and straddled me. My cock was poised just before the opening of those crotchless Christmas knickers. Her swollen lips poked through the open gusset. If I shifted forward a centimeter, I would be entering her. I folded my arms across my chest. She smiled. I would have murdered the world for that smile.

"You liked the idea of a strap on?" she asked me.

Oh, Christ.

"Do *you*?" I asked instead.

She scooted back and I laughed, pulling her forward again. The time of dom and sub, however confused and backward it had become, was ending. It was simply Ophelia and me, lost in each other again. The place I would always prefer to be.

"I like the idea of doing anything with you."

"And does the idea of me pegging you excite you?" She palmed my cock.

"So, you are asking," I began, my voice low, and accent an abomination of everywhere I had ever lived, "if I would like for you to be naked or in something of this sort." I pulled open the bow on the other breast. "Strapping on a belt with a fake cock, lubing it, and sticking it into my waiting ass while you use your soft hands on my own cock? You are asking if I would like this gorgeous selkie on my lap to fuck my ass and cock, while her wet, wet mound drips all over me—front or back? The question is if I would enjoy my ravishing queen giving me a double orgasm while being so turned on, she comes all over my balls?"

I flipped her around and pinned her over the sofa. Her pussy was glistening through the open gusset of her knickers. I ran my hands through it and over my cock before quickly ramming her with my cock. I slipped behind her and into her pussy effortlessly.

"Was that what you were asking?" I asked her, squeezing her ass cheeks as I railed her. I could see her breasts bouncing against the sofa.

"Yes," she hissed.

It was only then I noticed she wasn't hissing, fangs bared. My heart swelled with pride at her control. Of course, it would have been a wholesome moment, had I not been balls deep in her.

"That was what I was asking."

"The answer is yes," I said close to her ear. "I want your cock in me."

She pulled away from me and turned around, grabbing me by the hair.

"There will never be another's cock in you," she said to me. Her fists were full of my short hair. "Not in your mouth, hand, or ass. And you will never touch another woman either."

I allowed myself to melt into her. Her soft pale body pressed to mine.

"You are my one and only. I will never touch another. Never want another. There is only you until the ends of time." My words were more than that. They were a vow. A decree. A gilding of sentiment in the very firmament of the world.

She slowly turned back around and raised her ass to me.

"Then rail me. Hard and fast. Because I will bleed you dry after, vampire."

This time, I didn't last. It was all too much. The emotion, the vow, the arousal. I pulled out in time for her to drop to her knees and catch the release in her warm mouth. I could die the final death with my cock in her mouth. She swallowed repeatedly, massaging my balls as she did so. When it was done, she stood and bit my pec where I had sliced, and she drank from me until I was drowsy, pulling her body against mine, and allowing a short sleep to claim us. The world had been altered when she and I mated. It would never be the same again.

CHAPTER THIRTY ONE

I awoke with a start, realizing we hadn't checked on Sascha. Javi and I had torn each other apart and glued ourselves together all while my best mate sat barricaded in her borrowed room above us. I felt a bit shit about that. I pulled on my sweats again, kissing Javi until he woke up. We made our way upstairs, hand in hand.

"Hey, tart," I called through the door. "I'm less evil now, if you feel like letting me in."

The sound of a heavy piece of furniture moved across the floor.

"I've seen this film," Sascha said opening the door. "This is where I fall for the false normalcy, and then I get eaten."

"I already ate Javi," I said. "I'm full up now."

"That's kind of hot. But also, ew."

"Would *you* like to come down and have something to eat, Sascha?" Javi asked her.

She shrugged and followed us down. We sat on the counter stools while my lover heated up this and that in the kitchen.

"Honestly. You cook more than any guy I've known. Which totally doesn't make sense because you mainly eat blood. Or drink blood. Whatever."

I laughed as Javi put a plate of gnocchi and pesto in front of each of us.

"I'm not even into food, but I would fuck you too if you made me food like this," Sascha said with a groan.

"So, my mum was in your flat," I said abruptly.

There really was no other way to segue into the conversation. A note was left. There had been a vampire or two in there, the smell of my mother's perfume, and someone who wanted Sascha to look after me. Sascha pulled the note from her breast pocket. I smoothed it on the black countertop. It was as if I had swallowed a football. My mum's lopping handwriting was written across a sheet of heavy linen stationary paper. The kind she always loved. Was it okay to feel heart happy that she was in my city once again? That she seemed to care for me? Was it okay that I wanted to have her hug me and envelope me in her island holiday scent? And was it okay to hate her? With a force like forest fire, I hated her for leaving me. For possibly murdering my dad. For irreparably fucking me up. I had been on twenty-two different medications for my mental health since my parents died. Because my parents died. Twenty-two. Over the course of ten years. None had worked. None had given me the focus I needed or the mood stabilization I required to fit in. None had calmed me enough to sleep properly or wake properly. Nothing until Javier. Until I was too poor to continue my business and had to sell myself as a blood donor to a vampire and become one myself, I'd never known love. Apart from Sascha, who had her own demon to manage. So that expensive stationary I remembered as being what sat where my mum graded papers, brought forth the need I had to see her and be held by her and to tell her I hated her with my every breath.

"It wasn't my mother," Javi said quietly, touching the paper. "And we are not the same person, so I cannot know how you feel completely. However, just recently, someone I had shared centuries with, for whom I'd harbored some sort of love, turned up very much alive."

Alicia. I knew what he felt must have been complicated. Not that he hadn't fallen for me or wanted me. But that total upheaval of what he knew must have been a web of complexities beyond what he could say. I laid my hand over his.

"Feel everything you need to feel, Fela. It's all valid."

That was something I had rarely been told. I had rarely been given validation. Just after my parents' deaths, of course, everyone told me it was natural to feel angry, sad, etc. I had one therapist who validated me. Who understood that my loss had changed me on a chemical level and that I wasn't making it up. My body could no longer process emotions properly because I had my world ripped out from under me and had no place to go. Could someone's body be altered like that? If stress could cause DNA mutation, wouldn't such a stressor—such a profound loss—rewrite my DNA? But then, the part of me that was meant to be a vampire hadn't been rewritten. So, was it just the human heart? Had I been fighting my vampire side until I drank the Kool-Aid of Javi's life? Goodness that sounded ridiculous. Yet...

"Who else was in my flat?" Sascha asked. I gathered our finished plates and set them in the sink before filling the kettle. "You said vampires and a human. I have a cleaning lady. Could it have been her? She last came, I dunno. Maybe the twenty-third?"

Javi said it could have been. I nosed around in his cabinet for the herbal tea he liked and placed a bag in each mug, waiting for the kettle.

"I didn't recognize any of the scents. I did recognize the perfume; however, it had been the one in the shop where Ophelia bought the candle. So, I figured it was that sort of thing. It didn't register as being a perfume."

The kettle clicked off and I filled the mugs, steam

billowing from the cups, releasing notes of rosehip and lemon balm. Javi looked at his phone and told me it was Alicia texting. He left the room while we sat with steeping tea.

"I don't hold any hard feelings regarding you and Alicia," I told Sascha. "I appreciate your loyalty to me. Always. But you are my only friend, and I want you to be happy. If that's with vamp bitch, then it's with vamp bitch." I punched her red satin shoulder. She smiled.

"We'll see." She sipped the tea and pulled a face. "This would be better with gin. I know, I know. New Year, New Me and all that rubbish."

I mumbled a mmhm and drank my own tea.

"This new year, I certainly will be a new me," I said.

She spat out her tea. I felt mine threatening to come out my nose. We giggled.

"All you wanting to lose a stone or quit smoking, I've got you one upped. I literally became a new creature. Suck on that." I barely got the words out, we were laughing so hard. There was lemon balm and rosehip tea sprayed over the pristine counter.

"We should leave in the morning." Javi came in as solemn as we were happy. "Alicia found the rest of the boy."

The giggles evaporated between us. The boy. The rest of the boy. Like he hadn't been a person. Sure, Connor had been awful. A real example of how not to human. But he had been torn apart. Scattered in two places. I did not mourn him. I never would. But he was a person, and the cold way Javi said that phrase, *Alicia found the rest of the boy*, rang a furious bell in my mind. I kept my mouth shut while Javi told us he had been found outside a club in Manchester. That was quite a distance from where his head was.

"The body, like the head, was likely moved some distance before it was placed there as well. Why someone would bother, we don't know. It's not as if it's a simple robbery or overdose when the head is gone. A group of club kids had said something about it but were too high to make sense. Alicia had been following the scent of another creature she didn't know. Which is how she ended up that way. The kids were all enthralled, so it's clear. Alicia and Pietro moved the body to an incinerator owned by one of her tenants."

I looked at him aghast. His face was a tired show of exasperation.

"Ophelia, we are not humans. We are vampires, living in a human world. Our food supply is the very populace of the world. It has been and always will be in our best interest to have allies, places of refuge, places of containment, and ways to problem solve. Feedings aren't always perfect. There is no recourse for us. It is a lesson you are learning, albeit, you have the security net of Alicia and me. I am not asking for your gratitude. I am asking to not have your disgust. I do my best. It just most often isn't good enough."

I was ashamed of my reaction and a bit embarrassed by my seeming naivety, so I excused myself. Sascha trundled after me. I still didn't know where we were to head in the morning, but it was winter in England. I only had winter clothes with me. The rest were in boxes at Sascha's, so I just went back into the room where Sascha was now staying and my clothes still hung. We packed up our things together silently.

It was after two in the morning. I couldn't see straight. My body was physically spent. I knew I nodded off, folding my last jumper. The next I knew, it was early morning and Javi was waking me. Next to me, Sascha snored with her matching red silk mask over her eyes. I sat up, rubbing my eyes. I was crusty from my lashes to my nether regions and needed a shower before anything else happened. Javier kissed my forehead and told me to try to be ready in an hour. I turned my phone music on full volume and placed it under Sascha's pillow while I went to shower.

Winter mornings here sped past the window on the M5 in sheets of icy rain and gusts of wind, which loomed like angry ghosts. The weather raced past the car window as we crossed the bridge passing Bristol and into the Cotswolds. None of us had been particularly talkative over the course of the drive. I huddled into my fleecy jumper, snuggled against the heated seats. Sascha snored in the backseat. I decided I did not need to know where we were going. I didn't care. I needed to be away from everything.

We skirted London, bypassing the city altogether. I blew out a breath once we had truly cleared it. If I could manage, I would never return. We headed north. That was all I knew. The cities thinned as we took smaller motorways. I knew Manchester was the other side, so I didn't think that was our destination. Which of course made sense. Why would we be in Manchester? The cities I knew dropped away altogether as we crossed the border into Scotland. The day was full dark already, yet still we drove. I nodded off here and there but was awake when Javi shut the lights off the car and drove in total darkness the rest of the way. It was majestic moving through dirt roads and fields, knowing he saw as well as head-lamps. His fangs were out, eyes reflective green. He must need to be in demon mode to see this well. I tried to call my own and try my hand at night vision. It seemed that no matter how I tried to will my demon self to pop in for a visit, she was otherwise engaged. Javier cleared his throat gently.

"I think you will like it here. I hope so. It's calm. Hidden."

"Because it's so far in the wilderness?" I asked.

He looked at me and smiled his sweet, calm smile. "That, and it's protected by wards placed by mages. Many years ago."

"Like the resting place in Tuscany?"

He nodded in the dark, but I saw it. He drove on for

another hour or so, the car moving through the late night like a falling star. It wasn't until even I could see a silhouette of a building on the near horizon, its back fortified by granite cliffside, that Javi switched on the lights. Once on, once off. A signal, I realized, to whoever was in the building.

I sat up, winding my scarf around my neck. My back ached with sitting for so many hours. We had stopped twice, only by the side of country roads, to have a quick pee. Javi apologized for it, but we were trying to stay off CCT and off grid generally. He hefted the bags out of the car, carrying them up the steps. Alicia opened the door and ushered us in. I was strangely glad to see her, and based on Sascha jumping up and wrapping both legs around her waist, she was as well. Javier moved the car to a garage on the side, so that wards or no wards, there was no car out front.

The front entrance had a mud room we passed through and once the door shut, lights were on everywhere. Black and white checkerboard tile ran through the halls and what looked to be a few rooms. I was starved, so we gathered in the kitchen where roast chicken and potatoes were waiting in the warmer. I didn't know who had cooked them, but I was thankful and ate my fill, washing it down with a goblet of red wine.

"I know you are mad at Javier, Little Flower," Alicia said to me. "But we as vampires need to do what we can to keep ourselves and those we love safe." She gave Sascha a pointed look. My friend rolled her eyes, but I knew from the rapid movement of her foot near mine under the farmhouse table, that she was caught off guard.

I said I wasn't mad at Javi. He raised both eyebrows at me.

"I'm not. I'm overwhelmed. My nerves are shot. I'm offended by my life, really. If we are being honest."

Alicia poured me water from a pottery jug. She

commented that we were always being honest now. Our lives depended on it.

"I hate what my life is. Everything about it since finding out about my parents' deaths. Which apparently was a hoax. Well, everything except Javier. But then I'm a vampire. Which is cool and hot on you lot, but like, what in the actual fuck even am I? Some weird chimera thing." I made a disgusted sound and finished glass number two. "My mum isn't dead. Or she's undead—who knows! It's a mystery mind fuck, kids!"

I stabbed two potatoes from Sascha's plate because she never ate while she was drinking. Thank God it was nearly dry January for her.

"For what it's worth," Alicia said, "I do not think you are gross."

I snorted.

"You are lovely, Little Flower. And Javier loves you. The rest we figure out." She blew me a kiss. It made me smile at least. Javier came around and wrapped his arms around me from behind. I leaned into his warmth.

"I'm not mad at you," I said again and turned my head to kiss his chest over his gray jumper.

OPHELIA

Sine Nomine Domus was a castle. Not a big house like you see in the countryside. It was a castle. Semi fortified, medieval. In the full dark, I couldn't see the breadth of the building on the outside. I did look forward to exploring in the morning. But on the inside, after we had fed and watered.

Javi showed us around. We were all limp with exhaustion after the last few days, yesterday's long night, and the hours upon hours of driving. Yet, stretching our legs and checking out the extraordinary place in which we were staying, was more than appealing. Checkerboard flooring gave way to rooms paneled with dark woods and draperies that could have been from another century. Perhaps they were, and the wards kept them from moths. I had much to learn. Alicia seemed just as interested as I was. So, I asked her if she had been there before.

"A very long time ago." Her face dropped. It was a look I would bet didn't appear on her face often. "I of course could not show up after I faked my death and all of that. Before that, it had been what, Javi?" she asked. "Perhaps a century? Before Victoria's reign, I believe."

Javi pursed his lips in thought and said that was probable.

"Who comes here?" I asked, touching a shelf where hundreds of books lined up, yet there was no dust.

"There are several of us who have access and there is staff. They will keep to their own quarters while we are here, and we can have our own privacy. It is more for their safety than our comfort." It made sense. When vampires were in residence, things could change like a storm on the North Sea. "Pietro will not be joining us. He is no longer welcome where you both are, and if I find him near you or working against you, there is no place on God's earth he can hide."

The room cooled dramatically with his statement, as though it were keyed into the severity of Javi's emotions. What a fantastical thought. Shelves of books lined the walls with desks and armchairs dotted around as well, a bar cart and cut crystal decanters in the corner. I pulled back a curtain, expecting to be told off like it was the Blitz, and we must keep the windows dark. Javi simply looked out with me.

It was a great plain of black, yet after a while, my eyes adjusted, noting small buildings, stables, and hillsides as far as the eye could see. That must be facing the side. I knew behind the castle was mountain. Unforgiving mountain born from hell itself. Or from the Scottish Highlands. Pick your poison really.

I asked what the name means. I was tutored by my parents in Latin and Greek. *Sine Nomine Domus* meant "nameless house". I understood on a basic level. But that would be like naming something *heartbreak cottage*. There had to be backstory.

"Ja, Javi, I'll tell her," Alicia said. I dropped the curtain and turned to her. We walked from the room into the next. It was another salon, with larger settees and coffee tables. It began to register that there were probably several more. Each decorated a bit differently than the last. Where the first was dark and masculine, as though a bottle of whiskey wanted its own room, this one was more like a French provincial country home. Comfort over severity. The settees were plush, the tables rustic. More sconces and electrical lights, lighter fleur-de-lis patterned linen draperies. Perhaps this one was a case of a nice vintage of wine, requesting a weekend away. I amused myself with the thought.

"*Sine Nomine Domus*," Alicia said, "obviously means 'nameless house'. I'm sure you knew that. Your parents taught classics here and there, no? I don't think it's very clever. We dithered on the name. Javier kept saying it was a secret place, so it didn't need a name. No one would know anyway. I argued that a castle like this deserved the respect of having a name. After all, it was supposed to be a safe harbor. Where we could go when the world no longer welcomed us. And so it went for the better part of a decade. He would say something about the place, and I would say, 'oh you mean *la casa sin nombre?*' And he would roll his eyes."

Javier smiled to himself as the story was told. A favorable memory, then. I'm glad to see those between them. Javier touched a bust of some person I may ask about, but who may be as random as any folly in a place like this.

"At last, when I arrived here on a night not unlike this one, it was sinfully dark, on the coattails of a winter storm that ultimately got caught in the valley over that mountain." She gestured to the walls beyond us. "The storm doubled back on us and snowed us in. We were white noise, as they say. Ghosts in our own between. We had created a space where we could just be. Exist without existing. Nameless, forgotten, ensconced within the walls of a place that would forever hold us in its protective womb. We were nameless between the wards of this fortress. *Sine Nomine Domus* seemed fitting for a place that never existed yet was so essential to our survival many times."

Javier pointed to the door, and we followed him out.

What a story. I really just expected it to be something along the lines of, why call it High Ghost Manor or something, when no one knew about it. I mean, I guess that's the gist of what she said, but far more eloquently. I was lost in the romanticism of them getting trapped during the snowstorm. But really, I also wanted it to be me in the story. I leaned my head on Javi's shoulder as we walked up the impossibly wide staircase. There was a legit suit of armor.

"I wish I had lived a lifetime with you," I whispered to him, feeling sappy.

He kissed the top of my head and started to say something.

"That thing had bloody well better not come to life and chase me round in my knickers," Sascha said, her voice pitched high. I giggled and felt Javier rumble with laughter.

"Only during the dark moon," Javier said.

"Only WHAT?" Sascha exclaimed, physically turning Javier. He was openly laughing.

"We made our peace with the ghosts of this place long ago. They keep to themselves and we to ours. It's pleasant on all accounts. Although," Javi said, waggling his eyebrows, "you both are the first living beings who have been here, so you never know."

"Fuck my life. You," she said, pointing a black nail in Alicia's chest, "will be accompanying me to the loo, shower, and are not even allowed sleep if I am sleeping. Fucking ghosts."

"Sascha, you are literally sharing an isolated castle with three vampires," I reasoned. "Surely the ghosts are the least of your worries."

"Nope. It's the ghosts. Vamps are hot. Ghosts are dead and creepy as fuck."

Laughter ran its course through us, lightening the mood on this darkest night. Javi showed us a few more alcoves and rooms, a shared bathing chamber, and then our bedrooms. He pointed out that he put Sascha in her own room if only for her things to be there, but she said there was no way she would be spending any amount of time alone in a haunted castle.

We said our goodnights to the other girls and flopped on the bed in our room. There were curtains around the four-poster bed and a claw foot tub on the far side of the room. A door to a bathroom with a shower and a large closet stood across from the bed. I was ready to get under the covers and call it a night. As soon as I did, I felt Javi's eyes on me. He was facing me in the dark, stroking my hair away from my face. We stayed that way for a time, looking at one another, unbridled by light or outside forces, and not within the odd confines of the house where we had begun our whole current lives.

His thumb ran across my lips, brushing my chin. In the dark, I saw his slight smile. An unconscious muscle movement that spoke volumes to me. Here with me, in this place, he was at peace. Much like the ghosts lurking within the walls, he could call himself at rest. There was a drop in his shoulders. A softening in his countenance here. It was protected by walls and wards and the knit of this odd vampire family we built. If he felt he could rest, then surely, I could as well.

The softness of evening gave way to the dove gray of morning, enshrouded with mist and the promise of heavy rain. I hadn't slept. My mind had wandered all night. Worry and relief. I had felt safe and comforted in Javier's arms as he slept not so much beside me, but as a phantom part of me I never knew existed. I just couldn't turn my thoughts off. There was a reason we were here, beyond Connor's body and my mum's visit to Sascha's flat. Neither Javi nor Alicia had said a word about it. Why it was time to seek refuge in a fortified castle deep within the Highlands of the country to the north. We had driven from the top of Cornwall to almost the farthest point of Great Britain. And I knew it wasn't because of Connor.

Javi's breathing changed to a quickened pace. I touched his cheek, knowing he was waking. He opened those hazel eyes and smiled at me, wide and stunning. No one had looked at me like that before. Especially not first thing in the morning. My eyes were surely marked with thumbprints of purple, my hair tangled, and there was a definite possibility of morning breath. Yet, here he was, looking at me as though I were the goddess, not he, the god himself before me. His hands slipped under my pajamas top and explored.

"I want to stay here for a bit, but it's probably time we all had a talk about what it looks like the situation may be." His words were breathy. Like a rocky hillside somewhere in Italy or Spain or Argentina decided to speak through the wind. I shivered.

"Talk about why we are here?" I clarified.

He nodded and leaned over to kiss my collar bone.

"Before we do that, and after how...intense the past few days have been. Between us I mean..."

He looked unsure. I smoothed his dark, heavy brow with my fingers, and kissed his nose. He drew me closer.

"These times with you were beyond the scope of what I could have imagined."

I smiled. He had been and done far more than I could imagine. His face fell. I felt uneasy then. Like this was a strange let down. If it had been so great—which I thought it was—then what on earth would have to be discussed. Right now. In this warm bed, within a cold, ancient castle, with his ex-wife and my best mate down the hall.

"Javi," I said without any follow up. He placed a finger to

my lips. I felt tears prick at the back of my eyes and I wasn't sure why.

"Fela, we fucked and fed like our lives depended on it. And perhaps they did. It was consuming. I wanted it. More than anything I have ever in my life wanted."

My stomach rolled over. Was this a breakup? Seriously? Was he breaking up with me while in bed with me, in an isolated castle in the middle of fuckknowswhere? Tears ran down my face. He brushed them away and pulled me closer, kissing the tear tracks.

"What the hell, Javier," I said through a movement of my lips I wasn't sure had made a sound at all. He shushed me.

"What you wanted was a bit more up and down. Things seemed to be swinging wildly."

I tried to sit up, but he held me in place.

"What I mean is that as partners, our communication with sex is unprecedented. We have been more or less limitless. I'm in a state of shock, to be quite honest."

"Is there a point here, because all I hear in what you are saying is a rather large *but*."

"But," he said, and I saw red, "I don't think it will necessarily always be like that. It may and that is wonderful. But," he said again and smiled, tucking a stand of my messy hair back. "You need to know that I don't always need you so...intensely."

My heart was racing. I had been so wound up, not knowing what in the ever-loving hell he meant. I was drowning in my own projection of grief. He put his hand to my heart and widened his eyes.

"My love. I am such an idiot." He shook his head and kissed me. "I didn't know how to say that. I meant I want you like this. Quietly. Softly. Slowly. I want you like this, just as much as I want you beastly." He kept kissing me, hands over my skin under my shirt.

"So, this wasn't some weird breakup to leave me stranded in a creepy castle, alone?"

He laughed.

"I dare say it was not. It was me wanting to make sure you knew you are loved in every circumstance. With every sort of mood and with every beat of my heart."

"Oh."

"Oh." He moved on top of me and slid my pajamas down. Long fingers drew featherlight lines up and down the sides of my hips. Each movement of him over me was as though breath impersonated action. There was an intent in his eyes that kept tears rolling from my own eyes. One such stroke of his fingers drew inward, playing between my legs like an instrument.

"*Ohhh*," I repeated in a decidedly different tone. My head fell back on the pillow, a gasp escaping me, not knowing such a ghost of a touch could evoke sensation like the explosion of sparks in my core. We rocked together just as quietly and softly as he had said. A cadence the two of us had not yet experienced. The joy I found in my release came with more tears and clutching him to me as I cried. This was all so new to me. To think it might be new to him, after hundreds of years, was comforting.

CHAPTER THIRTY THREE

Every so often, the being I was required a death or a way of cutting the apron strings from whatever life had given me comfort for a time. We didn't age. It was a fact of my existence which meant, in this human world, I was forced to leave the life I'd built. Mostly, it had suited me to come here, to *Sine Nomine Domus* and lay low for a while. Things were simpler before the immortality of the internet. Humans had short term memories. I could disappear for a time and reset the last twenty to thirty years, then resurface somewhere without the worry of being discovered, ageless.

Nowadays, high-definition photos remained. Voice recognition remained. My fingerprint on my keyboard. Facial recognition on my phone. All these things seemed innocuous, until you were tasked with the idea of needing to remove yourself from the known world. I couldn't simply stay in *Sine Nomine Domus* for a few months then leave for Greece or Cuba. I had to fade away or die. I had to snuff myself out completely.

Before I hired Ophelia, I had been starting to think about my next move. I had been in our small university city for the better part of ten years. There should have been a good ten more before I needed to be gone. Much could happen in a decade, so my thoughts were yet just notes on a page. My heart sank thinking Ophelia would have to do the same. Which would mean giving up her city, her business, her life. Still, she had longer than I did. With the advancements in antiaging and the lengths many women went to stay young, she could feasibly get away with almost double what I had in the past. I'd seen many women nowadays whom I couldn't tell if they are twenty-five or forty-five. The world was so very different.

We had woken with a day that held weather in its bosom. The ever present mist in this valley was heavier, the smell of ozone thickened the atmosphere. I smiled, knowing the ghosts would be milling about when the weather broke. I felt a bit sorry for Sascha, who was not afraid of anything. She was a spitfire, the likes of whom I haven't seen since Alicia. They were well suited. Yet, somehow, this fearless sprite of a woman, was afraid of ghosts. We all had our bugaboos, I supposed. Ophelia marveled at the paintings and tapestries on the walls which were far easier to see in the water-colored daylight, than in the shadowy sconce-lit night as it was before. She was bundled in a thick black polo-necked jumper and jeans which tucked into her winter boots, ready to explore the grounds. I fried her an egg on toast for breakfast and watched her eat as we both sipped at tea and spoke of things I had done in my past to warrant a quick escape to this hidden harbor. Her face was paling by the moment. She needed blood but with her being so new, that meant we would probably get caught up in the debauchery of our desires, and I knew she wanted to explore before the weather caught us up. Against my better judgment, and that of a cock that wanted round two of our morning tumble, I led us out the back door and into the kitchen gardens.

Winterized vegetables and other plants, covered with plastic tarps, braved the season with frost on their tips. Stalwart soldiers understanding the assignment. Ophelia mean-dered between rows of crops, occasionally reaching a hand to touch the tarp or a frozen crystal of dew which hadn't sluiced from the abominable synthetic material in this lonely, wild place. From the gardens, I led us across to the stables where sadly I no longer kept horses. Perhaps one day again, if Ophelia wished to spend the liminal time with me here, we could get horses again. Companionship and means to exercise and move about. It was a thought. I pointed out the servants' home, which was a large manor house at the very edge of the property, bordering a tree line that fell into a gorge so steep, no man I had ever heard of, had scaled it.

I knew each type of fir tree and wood which hung about the perimeter, giving this place a frontline of defense in case the wards did not hold. All the while, the sheer granite behind the castle made up the rest.

"What's up there?" Ophelia asked.

I looked to where clouds blotted the summit of mountain behind the castle. "More forest, a brook, a bog, bears, and several miles to the north, a nationally protected forest. Plus, wards, of course."

"I was wondering because it seems so much land up here has been snatched up by investors and holiday-home buyers. I know it's been a contentious debate between the government and the people, allowing the highlands to be pillaged like that."

For years I tried to work against the government allowing that sort of gentrification of lands. It seemed I was working a double standard, yes. I, a foreigner, having this property that once belonged to a highland lord. However, I was as much a part of this land now as most who claim clan ancestry. I am a citizen of each place, making my home for a time and doing my best to leave it the same, if not better, than when I had arrived. So, it was with great effort I managed to get thousands of acres of land surrounding mine to be protected by both Scottish rule and the UK. It gave *Sine Nomine Domus* more protection and autonomy and gave the lands themselves more breathing room.

I explained this to Ophelia as we hiked up a gnarled bramble path. Thorny thicket snagged at our ankles, thinning out the higher we trekked. Ophelia's cheeks and nose shone bright pink in the early morning air. I smiled at her, loving the way her eyes crinkled at me when I did. Could this goddess really be mine? The last boulder we clambered over ended up being where we sat, at the top of the cloud line, high above *Sine Nomine Domus*, feeling like nameless spirits ourselves, possessing these wilds.

She took in her surroundings, concentrating on seeing beyond the fog which was dropping lower and lower. We had very little time now before the storm made the descent miserable. Her concentration looked similar to how it did last night in the car. I could tell she had been trying to will her vampire sight to present itself on the drive in. She had clocked my own demon at the wheel and worked for a long while to make her own appear. In time, she would master it. I was downright shocked with how well she had already done in the few days since turning. Ozone crackled around us. The lit fuse before the storm. The tiny hairs on Ophelia's neck, which weren't covered by her jumper, rose. I smiled, knowing how it felt. Her fangs dropped. It took me a second to realize she was circling into vampire mode.

"Fela?" I asked and put a hand on her back. Touching her was my tether. She turned to me, eyes like bourbon lit aflame.

"I need to feed, Javi," she said, voice distant. Different.

I took the moment to scan our surroundings. Was there a threat I hadn't registered? Something she did? I sensed no one. There was no scent I didn't know as well as my own and hers. Simply Ophelia and me and the great expanse of this place, high above the world.

"I need to be ready." The voice was not her own, and I really did start to worry. "Let me feed, Javi."

It was within the space of a millisecond that she had me on the damp earth, my jugular a burst pipe in the maw of her demon. I could not speak. My hands lifted her mac and jumper, finding themselves on her cold skin. I stroked her back, drawing infinite circles with my fingertip. She was taking too much. I would recover, I thought. But I might not make it back down for a long, long while if she kept feeding. The instinct to drink and kill was at its highest. Perhaps a result of being in a place with no rules but those of nature, which claimed its own.

"Fela," I choked out.

She paused, then chewed deeper. I was losing my mobility, my hand falling away from her body. It touched on her arm, and I used the last of my strength to bring her arm to my mouth. I bit down and took from her as well. High atop that mountainside, we were an ouroboros, pouring into each other what we took. Thunder played its bass notes in the sky. The fat drops of rain that hit us brought her out of her feeding frenzy.

"Javi?" she whispered. Then, "Javi. Oh my God. Javi. What have I done?"

She had her hand over my throat, which still bled and had yet to heal since she had fed more than I. She used her long nail and sliced her own neck, lifting me to her. I latched on, my forked tongue digging into the sinew of her neck. She moaned. It might have made me laugh, had I not been at the brink of a second, possibly true, death. There was something otherworldly about how she had spoken to me. Something which drove her to feed from me like a far older, more powerful demon than she was. Or than I had thought she was. I could lift my hands then and clutched her tighter to me, sucking at her neck. Our bodies pressed in as close as we could with the layers of clothing between us. The rain came down harder.

"We need to get off the mountain," I rasped, pulling from her. She looked at me in horror. I knew I hadn't fully healed. "You need to get us down, Fela."

CHAPTER THIRTY FOUR

OPHELIA

What had made my demon come out to play when I had been content sitting in the expectant morning air, enjoying my alone time with Javier? Why did I attack him when I knew he would always feed me. How did I allow myself to get so far gone I nearly killed him. There had been something. Some feeling of discontent that drove needles of apprehension into me, requiring I be at my strongest. Except if that were the case, I had reduced my strongest ally to his weakest, which would help no one at all. If I called out, would Alicia hear me? The rain seemed to swallow any sound I made as though the words themselves were stone, tumbled under raging rapids.

"Javi, get up," I urged. "Alicia!" I screamed. "Alicia!"

Thunder boomed, cutting off my next call. I dragged Javi over the boulder. We were at the precipice of the steep uphill climb we made earlier when the path was hindered only by bramble. It was quickly becoming a river.

"Javi, please," I begged, choking on tears.

His face, always more masterful oil painting than human, had the ghastly look of a dying man. His fangs sprouted from a drawn, graying face, his hazel eyes, so animated and amused, were now the color of the mud puddling under us. The wound I had created on his neck was barely healing and not enough to keep his face from weathering further.

"No. No. Javi. Please." I was sobbing, pulling him to me. He hadn't taken more of my blood. It was properly storming now. Winds ripped at us. My mac blew behind me, freezing stiff in the wet mud. "You will not die on me," I yelled at him. "Alicia!" I screamed her name over and over, tugging Javier foot by foot.

The path dropped. I remembered thinking it would be precarious coming back down as I'd been nearly on all fours coming up. There was nothing for it. We couldn't stay up here. If I left him, he would die. The exposure was too much when he was drained to this extent. I tore at my hair and face. That's when the snow started. Lightning speared over the top of *Sine Nomine Domus*. Zeus's bolt across the white blanket of winter. A rare occurrence of thunder snow, said to be a portent of great change.

Path and cliff drop were quickly becoming obscured. It was now or never, and I refused to let him die. I wrapped my arms under his and hefting him with all my strength, falling. Falling fast. We hit the ground, slick with ice. Our bodies slid on the path, catching on sharp rocks and hedge, yet we kept sliding. My arm cradled his head, and I tucked mine down, thankful I was still mostly on my back as we moved at this neck breaking speed. There was nothing but white forever in the distance. We hit a rock that veered us off the path and landed us against a different boulder. I sat, stunned, not knowing if I could inventory any injuries yet. Javi was totally unresponsive in my arms. Someone called to me. I heard a voice and tried to croak back.

"Help." My voice was a shout in the void. "Alicia." I thought maybe my arm was broken. Or my leg. I felt like I couldn't move. Were we almost at the bottom? Would they be able to find us now? A voice called my name again.

"Lily," it called. Sascha? "Lily, love."

"Sascha," I croaked.

Hands found me, covered as we were, in snow and ice. They found us. Javi would be safe. I felt tired. So very tired, yet I would not rest until Javi was back in the house, warm and healing. Because if he died, there was little for me now. I could not navigate this demonic path on my own. We were being pulled across snowdrifts. A door opened. Not the main hall doors. A single door like the one through the kitchen, but there were no kitchen smells. Warmth hit me.

"Sascha," the voice called. Sascha? I may have repeated it. But wasn't it Sascha who carried me? Footsteps ran at us.

"Holy fuck, Lil!" Sascha's face was in mine. Her hair was mussed from sleep. I tried to smile. She was not a morning person. "What the fuck?" she said. "What the fuck. Oh my God. Get the fuck away from her!" Sascha was screaming.

A different door slammed and without the sound of footfalls, there was instantly another with us, hissing and growling.

"Out!" The three-letter word was said with more force than a canon shot. Alicia.

"Please help Javi," I managed. I could pull my arm from his head and sit myself up. Sascha warily replaced me in keeping Javi's head from the ground.

"Let me help, please," the voice said. I turned my head. A sob wracked through me.

"Help her then," Alicia said. "If you make one wrong move, I will tear you apart and throw you to the four winds."

I had never heard Alicia sound like that. The apex predator she was. I was suddenly very glad she was on my team. Alicia lifted Javi like he weighed nothing. Sascha grabbed me and held me to her, eying who was behind me.

"Lily, love." The voice strained. Worn threads pulled to their maximum.

"Mum?" I squeaked.

OPHELIA

The lights were far brighter than necessary. I was uninjured, only bruised. Someone had removed Javi's and my clothing, laying us together and twisting our legs so we were entwined. An ouroboros once more. I pulled back to look at him, steeling myself for the decrepit rapid aging I had been seeing in him at the top of that blasted mountain. He was no longer that dying creature but Javier once more. Smooth olive skin and black fringed lashes that rimmed mossy eyes. Eyes that took me in. Lips, if a bit dry, poked up at the corners in a smile.

"Hello, little demon," he said.

I kissed him. Fully. A throat cleared across the room.

"Well, that was quite a morning you two had," Alicia said, standing over us. We were in our bed with its carved wood posters. The carvings were reminiscent of the thorny bramble on the path outside. "I will let you get dressed and feed and fuck or whatever you must do to get out of this room and down to the salon where the Little Flower's mother awaits. Ja?"

A look of alarm crossed Javier's face. Alicia said to not worry and take our time.

"Not too much time," she said and danced out of the room, shutting the door behind her.

"Alicia fed me earlier. Do you need to feed?" he asked me. I shook my head no, eager to get downstairs and understand why my mother was here. And how.

We quickly showered together and threw on warm, comfortable clothes. I wore my softest leggings and a baggy jumper with my wooly slippers. Javier kept my hand in his, knowing I needed that closeness.

Mum was standing in front of the window I had looked out of the night before. Her glossy dark hair hung in a long plait over the back of her tight-fitting jacket. She turned when we walked in, and a smile broke out over her face, lighting the room as it always had. She opened her mouth to speak, but I wasn't ready yet. I held up a hand.

"I don't know why you are here now," I said with far more strength than I felt. My legs wanted to give way. "I don't know why you faked your death and left me when I was most vulnerable. I don't know any of that or why you would kill dad. So, before you speak to me, understand that there is a whole lorry load of anger in me over you." I sat hard on the settee. There would be no feigning strength if I fell over from the nerves of this all. My mother looked at Alicia then back to me and stepped toward me.

"Lily," she said.

"Only I get to call her that now," Sascha broke in. "You gave up that name when you left her."

The woman before me, not a day older than when I last saw her, and come to think of it, not looking a day older than I do, let out a strangled sort of sob. Her lovely face as young and beautiful as it was in my memories and photos.

"I know I don't," she said. Tears ran down her pink cheeks, welling in her deep brown eyes. "Leaving you was worse than death. Believe me. Had I not known you would need looking after, I would have wished for my final death."

"Looking after? I was destitute. I worked my ass off though school and had such low self-esteem. I was in an abusive relationship for years before getting myself out. How was I looked after?" I wanted to scream but did not have the energy. My tone was almost bored.

"That is why I am here now. There has always been someone else after you, and we had to keep them from finding you."

Her words meant nothing. Or so I told myself.

"Well done, then," Sascha piped in. "So instead of using your vamp bitch abilities, you decided to kill her dad and fake your own death? I know I am not the university professor, but honestly that's a whole load of rubbish right there."

Sascha was in Mum's face. We stared at each other, the fire in the hearth the only sounds for a long few moments. Then there was a rapping at the larger front doors. Alicia and Javi looked to one another, brows drawn.

"I'll get it," she said and left.

I exhaled, not wanting Javi to leave, though an itch in the back of my throat lent itself to the probability that I would need feeding and fucking soon. There was rapid chatter from the foyer and hall that carried in drifts. It sounded like whoever was there was responding to Alicia's machine gun fire mix of Spanish, Italian, and Latin. It was a male voice responding in Latin. The two walked in, and I felt like I was going to be sick.

"Dad?" I managed.

"Halloo, Lily. Still silly?" he greeted me like he always had.

That damned nickname that stemmed from a mix of my birth flower and something about Ophelia that didn't have a decent diminutive—until I heard Javi call me Fela. My parents called me Lily for fun, saying day lily, lily of the valley, silly lily, all of them. We had been the goofiest, oddest family, and I thought as a child, there could be nothing that would shake our love for each other. Then I grew up.

I could have been standing at a window, a veil between yesteryear and today. I could see myself as a child, holding Dad's hand, skipping over the walk to Saint Michael's Mount in Cornwall, Dad reciting bits of poetry by Charles Causley. I liked the magical feel of the words, though never understood much of the poetry itself until I was older, feeling the words steeped in folklore. Dad stood before me today, next to Mum, tension and desire almost audibly buzzing between them. They were living ghosts. The same freckles on their faces, the same tattoo sleeves running up Dad's bare arms. Those two faces I knew all their students secretly wanted. The two bodies in constant orbit 'round each other.

Dad must have shed a wet coat in the foyer, as the weather was as unforgiving now as it was an hour ago when Javi and I were rescued. Carried down that damned mountain by my ageless mum. I focused on Dad's ink, knowing I hadn't committed them all to memory, as I believed I had. There were symbols and words, a sketch of a child's face, blurred by a selection of flowers. Lilies. Yellow day lilies and white lilies of the valley. A majestic calla lily, hydrangea, and a soft tea rose. The ones Mum loved. She didn't look soft today. The Mum I remembered in my heart had been the one wrapped in a white dressing gown, who loved sea glass and bright things. Not this stark brunette beauty with her wet hair slicked back, making her sharp cheekbones stand out in profile, wearing some high-end active wear that showed her fit body. Thighs more toned than I remembered, and lean muscles coiled into the tech fabric of her clothing. Dad looked the same. So much the same that I felt I could vomit. Same dad who had his own style that was somewhere between 1990s punk and Great War aristocrat. I couldn't look at either of their faces, so I stared at his houndstooth trousers. The wool tucked into mahogany combat boots with the top laces undone. He seemed as athletically thin as ever. Memories of his rowing on the Exe and running through the city fluttered through my nostalgic mind. He was physically a man in his late twenties or early thirties. He looked younger than Javi.

Dad's hand kept flicking the inside pocket. It was his nervous gesture I would know anytime, anywhere. The click and pop of him flicking open his pocket watch and shutting it. Over and over again. Some sound came out of me. One I wouldn't know how to describe if I tried. Javi and Sascha each had an arm around me, noting the shivering I couldn't control.

Dad ran a hand through his mop of dusty brown curls, then looked to Mum. There was something tortured in his eyes.

"Darling, it's time," he said.

They stood a pregnant distance apart, which to me felt odd. Not like them. My parents had always been magnetically close. Where one was, the other was, never lead and follow, but a constant orbit, spinning around one another. They mirrored each other's movements and anticipated the other's needs. They kissed openly, hugged freely, and I knew how special the words "I Love You" were because they were so often spoken by my parents to one another and to me. I had known when Connor said, "love ya", it was false, and I had never felt the need to say it to him. Perhaps once when I was drunk, attempting to say it for the sheer curiosity of the feeling. I could say it to Sascha, my sister in all but blood. I had never meant to say it to a partner. A man. Not until Javier. I knew what my parents had together was rare. That kind of fulfillment in another was not commonplace. So, to see them standing apart was not boding well with my memories. Which made me question whether my mind had replayed cut scenes for all these years. Not the real script.

"Before you say anything else," I said, "did you send Connor's head to me?"

"We did not," Mum answered. "I would never do that, my darling. I understand how I seem to you. How perhaps we both seem to you. But I assure you, everything I have done in these years was to keep you safe. All I ask of you at this point—"

I started to protest and say she has no right to ask anything of me at all, but she must have anticipated it. She held up a hand, a gesture I must have gotten from her.

"I know I have no right to ask anything of you. And yet, still I do. It is only to listen. And when you do, after you do, no matter what you may think of me—"

"Of us," Dad chimed in.

She looked to him, a small smile of gratitude and that near identical tortured look in her own eyes. "Of us, though I think you may see me more the villain. All I ask is that you know, without room for doubt, that I love you. We love you. More than this earth. More than our own lives. Anything and everything we did was to try to keep you safe. And that we know we fell short. We know ultimately, it didn't work." She gave Javier a look that could melt steel. "Will you take that to heart?"

I shrugged. She blew out an exasperated breath. A sound and look on her face I knew like I knew my own. My heart squeezed. Despite the anger and aching. Despite my parents looking like I had time traveled a decade—more, now that I realized they stopped aging long before I was born. Despite all these things, I still wanted to crawl in their arms. Javi's fingers found mine and squeezed. The faintest touch to comfort me.

Sascha poured what looked like whiskey into tumblers and handed them around. I didn't know what time it was. Javi and I had started on our ill-fated hike around eight. It must be noon or after at this point. The concept of time seemed foreign to me here, where day and night were a gray smudge, and I had nowhere to be. Whiskey was fine then. I sipped it, warming within seconds of it slipping down my throat.

Sascha used to say she and I were like a litter of free kittens. We stuck together, but if we were in pain, emotionally or physically, we would crawl off to our respective corners and ride it out alone. I had gotten good at curling into myself. Sascha was not an orphan by any means. Her family was loud and welcoming, overbearing, and had more money than they knew what to do with. They also did not understand her. They didn't accept her sexuality, her career choices, or her wardrobe. The only two things about her they accepted were me and her drinking. The whole lot of them drank to excess, and to this day, they never noticed that Sascha was always one drink ahead of everyone else. She always ended the night three sheets to the wind, insisting she could drink all night, and no one ever knew the difference.

Sitting in that overly large salon with its dark paneling and leather covered everything, I wanted to curl into my ratty cardboard box and lick my paws until I healed enough to walk my stray-cat self back out into the world. Sascha knew by my body language that was what I wanted to do. She pressed her hip into the side of mine, locking me into the sofa, squished between her and Javi, who then put both arms around me. The scent of him. That airy yet masculine scent that made him *him* wrapped around me as well. I could smell the laundry liquid on the T-shirt he wore under his jumper that smelled like expensive cashmere. I could smell the face wash he used and the shampoo in his hair, which I had used as well. His scents were grounding me in the here and now when my mind was wanting to see the two people before me —the people I had loved and trusted most in this world—and revert to my child self.

Alicia stood behind the sofa. She was like the massive mountain behind this castle, fortifying the three of us who sat down. Unlikely allies against unfathomable foes.

Dad and Mum took seats in the two armchairs opposite us. Seeing them three feet apart had my heart screaming.

"Why aren't you touching?" I blurted out, unable to contain myself any longer. They looked at each other from the sides of their eyes. I felt sick. "Are you not together anymore?" I asked. My voice was high. Childlike. I hated it. I hated them seeing me wistful for their older days.

"Perhaps it's better to start from the end," Mum said, biting her full bottom lip. Dad saw the action and looked down at his boots. *Click. Pop.* I took another sip of my drink and saw that everyone else did too.

"Yes," Javier purred. "Do tell me how you managed to find us and circumvent my wards."

"We know Ines. Your mage," Dad said. Mum's face was impassive at Dad's admission.

"And she told you where to find my very well-hidden refuge?" Javi asked. He crossed one foot over a knee. "And told you how to bypass the wards we had?"

Dad scrubbed a hand over his face. His fingers had starbursts and Greek letters tattooed on them. They both actually looked younger than I did, which felt a bit shit, really. Plus, I really didn't know how Mum could be so bloody fit and I had thighs that could strangle a man. The thought rushed heat to my core, which I immediately banked.

"I am not very good with linear details," Mum said, shifting in her seat. There was a look on her face I wouldn't be able to read if I tried, but it was akin to heartbreak. "My mother, Allegra," she said and looked at Alicia, "knew her. Ines, that is. It was Allegra who came to me and told me to look out for you."

Alicia made an impatient scoffing sound. Considering Alicia thought Allegra to be dead, this was all rather confusing.

"She told me the details of this place and how to bypass the wards without"—Dad waved his hand in the air erratically, his mind always faster than his mouth—"I don't know, messing them up. She had your safety in mind, I can promise you that."

"Why," Javi tried again, his voice like silk, and I shivered, "would my mage, who I have known for centuries, tell you how to dismantle my wards?"

"Not," Dad said, mussing his hair and shaking his head. His body vibrated with nerves and tension. *Click. Pop. Click. Pop.* His mannerisms had always been shifty and unsure of himself with other people. Never with Mum and me though. We were his people. Were. Past tense. "Not dismantle. Bypass. As I said, I did not want to mess them up. They are in place for your safety, and I appreciate that. More so, we knew they would be a safe haven for our daughter." He looked at me. "Ines told me how to bypass them."

"I was not aware there was a bypass." Javi's words were casual, and he was speaking off to the side, not looking at Mum nor Dad. There was a brick of tension in his corded arms though.

Dad held up a finger and fished in his pocket for his phone. He pulled it out and opened his photos then stood to walk to us but halted and moved from foot to foot, as though asking if it were okay, his waist chain swaying with the motion. I took the phone. There was a photo of a wooded pass. An autumnal jewel box. The leaves looked wet, and more brown than gold. The photo was hazy, unfocused.

"It's not unfocused," Dad said, tapping the phone. The picture switched to another, further back. There was a gap between two boulders. "D'ya remember, Lily, when I taught you to sew a blanket?" he asked me. He had taught me first how to hand sew, then how to use the machine. He had worked in a factory during school, saving up for university. "You know when you sew the whole thing inside out, but have to leave an opening to turn it right side then you need to be really careful, stitching up the last bit?" I nodded. He looked at Javier. "This is that last bit." Javi leaned over and peered closer. "Ines sewed up the whole place. But she needed a spot that she could exit. I suppose her magic has to be done from the inside? I'm not really sure, but that would correspond to many tribal magics I've studied. Magic is a grasp on nature, and wards like these must be made from the nucleus. Creating a new cell. Here, the nucleus is this house. Castle." He gestured around, then stuffed his hands in his trousers. *Click. Pop.*

The dark-brown waist coat he wore buttoned over his T-shirt was classic Dad attire. He always looked a bit steampunk in my memory, I guess. I loved it as a kid. He never looked like the stuffy old professors I would see around town. My friends would sigh and whisper, "Hot dad alert," when he was around. And now, Mum looked even more his perfect counterpart, yet somehow, they were not partners.

"This building is the inner walls of the nucleus. The strongest wards are here. The protection radiates out from here, using nature as its stronghold. Like tent stakes holding it in place." Dad's caramel eyes lit up with excitement. He hadn't been lecturing all this time, I realized. The nerves were because he wasn't doing what he loved. And here he was, lecturing again. "There are stronger wards above as, of course,

you don't want anything seen from the skies. But right there"
—he pointed to the photo again—"about thirty-six inches
high and a bit less wide is where she had to leave and sew up
the wards."

"And nothing could keep that shut?" I asked.

He looked at me. "Something could. Javier's blood." Dad
backed up. "Which is also what can bypass it."

"Sascha's flat," Javi said.

I didn't understand. Javi's blood was never in Sascha's flat.
Oh. Javi looked at me. That night. The one where he bit
himself whilst feeding from my inner thigh. I really mustn't
think about that night right then. With my parents in the
room. Well, that was sorted out. The last twenty-four hours
were cleared up. How about the preceding decade?

My eyes must have been daggers, staring at my parents. I
had to get up. To move. I pushed Javi's arms off me and
moved with lightning speed to the bookshelves. Something
to do.

"When I was little, my mother gave me blood." My own
mother's voice was icy. Not the warm Mum voice she used
with me. "My food was doctored with it. I didn't know this,
of course, until I was older. About eighteen or so. Then she
got me drunk to celebrate my uni acceptance, and she bit my
wrist. I was scared. So scared and angry. She showed me her
fangs and her eyes—bright orange—as I expect yours
must be?"

I nodded.

Mum stood and walked slowly to me as though nearing a
beast. "I was drunk and paralyzed with her enthrallment. She
drank from my wrist—"

"Allegra was human." Alicia stormed to us. Her fangs were
out, eyes flashing. "I raised her. I knew her."

"And yet, she was not human. She was as I am. Vampire.
My father died when I was very young. I never knew why.

They always said he was sick. Cancer. Something of the sort. It was not true, of course. My father was also vampire. They met I don't know when. She wrote to you she was safe. He lived life as a human. Stayed off radar. Then she killed him."

"No." Alicia was backing into a crouch. Javi jumped up to hold her.

"I'm so sorry. As a mother—"

"I never left my child." Alicia's words were icicles. "I left my husband for my child. She decided to leave me and live as a human."

"She decided to leave you and live as a vampire who could birth other vampires. She was very good about concealing who she was until the time suited her. And she always got what she wanted. I was her only child. It seems it only works once. I transitioned that year."

Alicia wrestled her way out of Javier's grasp and sprung onto my dad. She bit his throat. I screamed. Mum launched herself at him. She slashed her nails across Alicia, who dropped Dad. He was mumbling that he was okay, though he was bleeding quite a bit. Mum pinned Alicia down, a hand around her throat, her knees on her chest.

"I am here for my child. Your great grandchild, I might add. So, if you would listen to reason, we could sort this out. You do not have to like me, but if you attack my husband again, I will destroy you. *Hai capito?*" Italian for 'have you understood'? Alicia looked at me and her eyes shifted back to their lovely brown. She nodded. "Are you healing, Angel?" Mum asked Dad.

"Yes, thanks." *Click. Pop.*

I did not miss the lift of his lips hearing her call him that old nickname. His cheeks flushed nearly as red as the healing wound below it.

"Are you still married?" I asked. Honestly, right now, I was a child enough to think it was of utmost importance.

"There is no divorce in death, Silly Lily," Dad said with a wink. *Click. Pop.* Mum made a sound that was almost a sniffle, almost a chuckle.

That was not the answer I was asking for, but I thought if I pressed right now, I would cry. Then I would get angry and need to feed and this was a rather unpleasant vicious circle. Alicia had told us Allegra died as a human. Or so she had assumed. I could not imagine all she was feeling. She had left Javi. Faked her own death to raise Allegra, who took a teenage rebellion a bit too far. Then in turn, faked her death too. Jesus. I rubbed my temples. And then, my parents faked their deaths.

"This is a horrible family," I said.

Mum and Dad gasped, which was so bizarre, I had to blink rapidly to think again.

"You"—I pointed to Alicia—"faked your death to leave Javier so you could raise your little vampire baby."

Sascha shuddered. She had poured an additional knuckle of whiskey into her glass.

"Then teenage riot vamp baby goes off and fakes her death so she can have her own little vamp baby." I turned my baleful eyes on my parents. I was getting angry. My gums burned. I willed the fangs to stay in, but they dropped anyway. Fuck. *Click. Pop*, went Dad's pocket watch. "Then you play house for years and fake your death, leaving me by myself wishing I were dead!"

"I would never have left you," Mum began, slowly. She spoke as though trying to moor a fire in her chest. "But I killed your father," she said. "And when I turned him..." She was openly crying.

I wondered, if this were all true, if she had ever spoken this aloud. She wasn't looking at him. She stared at the floor. He took a step toward her but stopped before he was in touching range. I felt a gut punch with that. *Click. Pop. Click.*

Pop. In rapid succession. The air around them sizzled with unspoken emotion.

"It was my fault," he said. "I asked you to keep taking."

"It was *not* your fault. It was *never* your fault." She wasn't looking at him as she said it. Her head bobbed up and down, speaking to her feet. "I didn't have to use you as my donor. I didn't have to marry you and make a life with you only to kill you."

"I don't understand you two. Why did you have to leave *me?*" I shouted. I was a petulant youth again, but I needed answers.

"Because I called my mother to have her help me transition him. She hadn't known about you before that, Lily Love. Or so we thought." She turned her eyes to me. "She threatened to take you away. She wanted to use your blood to create more vampires. See how others could be born. Since you were half, you are a marvel. Unprecedented. A miracle. But you were mine. Ours."

"Please, do explain how leaving her to fend for herself at aged eighteen was a better solution to having a blood-thirsty mad-scientist granny on her tail." Sascha was the one to ask, though we were all thinking it. Javier I could tell was simmering with rage he was doing his best to keep in check. It was an inconvenient time for me to be switched on by his rage.

"I did not transition well," Dad said. His cheeks sucked in, making the tattooed veins on his neck pulsate. "I was, for lack of a better term, in an extended episode of psychosis. I was murderous. Vengeful. Always hungry. Always..." He waved his hand around again.

I thought I might get what that unspoken word was and did not need to hear it from his mouth. Ew.

"Mummy had to get me away. Immediately." *Click. Pop.* "We could not risk hurting you nor anyone else with my mania. After a few years, I was better. I'm better now!" He nearly yipped it. "I'm not mad. Well, no more than I was as a human." He winked at me. Mom sniffed a bit of a laugh. "But it was awkward trying to figure out how to reintroduce ourselves to you when you weren't in this world of blood and gore. I didn't want my baby girl to have to be in this. So, we were on the defensive against Allegra. And things between Mummy and me...they were different. And we were afraid of that as well." He stepped toward me. *Click. Pop.* "And then you met Javier. You stumbled right into this life we had tried so hard to keep you out of."

"Because I was broke. I needed money."

"You don't need anything anymore. Not from him," Daddy said pointing a black painted fingernail at Javier. "Not from anyone."

"I love him," I said. "Completely and endlessly. He is not in question here." My words were final. Dad nodded.

"I understand. For some of us, there is only ever one person."

"And she is mine." Javier broke his silence and took my hand. We were all standing in this room of six thousand upholstered seating agents. Well, all but Sascha who was wide eyed on the sofa, legs tucked under like she was watching a Sky Drama.

"We know," Mum said. "There is no air between your auras. You have become one.

"I will need time," I said. "I don't know how long. I'm feeling so many things right now. Not all are good. Some are. Some are more painful than I thought they ever could be again. I'm also so sad about you two." *Click. Pop.*

I needed air and said so, starting to walk out of the room.

"It was Allegra who sent the head." Alicia said it as a statement. Not a question.

"She did. She has been aggressive lately. It was wise to bring Lily here. Thank you." Mum swallowed hard.

Dad was looking at her like all the air had gone out of him. Like he had been filled until this moment, but the moment was over, and what was left was a husk. I saw the tears and had to hug him. He crumpled over me, holding me against him. He smelled the same. That citrus and black tea cologne and his three showers a day obsession. I could have stayed in the hug forever. But he pushed me off and turned me to Mum, who did not wait for me. She took me in her arms and held me tight. I was a mess of hot tears and the need to eat.

"I am so very sorry, love. We are here now." She pulled back to look me in the eyes. "You have a home in all of us."

I kept nodding and left the room.

Javi followed me and led us to the kitchen where we had eaten the night before. He pulled out a loaf of bread and sliced a few good hunks of it, grated what looked to be cheddar over top, and broiled it. We didn't speak. He made me tea and set the cheesy toast in front of me, then kissed my head and sat beside me as I ate. We heard Sascha insisting Alicia take a break. I could not imagine how Javi's ex felt then.

"She will be fine," Javi said. "Alicia is not one to stay down. She will be fine."

CHAPTER THIRTY SIX

SASCHA

Honestly, I had to nearly drag Alicia back to our room. She was in full on vamp bitch mode, and I thought each of us odd couples needed time to breathe apart. It had been a mind fuck of a morning. Made me appreciate my drunken dynasty of a family. The worst bit was that Lil's parents were out of sorts. Like they were on scales which should be balanced perfectly yet kept tipping away from the other. It made me need to kiss Alicia. Which, of course, I did once we entered my room. She pushed me away.

"Ja, Sascha. I am in no mood."

I was stung.

She patted my cheek like I was her pupil who had done well on an assignment. I went straight for the bar cart in our room.

"This place feels like time does not exist. It is easy to get lost in bad habits." She pointed to the bottle in my hand.

"I was trying to get lost in you," I retorted. "Now I'm just bored. There isn't even a telly in here, and if I go on my laptop, I'll have to pay bills. Which doesn't sound particularly fun right now."

Alicia looked out of our window, which faced the front of the estate. Snow was thick on the ground.

"Shall I leave you alone?" I asked.

She turned to me, a confused look on her face.

"Come." She held out her hand. I took it. "See there," she said pointing to the absolute darkness that had fallen so early. A massive tree stood off to the side of the driveway. I squinted, hoping she didn't see that I really needed contacts. There was a split in the tree it seemed. "Sometime in the eighteenth century, we were here. Javier had been helping out the Jacobite king. It was a bit of a cluster, as you say. Javi was an envoy and there was a shipwreck. Gold was lost. Or silver. I do not remember. Truly a disaster. Well, we had to hide out here for a few years. It was dreadfully boring. But that tree went from a normal tree to how it is now overnight. We inspected it, and Javi told me not to go in. He was afraid it was a fairy circle." She smiled at me, her glossy lips reflecting light from the sconces. I licked my own. "Well, I went in. He followed, of course. It's Javi. I don't know what to say it was. Or is. But when we entered, it felt as though the world outside did not exist. It was a breath of a moment before Javi had my skirts over my shoulders, his cock spearing me."

"You wicked vamp bitch," I said to her ear. She shivered. "You should wear skirts more." I undid the button on her trousers and slipped my hand in them. Oh, she was wet for me. I stroked her, teasingly. "I didn't bring my strap on," I said, flicking her clit. "So, you will have to just have me." I slipped two fingers in her and she rode them. My hand was around her throat. Her soft peachy skin felt like heaven. I wanted to fuck her forever. The thought made me stop pumping my fingers.

"What is it?" she asked.

I shook my head and nipped at her neck, and she moaned.

"Drink from me," I said.

She stopped riding my fingers. I knew she had been wanting to. I knew it physically pained her that she hadn't.

Sure, a taste here and there. Enough to get me edged. But she was never fully sated. And neither was I.

"Don't overthink it. Just drink from me. Make me yours."

Before I'd finished, she had me pinned to the window. She tore my trousers down and opened the button-down shirt I'd been wearing. Her hand found my breasts, and she pressed against me from behind. A noise of frustration came out of her, and within seconds, her body was naked. I lost my shirt too. Our faces and my tits reflected in the dark window. I saw her vampy eyes glow. I made an odd sound and felt wetness between my thighs. She dropped down and licked at it. She fed from my cum from behind me. Under me. My hands flat palmed the glass as I rode her face where she knelt under me.

The first puncture of her fangs next to my pussy lips strangled me. When she drew blood from it, I thought I might faint. My body was on fire, ready to explode. I bucked and thrashed against her, fingering my own clit as she fed. Her fingers kneaded my breasts and ran over my ass. I came hard on her face as she finished drinking my blood. I saw her slide those hot little fangs out, dripping with my blood, her porcelain face covered in my cum, and I shoved her against me again.

Once I caught my breath, I led her to the bed and traced every line of her body with my fingertips. I kissed her nipples, one by one. Kissed her belly button. Her hips. Her fingertips, which still tasted of me. Her face, which was a sticky mess of me. I moved down and licked a long line from her belly to her crease. For moments, I circled her clit with my tongue. Her body was bouncing from the sensation. I giggled and tongue fucked her. My tongue darted in and out while I rubbed her little bud until she grabbed a fistful of my hair and cried out, slamming her cunt into my face three times. Four. Then her body dropped and relaxed, pulling me against her.

"I want to fuck you forever," I said to her—the thought I'd had only a few minutes earlier.

She pierced me with a glare.

"No."

"No?" I asked hurt.

"I won't take your life, Sascha. It most often does not result in a vampire like Ophelia. Her dad is a more common example. I was very similar. A danger to society. I was locked up for five years."

"You were what?"

She nodded. "I would be let out only to kill immediately. It took five years to tame me. I won't go through that with you. You have a lovely life. I want to keep you. You. Not a different version."

"I will get old and die."

"And I will love you and mourn you."

I felt confused. I couldn't be hurt. I couldn't be put off. She wanted me as I was. For as long as I was. And I supposed, in my self of selves, who drank to excess and took diuretics to shit my extra weight away, the sexiest thing anyone had ever told me was that they wanted me as I was. So, I was okay with that. For now, at least.

CHAPTER THIRTY SEVEN

Ophelia retired to our room for a nap. If I could nap, I would have. It had been a hellish morning. I almost died, which was one for the books. I walked by Alicia's room when I left Ophelia to sleep and heard some nasty noises from behind their door. It nearly made me turn around and go see to my own girl. Instead, I took a breath and walked back down to the salon.

My feet in this castle were cat like. I never made a sound. Ophelia's parents did not hear me when I crept around the corner. Their voices were low and hushed, so I thought it might do to employ a bit of reconnaissance. I stood behind a hanging tapestry which was used to keep drafts from room to room.

"You should not blame yourself, Lincoln," she said. "This was all me. Or my mother. Or this shit world we live in." I could hear the choke of tears in her voice.

"Had I turned better—"

"I killed you." There was a rustle of fabric. "Had I not taken so much, you would not have died. The turn would have been irrelevant."

"Annabella," he said. "I had been asking you for many years to turn me. So we could be together. Do not shift the narrative. Had I transitioned better, we could have looked after Lily better. Eased her into adulthood. Given that piece of shite Connor the scare of his life earlier on."

I heard Annabella sniffle what could have been a laugh. Feet shuffled. I peeked around the tapestry and saw her turned from him. He hesitated then placed his hands on her shoulders. She shook.

"Had I not been such a piece of shite myself and taken so many lovers when I transitioned, we would not have fallen apart." He said the words like they had never been spoken before. She sobbed, leaning into him. I heard the catch in his voice. "I will never excuse myself. Just as I will never forgive myself. Nor will I ask it of you."

"I know what it is to turn a vampire. I know the need in transition. I was different," she said. "I knew there was a chance that would happen."

My heart ached. I rubbed it. I had been afraid of that with Ophelia. It happened to me. To Alicia. To every vampire I had ever known. The need for satiety was maddening. And it seemed Lincoln James was predisposed to it a bit more. And it tore them apart. Any plans they'd had for their daughter. For them. All ash on the wind. I sent a thanks up to the God I somehow still believed in that Ophelia had been different. Changed differently.

"And still, it was me who destroyed us. Anna," he said, resting his head on her shoulder. He was not that much taller than she. Their forms and beauty so evenly matched. "There will only ever be one person for me. You are the only light in my sky. The only harbor for me."

She spun in his arms and wrapped around him, kissing him with the force of years apart. I backed up slowly, leaving them the rest of their privacy. It seemed by that intimate conversation alone, what they had disclosed was true. I made my way upstairs to see Ophelia, but the lights shut off. One by one, the sconces went out. The ever-present whirl of the heating and refrigerator stopped. It could be the storm, but I counted to ten and the generator had not come on. Neither did the backup generator. I ran the rest of the way up, hearing boots from below following, and knowing Annabella and Lincoln were directly behind me. I rapped on Alicia's door, not bothering to wait for her to open it. I flung open the door and startled her awake.

"Up, Fela, quickly."

She didn't ask why or doddle. She threw her jumper back on and slipped boots on instead of slippers. Clever girl.

A maniacal sort of giggle sounded somewhere in the house. The echoes of this place made it so that it was difficult to tell where sound came from. With the voice came an unusual scent. Someone I did not know mixed with one I knew well. Ines. And somewhere, the affected, noxious cologne that could only be Pietro.

"Lily, Lily, soft and silly tell me how you bloom
With sun light, soil, and love aplenty
Lily, Lily, lovely lily, tell me how you bloom
With heat and brimstone, soldier, and sentry..."

The voice became softer, closer, darker.

"Lily, Lily," it whispered, seemingly everywhere and nowhere. Six of us stood on the mezzanine above the ground floor, not knowing where to turn. My hand was a bear trap on Ophelia's arm. If I was hurting her, she didn't say, but she was clutching my waist.

"Lily, Lily, demon lily, tell me how you bloom!
With blood and ire, the terror of the century!"

The nursery rhyme arrived at its end with a face. One with features so much like Ophelia and Annabella, though blood-hardened and cruel. A female who could only have been Alicia's adopted daughter. Allegra moved faster than even Alicia, exposing her position nearest Annabella.

"Hello, daughter," she seethed into Annabella's ear.

Tears ran down Annabella's cheeks. Her eyes shone liked fired amber. Allegra tore a wound on her daughter's neck and tossed her aside, treating her daughter like a discarded doll.

"Tsk tsk. Lincoln, I had such high hopes for you. You could have been marvelous. We would have been a team."

The look on his face was pure disgust. Alicia's was moving between fear, hatred, and hurt. I did not know how to help her as she stood frozen. I could not attack this woman, who was a relation of my mate and my ex-wife. I could only defend. Stand and observe. It was not a long-standing observation, for the work of a minute threw us all into disarray.

"Mama," Allegra cooed. "I grew up."

She flew at Alicia, quick as a shot, and clawed my ex-wife's face. Flesh tore under her talon-like nails.

I let my demon take over, as did the rest of us. I wrenched Allegra off her mother and threw her to the floor below, harder than intended. She landed with a crack, her head splitting open. Sascha was throwing up into a planter in the hall.

A whistled tune came from below, then another from the darkened hall behind us. More whistling sounded from above. A tune I knew and hated. Greensleeves. It reminded me of Puritan rule. Religious fascism. It was definitely part of my past, and I knew of two people who knew that. Pietro swaggered from the darkness, whistling the song in time with whoever was downstairs and up. It seemed Allegra truly was the highest bidder. All my threats of retaliation, and Pietro still did not grasp the magnitude of the lengths I would go to protect Ophelia. My mage appeared, walking in a trance, her arms bound, eyes full white. She was whistling, wending the tune under my skin like a hot knife, flaying my humanity with each betrayal. Ines, the mage I had befriended centuries before, working with the likes of Allegra and Pietro. Below us, the spot where Allegra had been was vacant. Only a pool of blood to show she'd ever landed. The pitter patter of ghostly feet ran up the stairs as though the child ghosts in this place feared whatever was coming. Sascha's retching began anew with a whimper of fear between gags.

"Lily, Lily," Allegra sang once again, whistling behind Ines. She grabbed the mage, viciously tearing out her throat. Sinew and flesh sprayed against a portrait of some long dead lord. There would be no healing from that. Ines was not vampire.

I yelled, reaching for her, as though she had not tossed years of trust into the grave. Lincoln caught the mage, ripping open his own wrist.

Before I could protest, Annabella screamed, "No!"

He stopped and looked at his wife, dropping the mage. Annabella stared at him and Ines, a shock of hurt cresting over her before she pulled Lincoln to his feet.

"Lily," sang Allegra again. Her arm was linked with Pietro's as they turned from the back hallway. "Ophelia. Fela. Little Flower—Oh! Like Saint Theresa," Allegra said. "Did you know that Saint Teresa was the patron saint of headaches?" She cackled. "Mama, you are too funny."

Allegra came toward Ophelia, Pietro closing in behind us. I caught Alicia's eyes, then those of Ophelia's parents. Pietro had little to gain in this situation, and it seemed that realization was finally dawning on the poor sod. He was a sad little man who had managed to survive these years as parasites tended to do. Latching on to a stronger host. This time, however, he'd picked the wrong side. Perhaps he could never have seen Alicia and me being civil. Perhaps he thought in infiltrating Ophelia's life, he would gain from Allegra. All the retrospection in the world could not save him now. Not when I had given him fair warning months ago on the green of Cathedral Yard, the monstrosity of stonework and stained glass at my back. Pietro had reached the end of his lecherous second life. In my eyes, I knew he could see a resolve like no other. Allegra's arm tightened on his, locking him to her side.

"With me," she sang, "Little Flower, you will be a headache no longer. I will show you how to live as a vampire." She spun in a circle, arms outstretched, releasing the leech.

I lessened my grip on Ophelia, ready to pounce. She grabbed me harder, so I ran my thumb over her arm to tell her it was okay. She was frozen. Terrorized.

"I can show you. Come. Come with me, Ophelia. Let us start our family. No more doldrums of this life." Allegra whipped her head to Alicia.

"Allegra," Alicia said, pleading, "I can open the tomb. We don't need Silly Lily to birth more. I figured out how to open it." Alicia stepped toward her daughter, putting her hand out. Allegra's eyes widened. She leaned in. "

"I already did it. Razed the place to the ground. The body gone!" She cackled. "Ophelia's line is better. Improved. We have weeded out the issues." She laughed again and lunged for Ophelia.

Ophelia screamed, pulling at Allegra's grip. Alicia came up behind her and yanked Allegra's head back while I took Ophelia fully into my arms. Pietro came at my left in a last-ditch attempt to escape. Using the weight of Ophelia's and my bodies to crush the other vampire to the wall, I aborted his flight. Sascha's screams were a backing track to the utter melee, the sounds uninterrupted where the only human huddled against the wall in fright. Annabella ran to her and held her while Lincoln took Ophelia. Pietro's face quivered with fear. A stark, undeniable awareness of his end. With the power of centuries behind me and a love for Ophelia as fierce as the winds beyond these castle walls, I thrust my fist into Pietro's chest and tore through, pulling his heart from inside, and clearing it from his body, ribs splintering. Alicia sliced the knife she always kept on her, across Allegra's throat, then dragged her daughter down the stairs as she bled out. No words were exchanged as I pulled Pietro down the curved staircase, barely registering the knock of his skull on each stone step. Together, Alicia and I tossed both bodies on the frozen ground behind the castle as we lit the wood burner.

Ophelia was shaking in her father's arms when I returned, Sascha doing the same in Annabella's. I came up the stairs, three at a time and Ophelia ran to me.

"Ja, Fela. It is done. We are all safe."

"What have you done with them?" Lincoln asked.

"We have put their bodies in the wood burner. It will be a bit longer. But they will be gone."

I looked around. The rugs would be burned too. I asked Annabella to take the girls to a room. Any room. And give them a drink and stay with them as I scrubbed this stain away. I wanted to clean any memory of this evening from the annals of time. The lights came back on. Alicia had fixed the power too. I trudged down, carrying Ines as gingerly as I could. I felt the weight of her in a singular spark I knew would fly free as was the custom with her kind. My friend. My protector. Why would she have betrayed me? Had she been enthralled? I would never know. For my own sanity, I had to assume that was the case. She would have her own pyre, reverent and solemn, nowhere near the likes of the others. But first, as per her beliefs, she must be laid upon the forest floor for three nights.

CHAPTER THIRTY EIGHT

OPHELIA

A countdown to our official opening commenced with the snipping of a confetti filled balloon. It rained pink and red heart-shaped confetti all over the lounge of my hotel on February thirteenth. I had needed a new architect, of course, but the weeks before opening were surprisingly free of major hiccups. I had a team of many now, though, and it felt like for the first time in my life, I was a part of not only a family, but of something bigger than me. Mummy and Daddy toasted me with their rosé champagne and kept to the shadows as I made my rounds. Alicia kissed Sascha on the cheek and squeezed her arm. I could see that Alicia was proud of her. I was too. Sascha had endured so much in the past months with me, and here she was more boss babe than ever. Her entire family came to celebrate, talking to their society friends about our new boutique hotel, catering not only to university elite, but to younger couples and families.

I hugged Javier, knowing he did not love parties but remembering how he had still come to see me at my Christmas party. I kissed him quickly, continuing to engage with my guests until the last filed out. When the hotel was clear of all but my business partner and me, and our own two partners, Javier led me away.

"It would be a shame to not christen a room here, would it not?"

"You are a man of God, not me."

"It would be a sin."

I opened the room he led me to and saw with a laugh, Voltaire sitting on the bed, a new strap and harness next to it. Javi shrugged and began disrobing. I took off my blazer dress and stood before him, wearing red lace lingerie and garters, the glass necklace he had made me decorated my collarbone.

"Mm, Fela. However will you take me?" He pushed my breasts together, burying his face in them. I felt his forked tongue slither into the cups of my bra. I put his hand at my pussy, letting him feel how wet I already was. Just seeing the damned strap on had me damp. I pumped his cock before dropping to my knees to take him in my mouth. My fangs came out, and he moaned.

"On your knees, vampire," I said around the massive cock in my mouth. I could suck him off all night, but it seemed we had a bit of a mission. The harness took a minute to figure out, but once on, Voltaire popped into place, I switched him on to my favorite setting, and came up behind Javi. His beautiful arse was high, and I bent to lick it, running my tongue and hands down, then cupping his balls.

"Fela," he drawled, "are you going to play all night or fuck me?" His words were slurred, heavily accented, and hissing through his fangs. For that comment, I bit down on his ass, sucking at the wound. My knickers fell to the floor as I lubed Voltaire and got ready to mount Javier. My hand came around him and ran the lube over his shaft too, and he rewarded me with a groan. My tits brushed his back, making me wince from so much heated friction. His cock twitched in my hand. I inched Voltaire in, asking Javi if he was okay. My fingers massaged his tight hole as my other hand stroked his long cock. Voltaire was vibrating softly. Javi started to shake.

"Fela, I can take more than that," he said, reaching behind us and pulling my arse closer. Voltaire slammed all the way in him, and he yelled in a sort of ecstasy of pain. The mechanics of this were a bit more involved than I had imagined, making me worry I was being too sloppy. Too inexperienced. Yet with the sounds Javi made, my worries subsided. With each thrust, my confidence doubled. I began fucking him, my pussy dripping as my clit rubbed over his bum and felt the vibrations from Voltaire.

"More Fela," he said, backward fucking me. Starbursts blew in my eyes. Nothing existed beyond the two of us here and the impending orgasm. My hand grasped him tighter, tugging his cock more and more. I came with a howl, covering Javi in everything I had. He was close; I could feel him tensing. He started making low cooing noises I'd never heard, and his body shook. I ripped my wrist open with my fangs and placed the bloody wound over his mouth so he could suck as he rode the prostate orgasm, then with a final thrust, he spilled all over my hand and the sheets I had picked out for myself. He kept moving in slow motion, suckling my wrist until I came again, going over the edge with a drop in my stomach and my heart full.

"We must do that again," I said, curled into him moments later.

He rumbled with laughter. "We certainly will. It has been a while for me however, so allow my arse to rest a day or so."

"So much for vampire healing," I muttered.

He laughed and kissed me. "Ophelia James," he said, tracing the slope of my nose and kissing it.

"Yes, papi," I said, batting my lashes at him.

"Happy Valentine's Day."

"Want to know a secret?" I asked him. "I hate Valentine's Day."

He burst out laughing. "I do too. It's a kettle of shit. But..."

I cocked my head to the side.

He kissed my nose again. "I was wondering if perhaps I could persuade us both to have better thoughts about it."

"How do you propose we do that, vampire?" I propped myself on my elbow and kissed his cheeks.

"By proposing, actually."

"Wait, what?" I sat up completely.

"Will you marry me?" he asked.

Was he serious?

"Yes, yes, of course!" I kissed him and rolled myself over him, laughing.

We stayed in that room all night, making love and talking about the future. I didn't know what or where it would hold, but in it, it did not take a seer for me to know that I had Javier and my family to spend it with. And there was no better thing to celebrate than that. It did not escape me that while my life had burned to cinders around me for so long, the Ophelia who rose from those ashes was a chromatic, beautiful thing, burning ever so brighter than before. And I was ready to light the sky with her for the indefinite future.

ACKNOWLEDGMENTS

Well, I suppose I actually published this gory little smut fest. The idea for BloodLily popped up when I was looking for a job and had lost all my clients during Covid. When you've been raising humans and working for yourself for 20 years, you find you are unqualified for many employment opportunities and honestly, why wasn't there a vampire who needed my very healthy blood?

I had never written this level of romance and spice before and I decided to approach it as an exercise in genre and feeling. I wanted Ophelia to be uninhibited. I wanted Javi to finally let go. I wanted two people who had been *not enough* for the people in their lives, to find completion in each other.

Just before the final act was written, my soul dog, Coco, passed away and it sent me into a really bad place. I was gutted. Shortly thereafter, we adopted Fiona, the dog no one wanted and gave away with broken teeth and broken spirit. The funniest, snuggliest, most difficult dog I've ever had. She and I wrote the rest of the book. I feel like as soon as I hit save, I sent it off to Emmie Hamilton, my amazing friend and fellow author, and Cassandra Thompson, who graciously offered to beta read it even though she has her own publishing house to run. Fierce females are my jam. I owe them more than they think since I really didn't know if I was capable of writing "this" kind of book. I also want to thank my husband, who REALLY encouraged me to publish it. He deserves a second shout out. He's worked overtime almost every single day for years in order to keep my fingers on the keyboard and I just don't know what else to say, other than, I love you, Damian. Thank you.

Thanks to the readers who not only pick up this book, but who understand that spicy romance is empowerment. Through any and all books, we have strength, and through those that express pleasure and fulfillment, even through our darkest days, we heal. We hold each other up.

Also thank you to my lovely editor, Friel. At some point, we will meet on that snowy hill and share that mezcal cocktail. To Natalie of Wonder Witch Boutique, a thousand thanks for putting up with me while we made this gorgeous cover.

Jessika Grewe Glover lives in Los Angeles with her British husband. She is the mum of two humans and a rescue bulldog. Jessika has a degree in Creative Writing (and some other stuff), a slight obsession with history, literature, and vampires. When she's not writing, she can be found traveling, lifting weights, and running in shoes that are never narrow enough. She is the author of Stars Like Gasoline, a contemporary romantic suspense, and the Another Beast's Skin romantic fantasy series.